Out of Sight

**Center Point
Large Print**

Also by Stella Cameron
and available from Center Point Large Print:

Cypress Nights

The Court of Angels Novels
Out of Body
Out of Mind

**This Large Print Book carries the
Seal of Approval of N.A.V.H.**

Out of Sight

A
Court of Angels
Novel

STELLA CAMERON

CENTER POINT PUBLISHING
THORNDIKE, MAINE

This Center Point Large Print edition
is published in the year 2010 by arrangement with
Harlequin Books S.A.

The text of this Large Print edition is unabridged.
In other aspects, this book may vary
from the original edition.
Printed in the United States of America
on permanent paper.
Set in 16-point Times New Roman type.

ISBN: 978-1-60285-861-9

Library of Congress Cataloging-in-Publication Data

Cameron, Stella.
   Out of sight / Stella Cameron. — Center Point large print ed.
      p. cm.
   ISBN 978-1-60285-861-9 (lib. bdg. : alk. paper)
   1. Large type books. I. Title.
   PS3553.A4345O993 2010
   813'.54—dc22
                                              2010018947

For Jerry,
My partner and friend.

Prologue

Sykes Millet had mostly enjoyed his reputation as an inscrutable man. He did not, so most said, show his feelings often.

Among the paranormal families of New Orleans, particularly those closest to the Millets, like the Fortunes and the Montrachets, Sykes was the powerful go-to talent they could rely on to keep his cool and find solutions under any pressure.

Not anymore.

Not as long as his family kept trying to run his life for him.

Underneath his calm exterior, he fumed. And he would do what he had to do to step out of his appointed role as the accepting, level one and into what he really wanted to be—what he was: a man pushed to the limit, whose anger simmered just beneath a smooth surface and was ready to erupt.

He was sick of being used.

From now on he would do what was right for him, preferably without harming anyone else, but definitely without depriving himself to make others more comfortable.

For months all had been quiet in the French Quarter. Just as many people trolled the streets beneath flashing neon signs. The truly drunk jostled with the drunk-on-anticipation. The bars and clubs, the fortune tellers and sellers of mostly fake voodoo paraphernalia plied their trade just as aggressively. Barkers heckled passersby, hawking topless dancing and whatever else they thought would bring the customers in. "Topless bikini," were words thrown out in one breath, followed by, "Lap dance." And the hungry—for whatever—rolled in. The initiated looked to the unnamed and hidden places to satisfy their more exotic tastes.

The reason Sykes considered the Quarter quiet was because there had been no new strings of murders bearing marks of the Embran, an alien tribe of shape-shifters with an empire deep beneath the earth's surface.

While police honchos and the city elders did their best to pretend there was no cause for panic, the Millets and their friends had repulsed two Embran attempts to take over New Orleans and enslave its inhabitants.

A sculptor, Sykes stood in the studio at his house off St. Peter Street in the Quarter and stared at the piece of green marble shot with gold he'd come home to find there—attached to a waist-high plinth—ten days earlier. He had not ordered it. He had known nothing about the thing until it appeared in the studio.

With the marble he had found a note bearing a few cryptic comments: "The stone is from the mountains of Morocco, subtle green-and-gold marble, and perfect for your task. Exquisite. I have the utmost faith in your abilities. Let your hands and inspiration guide you to find the form inside the stone. It will help in your quest. I will be in touch."

Of course it was unsigned. Jude Millet, otherwise known as the Millets' Mentor, Keeper of the Millet Book of the Way—or the rule book—knew Sykes would recognize the marble as coming from him. After all, Jude, gone from human presence for three hundred years, was still a Millet and shared the same erroneous belief as the rest of the clan, that Sykes could be controlled, manipulated and would always put family needs first.

"Just wait," Sykes said, walking around the foot-and-a-half-high lump of stone. The veins of gold glittered. "All of you—all my manipulating friends are going to get a shock and you won't like it. Finally I know what *I* want and I'm going to get it."

Love and death had a lot in common.

Both took something away and replaced it with . . . something. Sometimes the alternative was a void, emptiness, sometimes peace, even euphoria, but always the feelings were intense and someone was forever changed.

Sykes knew a good deal about death. Not so much about love. He had managed to escape needing a permanent woman in his life. As a passionate man, compatible female acquaintances had brought him pleasure but not the kind of satisfaction he had come to long for.

He wanted one woman, his woman.

But he had been branded a curse. This supposed curse threatened that a man like him could bring disaster to the Millets. This was because he was a dark-haired, blue-eyed male in a paranormal family that had an almost unbroken line of red-haired, green-eyed people.

Talk of the curse, and the fear it brought, started three hundred years earlier when Jude Millet—yes, that Jude—had lost his fiancée and on the rebound married a flamboyant woman in Belgium. Through the attention she brought in Bruges, the accusations of witchcraft, the Millets had come close to complete destruction. They had been forced to flee, first to London, then to New Orleans where they had lived relatively quietly until links were made between them and a string of unnatural deaths.

So far Sykes had seen no other proof of this curse, no documentation, and the deductions were drawn from one event, but his father was convinced that if his son ever took his place as head of the family and married, they might all be on the run again. The truth of it had never been tested—in good part because there had not been anything but red-haired descendants, until Sykes. And Sykes had started to feel rebellious.

His father's decision to turn over control of the family business to his brother Pascal and go in search of "a solution to the curse" didn't help.

Antoine Millet and his wife Leandra had taken off twenty years earlier leaving unwilling Pascal to assume what should have become Sykes place once his father either died or stepped down.

Sykes had endured the curse up to his ears, and his uncle Pascal felt pretty much the same way.

One fact that seemed to be ignored by Antoine was that the woman Jude had married three hundred years ago turned out to be an Embran in disguise. Not a mistake Sykes was likely to repeat. And the real curse they all faced was the result of those subterranean villains, a marauding race of shape-shifters, believing that the eventual return of the woman to her home had brought an end to their former immortality. They were slowly dying, much too slowly for Sykes and others who would celebrate the total extinction of these parasites.

Sykes didn't spend much time considering his own strong paranormal powers, or those of the rest of the Millets, the Fortunes, the Montrachets and several other families in the city. Occasionally he did wish he wasn't expected to follow the rules set out in a book he had seen only when it had been shown to him by an apparition of the mystical Mentor who supposedly watched over the family.

The book also hung somewhere between a real manifestation and an apparition, not that Sykes had any aversion to such things. But, in fact, he had never seen rules written on the pages he had seen, only pictures and a few words. But he had seen the book with its heavy gold cover encrusted with gems floating before him. So had his sister Marley and her husband Gray, his sister Willow and Ben Fortune who was now Willow's Bonded partner.

The gold keys he and Ben had found prior to the sudden and uncanny absence of the Embran in the city were absolutely real. So far there were three of them, thin, small, at first glance all the same. They bore the inscription Bella Angelus— beautiful angel. But they were not the same. Each one had a subtle difference, meaning, he thought, that they fit different keyholes.

He was certain these keys, which he now kept safe, were an important—even the most impor- tant—clue to whatever mystery dogged the Millets, and perhaps some of the other paranormal families.

Sykes assumed the state that brought him the most comfort: invisibility. He phased out and sur- veyed his studio, in particular the piece he was supposedly working on.

Seated on one of the long benches where his tools lay, Sykes looked down at the chisels, picks, mallets and chips of stone his human body would have concealed, had he chosen such an uncomfort- able place to sit. On occasion that state diverted him to get lost in insignificant silliness.

He surveyed the piece of marble again. He had been looking for "the form inside the stone" every day since it arrived. His hands seemed to guide his efforts yet he still had no idea what he was making.

To keep entertained, Sykes brought himself to the partial, ghostlike silhouette that was visible only to his own chosen few. He enjoyed adopting the form around his sister Marley who alternately felt honored that he rarely showed this side of himself to anyone else, or aggravated if he played games when she was otherwise occupied.

He reached to punch on some music and "Egyptian Fantasy" made him smile and sway.

Not for long. Cracking, faint but not so faint he didn't hear it over the music, made him frown and search around. From the edge of his vision he caught a suggestion of movement and jumped to the floor, staring at the work in progress.

While he watched, a small, perfect and very female hand formed. Relaxed, most of the fingers curled into the palm, it seemed to point upward, and the material discarded fell to the floor in a scatter of fine rubble.

1

Poppy Fortune edged through the crowd of partygoers in the spectacular St. Louis Street home of Louisiana senatorial hopeful Ward Bienville. She had just arrived—very late—but the only thing she knew for certain was that she wanted to escape again.

That was out of the question. She was there because she had to get out among people in the know. The hints and clues she needed would not be found by spending all her spare time alone or with her family.

Months earlier Poppy had made a foolish mistake but she had tried to put it right, and now, since the man whose forgiveness she wanted most despised her, she was determined to dig her way out of the mess by making herself invaluable. Poppy was set on finding a way to help solve the growing threat New Orleans faced—even if the citizens didn't seem to know its magnitude. She might not be as strong a paranormal talent as her three brothers, or some of the others they knew, but she had an unusual skill that might save all of them.

Familiar faces circulated around her, people she had seen at her family's club, Fortunes, and in photos from society events. Poppy didn't see anyone she would call a friend. She did get distant glimpses of one or two of Ward's close advisors among a tight group of people at the far end of the room.

What she did see, bursting from among the crowd, were more superalpha brain clusters than she had ever seen in one place. In fact, she had never seen more than one at a time and very few of those. Okay, maybe just one or two altogether. But she frequently located clusters of superior but lesser strengths than these, and she translated the motives that drove the host minds. Love, hate, avarice were all very common. There was a very uncommon degree of heightened stimulation in this room.

Slowly, swallowing hard to moisten her dry throat, she picked out first one, then another person with the telltale glowing chartreuse circle pulsing amid tight clumps of shocking violet spheres no bigger than fine dots. There were four superalphas, two men and two women and she didn't know any of them.

Poppy gasped.

They all had the same emotional trigger.

They were desperate. They wanted revenge and power. They wanted their own way.

They were afraid of failure.

She turned aside, breaking the intensely uncomfortable contacts. Of course there were strong-minded people present, ambitious people. After all, only those interested in shaping politics and events would come. . . .

She was here because she and Ward Bienville had met at Fortunes, which she managed for the family, and he had behaved as if she were his personal goddess ever since. Gifts, phone calls several times a day, invitations to accompany him to faraway places and to be at his side in just about everything he did. Despite not being wildly attracted to him, Poppy was a little flattered by

Ward's attention. That could be because her life felt like one big, disappointing flop.

And it made her mad. Sure, she had done something seriously wrong and come close to hurting innocent people, but she was sorry. She would never stop being sorry, but things had turned out fine for her brother Ben and Willow Millet, his Bonded partner as the Millet family referred to making a lifetime commitment. Other people got second chances so why not her? The answer made her eyes sting. The one person she really wanted to be with was unlikely ever to forgive what she had almost caused.

Ward was fun to be with, his charisma and drive fascinated her, but she wasn't falling in love with him. She wouldn't allow herself to think too hard about the man she did want. But there was another reason for her hanging around with the senatorial hopeful—she was aura sensitive and not in the simple way the uninitiated thought of the gift.

Poppy could see brain patterns like the ones that had just shocked her—but usually much more ordinary patterns. They emitted heat that created a spectrum of pulsing colors, some so brilliant they hurt her eyes.

Ward Bienville had the kind of wide circle of friends and acquaintances that brought her in contact with artists, professionals, industrialists, financiers, people with the will and capability to achieve. And among these the brain patterns were the most diverse she had seen in one place. She had even seen one or two she could not type.

Paranormals were a different matter. Poppy longed to know what their brain patterns might look like but they were either absent or not apparent to her.

If paranormals showed their brain patterns to anyone, it wasn't Poppy and she had tried hard to see them.

A brunette with a voice like Diana Krall sat at the piano wearing a skimpy silver dress. The bottom of the skirt didn't reach the edge of the piano bench, and the bodice hung on to the tips of her breasts as if glued there. But she could sing, play and she was beautiful.

Ward was always surrounded with beautiful people, male and female, which made Poppy a little uneasy about holding her own in such company. She wasn't a shrinking violet but neither was she vain. Her own looks were complimented often enough, and some expert opinions had assured her she had a killer figure, but since Ward could have anyone he wanted, why her?

More important than any reservations she had was the opportunity to mix with the kind of New Orleans citizens the Embran were known to prefer.

This was the first time she'd been to Ward's home. Not that she had not been invited—frequently.

Aubusson rugs graced dark, glinting wooden

floors. Gilt-framed mirrors tossed around images of New Orleans's rich and famous, the glitterati of the city. French Empire chandeliers, their lights supported by gold swans, and a series of Baccarat crystal wall sconces brought blinding prisms searing from the women's jewelry.

"Ms. Fortune?" A white-jacketed waiter at her elbow offered her champagne, and she took a glass from his tray. He bowed and gave her a serious, deferential look.

French doors stood open to the gallery. Poppy peered outside and found what she expected; it was empty. No guests could bear to risk missing a little of Ward's golden attention. So far she had managed to stay out of his line of sight but she already knew he had been asking if anyone had seen her. She wouldn't be free of his attention much longer. She had ignored three calls from him on her cell phone, and when he asked why she had not picked up, which he would, she intended to be honest and tell him she had needed some solitude.

Poppy smiled a little. Ward would only be more anxious for her approval if she thwarted him occasionally. He expected to get what he wanted in all things.

She stepped into the warm, fragrant night and closed her eyes for an instant. The gallery was dimly lit and relatively peaceful, despite the noise behind her.

When she approached the grillwork railing, cold slipped over her skin. Her heart speeded up and she wrinkled her brow. Rather than finding peace in the open air, agitation exploded through her. Sweat broke out along her spine and between her breasts. Her brow was instantly damp.

Voices rose from the street below—laughter, high-pitched female yells punctuated by male bellowing. St. Louis wasn't a main party street. People tended to wander through on their way to Bourbon Street and the center of the French Quarter. The group down there went on their way and relative quiet filled in behind them.

Suffused light showed through shutters at the windows opposite. Overhead, blood-edged inky clouds slunk across a thin white moon.

Breath caught in her throat.

She wasn't alone.

Champagne slopped from the glass and over her trembling hand. Of course she was alone. She looked right and left, peered into every corner. Nothing on the gallery moved other than hanging flowers caught by the faint breeze.

"Hi, Poppy. You seem edgy," a familiar deep voice said.

Poppy jumped and her knees locked.

Sykes Millet wasn't a man she would fail to recognize, even in darkness. "What are you doing here?" she said. "You weren't here seconds ago."

"Of course I was," he said with a hint of laughter

in his voice. "I saw you come out but you seemed preoccupied. I didn't want to make you jump."

He had done that anyway.

Very tall, his black hair slightly wavy and grown past his collar, he sauntered toward her from the left, from the farthest reaches of the gallery. He wore a tux. She saw the snowy shine of his shirt in the gloom. With his jacket pushed back and both hands in his pants pockets, he took his time reaching her, enough time to give her a chance to consider fleeing inside.

"Nice dress," he said, arriving in front of her. His eyes passed over her body in a way that made her feel naked—or wish she were.

Poppy turned very, very hot. "Thanks."

"Where have you been hiding yourself?"

"I've been around." And she was surprised he would know or care where she was.

"You spent time in northern California with your folks."

The glow from inside the condo illuminated his face. Every feature had its own shadow. Winging black brows, heavy lashes around his eyes, high, sharp cheekbones and a square jaw. And his mouth. The outline showed clearly, a fuller bottom lip and corners that tilted up a little even when he was quite serious. He was serious now but she saw him suck a long breath.

Sykes Millet was something else.

"How long have you been back?" he asked,

and she realized she hadn't responded to his last remark.

"Months," she said. "I was only away for about a week. The club needs me around."

She was, Sykes decided, thinking about the last time they met when she had confessed to him how she had tried to break up Ben Fortune and Sykes's sister Willow. "I think Liam and Ethan need you, too," he said of her other brothers who were also involved in the business to much lesser degrees.

"You didn't say why you were here," she said, visibly relaxing enough to sip her champagne. "Are you a friend of Ward's?"

"Nope. But I know who he is, everyone does by now. When I saw you I hoped you might be able to tell me why I would be invited. The invitation said something about my attendance being an advantage—to me."

She gave a short laugh and tossed her long, dark hair away from her shoulders. Poppy's skin was olive and smooth, her eyes almond-shaped and almost black. Sykes couldn't see her without thinking she looked Mediterranean. By the time this long-legged woman turned fifteen, she had flowered into the pattern of what she would become.

"That sounds like an invitation Ward would approve of," she said. "Confidence is his watchword."

How well did she know him? Sykes wondered. "He must be an old friend of yours."

"Fairly recent, actually."

And yet she felt she knew the way he thought?

Disappearing at the sight of Poppy had not been a mature thing to do, but he had needed time to collect himself and think. And to watch her. That had been a pleasure for longer than it probably should have been.

"I gather Ward Bienville is thinking about a run for the Senate."

Poppy swirled the champagne in her glass and looked up at him. "That's what he says. And that's what all this is, I'm sure." She waved toward the crush inside the condo. "He's starting to test the waters seriously. Finding out his chances of getting the kind of backing he'll need if he goes forward."

"The Bienvilles are an old Louisiana family. They're supposed to be filthy rich in their own right. Haven't they had statesmen before?"

She raised one bare shoulder. Her black dress was demure enough, a sheath that ended at her knees, but it was strapless and Poppy had full breasts that rose softly above the top and showed the shadow of deep cleavage.

"You could be right," she said at last, "about the statesmen bit. But Ward hasn't lived the high life."

Sykes cocked a brow. "You could have fooled me."

She smiled and pushed her hair behind her shoulders again. "I didn't put that well. From what he's said, his branch of the family has been

22

more involved with good works. His parents were missionaries and he's lived all over the world in various trouble spots. He doesn't like to say much but I think his work has been mostly under cover to assist with advance intelligence for aid groups."

"Sounds impressive," Sykes said. "He must be quite a man."

He studied her expression closely.

"I'm sure he is," she said, noncommittal. Sykes didn't hear a lot of admiration in her voice.

He shouldn't be relieved. "So I'm here as a potential donor? And you, too?"

"I guess. What are you working on these days?"

Sykes frowned. He hadn't expected the question. "An interesting piece. We'll see if it's still interesting when it's finished." An urge to see her again didn't surprise him. They had unfinished business. "Ben and Willow sound happy. I'm glad they decided to stay in Kauai for a while. At least they can hope for peace there."

She had stiffened. "The Embran have been quiet here," she said almost under her breath.

Sykes gave a single nod. "Ben talked to you about that?"

"Not a lot. But I've seen Marley, and we've discussed what's been going on."

Marley had not mentioned Poppy to Sykes. He might feel like asking her why if he did not figure she had sensed tension between him and Poppy.

23

"Marley looks wonderful pregnant, by the way," Poppy said in a rush as if she could hear his thoughts, which he knew she could not.

Since he and Ben were young teens and Poppy a little girl she had complained that she could hear telepathic communications but not send them. And she only heard what full telepathists wanted her to hear.

At the moment she watched him too closely, he assumed because he was quiet. "She's nervous waiting for something else to happen," Poppy said. "Having a baby probably makes you more sensitive. It isn't just you and the world anymore. You're responsible for someone else."

Sykes inclined his head. She looked away from him. This introspective Poppy was different from the woman he thought he knew.

"Have you told Ben what I did?" she asked softly.

He almost felt sorry for her. Her brother Ben had been her closest friend and she must still fear he would turn away from her if he found out the truth. "He doesn't know a thing unless you've told him. Look at me, Poppy."

Her breasts rose with an indrawn breath and she turned her face toward him again. She was beautiful enough in an unconventional way to all but stop his heart.

"I told you it was up to you if you wanted Ben to find out. I would never step in the middle.

Willow already knows and if she doesn't feel like saying anything, why should you?"

"To start over with my brother."

Impulsively, he touched her shoulder and let his fingertips slide to her elbow. She shuddered almost imperceptibly. Sykes felt the atmosphere between them change. There was a connection. He wanted that connection. "Give things time," he told her. "Sometimes we get too deep into something and it takes a while to climb out."

She smiled and the glitter in her eyes might be moonlight on tears.

"There you are, Poppy. I only just found out you were here at all." Sykes heard the soft, Louisiana gentleman's accent and expected Ward Bienville's arrival. The instant Poppy looked at the man over her shoulder, Sykes withdrew along the gallery.

"You are a vision, honey," Ward said, coming through the doors. He turned Poppy toward him and held her by the arms while he kissed her forehead. "But you always are a vision."

Dark blond, tanned, built like a middleweight boxer, but sleek and with a perfectly straight nose and regular features, Bienville had all the physical attributes he'd need for any photo op. Thick hair, Sykes thought, with a little smile that didn't warm him.

He didn't like the possessive way Bienville behaved with Poppy. The greeting didn't sound as if it were coming from a casual acquaintance.

Poppy glanced in Sykes's direction but he had already made sure he was out of sight.

"This is a special night for me," the other man said. His hands passed up over Poppy's shoulders and circled her neck. "I want it to be special for you, too. You know how much you mean to me."

From where he was and in this light Sykes had to use his third eye to see their faces clearly. He blessed the power that allowed him to go beyond the ability of his human sight.

Lips slightly parted, Poppy stared into Ward Bienville's almost begging brown eyes. A dewy anticipation hovered around her. She didn't even blink.

"I've got to talk to these people," Ward said. "I know everyone thinks I've got steel nerves. They're wrong. I'm still new to this. Tonight I need to know I can look at you while I'm talking to them. I need to see you believing in me."

2

Ward held Poppy's hand tightly. She had never seen him agitated before but she could feel excitement running through him.

"I was afraid you weren't coming," he said under his breath. "I kept trying to call you."

"I know. I'm sorry, but I had a rushed day. I wanted to take my time. If I'd known you needed me I'd have been here earlier." And she would have. He was a kind, considerate man, and from the looks he got, a number of women in the room would cut off a hand to replace Poppy's in his.

As they passed the piano, Sonia Gardner, the lovely singer reached out to take hold of Ward's sleeve and smiled up at him. He bent over and kissed her lightly on the cheek. She whispered in his ear, and he laughed before carrying on to stand beneath a portrait of a woman in mid-nineteenth-century dress, who bore a resemblance to Ward.

He let Poppy go as if it hurt to be separated from her and moved to stand in front of an ornate marble-topped demilune table. Stacks of small boxes stood on the table.

A space cleared around him and Poppy tried to melt back into the crowd. The best she could do was a place beside one of Ward's advisors just behind those closest to Ward.

As wide as he was tall, this man was all muscle. His ascetic features and rimless glasses didn't match his tense stance, or the impression that he could walk through concrete walls.

The room quickly got too hot for Poppy. Overhead fans moved the air and a muddle of perfumes, but didn't cool anything. Poppy disliked being hemmed in.

When the chatter died down, Ward said, "Since I want you all on my side, I'll keep this short."

A chuckle went through the partygoers, and a smattering of applause.

"Is there anyone who doesn't know why they were invited here tonight? Other than because they are among the brightest, best and most beautiful in New Orleans?"

Another chuckle and a chorus of, "No!"

Poppy rubbed the space between her brows. She felt a little sick.

"I guess you could say I'm on a fact-finding mission. I need to know who my friends are and how far they're prepared to go to help me start turning things around in a big way for Louisiana."

That brought a cheer.

"Thank you," Ward said, meeting eyes straight on. "Whatever happens I want all of you to know that my doors are always open to you. If you have a question, ask. Doesn't matter what it is . . . well, it almost doesn't matter." He gave a charming grin and laughed with the onlookers.

"The people closest to me from the outset are here. They are your go-to people while we get ourselves off the ground—if that's what we decide we want to do. Bart Dolan is my public relations know-it-all." He pointed at a small, thin man with a sandy crew cut and darting eyes. "Con Willis is security. Raise your hand, Con."

The man beside Poppy put a hand in the air.

"Dolph Huddle is admin. Yeah, all of it at the moment. We really are a grassroots operation."

Blond Dolph stepped forward with a boyish grin on his all-American face. He had the torso of a swimmer and his thighs strained against his tux pants.

"Last but not least, the delectable Joan Lewis is our treasurer."

Small, dark, middle-aged and attractive, Joan Lewis ducked in a mock curtsey and wiggled her fingers all around.

Dolph Huddle placed himself to Ward's right and held up both hands for quiet. "We aren't going to start talking money this evening," he said. "That'll come soon enough."

More laughter, the knowing kind between people who didn't talk about money, they just had it. The Bienvilles were certainly well heeled.

"But we are asking those of you who want to join us to take one of the zippy black boxes on the table behind us here." He grabbed and opened one and held out a gold pin reading WWW. "Discreet, but the message says it all for us. Win With Ward! Those who are with us from the beginning will be the only ones to own these limited-edition pins." His voice rose and his words were echoed back from around the room.

"We're hoping you'll wear one of these—or two if you're real enthusiastic—and sign the book Joan has. We want it as a keepsake of this night."

This was how these things were done, Poppy guessed, but never having been part of anything political in her life, the whole performance embarrassed her.

"I've got one more thing to tell you," Ward said. "And to me it's the most important thing I'm going to say this evening. I don't have a wife."

Cheers went up and the next round of laughter lasted a long time.

"Now, you know if there's one thing that raises eyebrows, it's a single politician. I don't think I can fix that before you all go home tonight, but I can ask you to give me a little help with the problem."

He had his crowd in his hands, Poppy saw. They loved his delivery and the way he embraced them with his words and made them his nearest and dearest buddies.

"You askin' for volunteers?" a man called out.

Ward cocked his head to one side. He appeared in deep thought. Then he walked forward, reached between the people in front of Poppy and took her by the wrist. He pulled her gently through and turned her to face everyone.

The dresses, the faces, the movement, everything blurred before her.

"No," Ward said. "This is not the future Mrs. Ward Bienville. Yet. This is Poppy Fortune. Some of you know her from Fortunes in the Quarter and you know her fine family."

Had he lost his mind, or was she losing hers?

"I just wanted to share with all of you that she's the best thing that has happened to me. I never met a sweeter, more intelligent and generous woman in my life. So, the next time you encounter her I'd take it very kindly if you'd sidle up and whisper, 'That Ward is one fine man. You ought to consider him.' "

Poppy could no longer distinguish between sounds. She let Ward hold her hand because she might have fainted without the support. And she managed to smile.

She gazed around blankly, aware of myriad auras that blasted forth from the gathering. Powerful emotion and obsessive ambition radiated in the room.

Then she looked into a pair of electric-blue eyes.

Without saying a word, Sykes Millet let her know he disagreed with every compliment Ward had paid her.

3

Poppy Fortune was nothing. One way or another, Sonia would get her out of the picture with Ward. He must consider the woman demure, the perfect little shadow for a successful politician, but he was wrong. He needed someone who would shine, someone who could do the things that might be needed to pull in that special favor and make all the difference.

Tonight he had as good as asked Poppy to marry him. If he had even remembered Sonia sitting at the piano, and what they meant to each other, he didn't care.

Sniffling, tipping her head back to stop the tears from streaming down her face, Sonia blinked against the mascara stinging her eyes.

She could go and kill the little nothing. The gun in the drawer by the bed was loaded and ready to go. It was meant for self-defense.

This was self-defense.

Why couldn't Ward have chosen her? They were good together. She made him more than happy, she made him beg for more of what only she had ever given him.

Exactly what he wanted.

No one else knew what turned Ward Bienville wild with lust. Sonia did and she was damn good at it. She yanked the loose top of her silver dress beneath her bare breasts and looked at them. Cradling each one, she held them up and laughed. Poppy—the mouse—Fortune, didn't have anything like these in her bag of tricks and if she did there was no way she knew how to use her body the way Sonia did.

She needed another drink.

Sonia started toward the big wall mirror but changed her mind. She didn't want to see the tell-tale splotches of mascara. She had cried all the way home in the car Ward had insisted that squat goon of his drive her in.

She smirked. From behind his silly intellectual glasses Con Willis's piggy eyes had the nerve to look at what could never be his. He had gone so far as to ask if there was anything he could do to help her and she'd seen the bulge in his trousers. For only an instant she'd lingered, looking over his massive muscles and wondering how he'd be in bed. The answer came mercifully quickly: like a slathering animal.

The only light she had turned on in her apartment was a table lamp and that was low, but she wanted to fuzz out her reality until the pain didn't show anymore.

She'd get it together.

The fight had scarcely begun.

She had begged Ward to let her stay over with him, but he had his sights set on new things now. Even hanging around for a couple of extra glasses of champagne after everyone else left his place had piled more fuel on her hurt.

Rather than drink, too, he had stood looking down at her, his legs braced apart, and his eyes roving the way that should have made her feel great. Only he wasn't planning what they would do next. He had looked because he was a man who analyzed constantly, analyzed everything, including women. And he tapped a toe, anxious for her to leave.

She would bet he wouldn't want to let the wonderful, pure Poppy go. He insisted he had fallen in love with her.

From what she could see, Poppy was the wise one. She left early and kept that deliberately wide-eyed innocent look on her face. The voluptuous mouth and the way she looked up at Ward gave her away, though.

Bitch.

Sonia heaved and pressed a hand over her mouth. She should have eaten before drinking so much.

She walked across the polished-wood floor, turning her ankles with each step. The very high silver shoes went perfectly with her abbreviated dress. In the kitchen she still avoided turning on anything but a dull strip light under some cabinets. Fumbling, she found an open packet of crackers and stuffed several into her mouth. She chewed and breathed through her nose, holding herself up on the counter.

The crackers scratched her throat as they went down. A sip from an open bottle of red wine turned the next batch of crackers to a lump of dough in her mouth and she gulped it down in a series of damp masses.

Coughing, choking until she could gasp in more air, felt good because she couldn't think about feeling sick.

She had to make a plan and put it into action.

Demure?

Okay, she could be demure. She had the clothes and knew how to dress down. She would do it.

Tomorrow.

And tomorrow she would go looking for a

useful gig, somewhere that would put her in the middle of the action where Ward would keep seeing her. She would use quiet smiles, deference, be sweetness and light to Poppy and wish her and Ward well. And every time she had the opportunity, she would give Ward a signal he would have to wonder about: had he imagined Sonia was offering him something, or was he just getting sick of being on a diet with the *demure* Poppy?

"Baby, you'll get hungry real fast," she whispered, turning off the kitchen strip light and wobbling back toward the sitting room.

When she went through the doorway, the wine bottle still in her hand, the table lamp went off. The little wall sconce inside the front door was already dark. She squeezed her eyes shut and opened them, but the blackness was intense. These places were old. The electricity needed an overhaul. This wasn't the first time everything had gone out on her.

Privacy was her thing and she almost never opened the heavy drapes over wall-to-wall windows. Even if they were open, this room faced a brick wall and that wouldn't help.

She took a step and tripped. "Shit!" Finally she gave up on the shoes and kicked them off. At least she could feel her way to bed.

One of the main reasons she'd taken this place was for the loft. The bed took up most of the open space. A walk-in closet was big enough to host a party in and the bathroom was even bigger.

I guess you're still not planning on having a family.

Ward said that every time they slept together there. This was a one man, one woman playpen and they both knew it. She kept plenty of toys to entertain him and he liked it that way.

Sonia made it to the bottom of the loft stairs and started up. Once she swung away from the banister and almost fell. After that she went the rest of the way on her knees, pausing only to slug more wine.

Her head buzzed, but the tears wouldn't stop.

She reached the top and felt her way forward on her hands and knees.

Someone pulled the wine bottle from her hand.

Sonia shrieked, then she fell to her back, rolled flat and spread her arms. And she laughed. "I knew you would come."

"You've had too much to drink. That was silly. Booze gets in the way of a really good perform- ance—you know that."

His voice came to her through a fog, but it wasn't angry. "Hi, baby," she said in the little girl voice he liked. "I was sad, so I had a little drink. It'll pass real fast. You wanna take me in the shower and help me feel better?"

"Maybe."

She rolled on her side, giggling, and put a thumb in her mouth. "I need to pee."

"So pee," he said.

She chuckled and hauled herself up, staggered against him. He smelled of a new cologne. Good.

"Help me, lover," she whined. "Nobody takes off a pair of panties like you do."

He hooked a hand under her skirt and ripped away her thong. "That'll make it easy," he said.

"Those . . . My silver thong went with my little dress, baby. Now you've ruined it." He would have a dozen silver thongs sent to her in the morning—he loved doing things like that.

"C'mon," he said. His fingers dug into the flesh at her elbow and he dragged her along.

"I can't see," she said, trying to wrench away. "You're hurting me."

"I can see just fine," he said, sounding amused. "Let's do all this by feel. How much fun will that be?"

"Fun," she said, wiping the back of her free hand across her mouth and hiccuping. "Fun, fun, fun."

He wrapped a hand under her bare bottom and moved her so fast her feet hardly touched the floor. She slammed down on the toilet seat, and he stood over her, silent.

Sonia shrugged. It wasn't so easy to go when someone was waiting.

"I thought you were desperate," he said.

"I—"

He pushed his hands inside her dress and pinched her nipples until she squealed. He pinched and rolled, bent over and sucked hard enough to make her yell.

"That help?" he said.

Sonia peed and tried to stop him from tearing the top of her dress.

"We don't want to keep those things covered," he said. "What a waste."

They made it through the bathroom and back into the bedroom.

"I want to make it different," she said, working on sounding sultry. Her mouth felt full of wax.

"It's my turn to make it different," he told her, putting his mouth to her ear. "I've got an imagination, too, bitch."

She retched. "Why? You don't say that to me." Even when he felt mean, Ward was a gentleman.

"I say whatever I want to say to you. You told me I could have you any way I wanted, remember?"

His open hand landed across her face so hard her feet shot from beneath her.

His other hand, twisted in her hair, stopped her from falling.

Sonia tasted blood in her mouth. She cried out, but he hit her again and when she reached for him, his fist landed under her jaw, cracking her head back.

"Please—"

"This is what I want," he said against her neck. "Beg. I'm going to hit you and keep hitting you.

I want you to scream and ask me for it. You know you want it."

The next breath she took wouldn't go past her throat. She grabbed for his crotch, gasping, grappling to get a hold on him. She knew how to put him under her control.

She got his pants unzipped and pushed a hand inside.

Sonia screamed, and laughed. He was a big man, but tonight he was huge and throbbing. He swelled into her hand, pressed her fingers apart. She tried to put him inside her but he held her off.

"Baby," she said, swallowing blood, not caring. Adrenaline pumped, and her heart thudded, her body pulsing with anticipation.

For an instant he released her, let her drop onto the rug. He loomed over her. She heard the heavy, almost animal sound of his breathing. In. Out. Then closer. He scraped her face with his fingernails, dug at her neck, drove into her breasts until she felt as if he skewered metal pins into her flesh.

Sonia cried. She screamed and sobbed and tried to catch hold of any part of him.

His fists came down on her, pummeling, first her chest and belly, her thighs, then he threw her onto her face and beat her back, methodically, working from the back of her head all the way to the delicate tendons behind her ankles.

Dull, blurring numbness seeped into her head.

She wanted to ask him to stop. Slowly, she got

her mouth open and whispered, "Love . . . me."

All she heard was a loud sawing sound between a groan and a bellow. Lights sparked in her mind, behind her eyelids. White, then so bright she sucked in and squeezed her eyelids together.

Points of fire raked at her.

She couldn't hold a thought.

Music played, grew louder and louder.

Sonia shouted, she screamed and fought. On her back again, a great weight came down to smother her, rolled her over and over, slashed at her.

She was going to die.

"Help," she cried around blood burbling from her lips. "Help me, please."

Every inch of her burned as if it were raw, and her exposed flesh screamed at the passage of the slightest current of air.

Cloth slid over her head. He yanked a bag over her hair. She felt his thighs spread over her. They flayed her.

"Now," he said, gurgling with excitement. "Now you make me happy. Understand?"

The last thing she saw before the bag covered her face were two staring white globes with molten centers so glaring she had to look away.

The last thing she felt was a massive rough thing thrusting into her, inside her, high, so high she felt him shove against her internal organs.

"You're . . . not . . . Ward."

He tore at her, and her world stopped.

4

Tapping on the door reached Sykes through the fugue state he adopted when he couldn't sleep and didn't want to be awake.

Tap. Tap. Tap.

"Sonovabitch, get lost," he muttered and put a pillow over his face. "You don't know I'm here, dammit." He had deliberately come to his flat in the Court of Angels to spend the night because he rarely stayed there and if anyone was looking for him they would go to the St. Peter Street house.

Ward Bienville looking at Poppy as if she was his next meal had ruined Sykes's night. He still couldn't decide what to make of the announcement Ward had made or Poppy's passive reaction.

He had to forget the whole incident.

Being close to family wasn't so bad, not when it was by choice. He wanted to spend some time with Uncle Pascal and show the kind of interest in the antique shop here on Royal Street that Pascal expected.

There was something else that was getting more and more overdue. Somewhere in the courtyard there was a special angel to be found. If the apparition of Jude was to be believed, that angel was more than important to the Millets and who knew how many others. Sykes had to get back to the search.

If the Embran stayed quiet, would Jude decide to take a rest, too?

Disappointment at that possibility didn't feel so good to Sykes.

He bolted upright in the bed.

The front door was opening. Slowly, creaking inward by the inch, he heard the hinges complain.

"Get out," he yelled. "Now." He wasn't himself. He never behaved like this. But to hell with it, he was only human—or mostly human.

He was all human. Sister Willow liked to pretend they were all not just human but "normal," or she used to until Ben came along.

A grunt reached him, and a furious whisper.

Next came either a herd of small elephants or Winnie, Marley's Boston terrier.

Sykes barely had time to haul a sheet over his naked body before Winnie launched herself onto the bed and ran over him with no regard for any tender parts.

With all four feet planted on his chest, she looked down into his face.

"Winnie! Come here!" Marley's whisper was loud enough to rouse a paralytic drunk.

The dog's round, black eyes stared into Sykes's and she licked him from chin to brow.

"Come and get her," Sykes shouted, wiping both hands over his face. "Yuck."

"Are you decent?"

Sykes held still. "Yes," he said through his teeth. "Get this beast off me."

"How could you call her that?" Marley's mass of red curls appeared around the door and her green eyes managed to look hurt enough to make Sykes ashamed of himself. "She loves you, Sykes. You should be grateful. Nobody else does, you nasty thing."

With a sigh, he jerked his head off the mattress and kissed Winnie on her wrinkled brow. "Now, get off me. I can't breathe. What are you doing here, Marley?" He worked his pillow back beneath his head. The dog curled up beside him.

As Poppy had said, pregnancy suited Marley. She had four months to go but was such a small woman it didn't seem possible she could wait that long.

"I almost didn't come in," she said.

"I should have been so lucky."

"Why are you so mean today? Don't answer. I think I already know. Why would you be mad at Poppy because Ward Bienville made an off-the-wall comment about wishing she'd consider marrying him?"

"He didn't actually say that." Sykes sat up and tucked the sheet around his waist. He crossed his arms and looked away. "But that's probably what he meant."

"Is it okay if I sit down?"

"Oh, for crying out . . . Sit down, now." He

almost forgot his unclothed state and leaped from the bed. "Do you need to lie down?"

"Don't be silly." She sat on the edge of a straight-backed chair. "I'm just fine. I love being pregnant and I never felt better."

"Good." He blinked several times and looked hard at his sister. "Who told you what . . . how do you know about the party last night? Not that it was really a party."

"It was a campaign kickoff," Marley said. "That's obvious. They have those at some sort of party, don't they? Not that I've ever been to one."

Sykes scrubbed at his eyes. "Where's Gray? Won't he be worried about you?"

"Gray left for his office two hours ago," Marley said. "Why don't you just tell me to leave, Sykes? You don't have to be kind." She gave a short laugh.

"Hell, I'm confused," he said. "I don't know what the . . . I don't know what I'm feeling or why. This isn't me. You know me. Mr. Cool."

"You've got it," Marley said. "The Ice Man."

He scowled at her. "Okay. That's it for the sensitivity session. I got a lousy night's sleep. I need coffee." He gave her a significant look. "If I'm allowed to get out of bed, that is."

A stricken expression came over Marley's face. She put a finger to her lips and came to prop herself on the edge of his bed. "Poppy's out there," she whispered in his ear. "I don't know what's

44

going on and you don't have to tell me but you'd better not be rotten to her if you don't want Ben on your tail."

Poppy was out there? "What the hell are you talking about?" he muttered.

"She's already been to St. Peter Street. She came to me because she thought I could help find you—maybe. Why would you be angry at *her* over what Ward Bienville said?"

"I'm not mad."

"Yes, you are. I can see it."

He looked around the plain old room with its built-in, painted cupboards and slightly crooked wooden floors. This was a very old building and he liked it here. He would probably be here every night if the whole curse business hadn't turned him into an angry man. "You think you know me so well," he told her. "Sykes is the even one. He accepts anything. Rub his nose in it and he just breaks out a new box of tissues."

"What?" Marley's face screwed up with confusion. "What are you talking about?"

"Forget it. Just get rid of Poppy and let me get on with my day. I've got a lot to do."

"Poppy said you're working on something new."

Now he really stared at Marley. He never discussed his work. "That's all I told her," he said.

"Sykes, will you tell me why you're so angry? I'd tell you if something was wrong with me."

For an instant he considered it. Then he shook

45

his head. "Nothing." This wasn't something he could share with anyone. He'd supposedly made his peace with being as good as disinherited over the color of his hair and eyes. If he started belly-aching now he'd feel small. "Why would Poppy come to you?"

"She told you we've become good friends."

"Good friends who made sure I didn't know about it."

Marley pressed her lips together. She pulled Winnie close beside her. "Poppy didn't think you'd like it. And before you ask, no, I don't know why. She's a really wonderful person but she's hurting. I think it's something to do with Ben but she won't tell me." She squinted at him. "Now I think it's something to do with you, too."

"Marley?" Poppy spoke from the hall. "Where did you go?"

Sykes looked at the ceiling. "She's been standing out there all this time. I'm being tested, but I don't know why. I've lived a good life. I'm a good man and I deserve better."

"You're not and you don't." She turned toward the door. "In here, Poppy. Come on in."

"*Marley!*"

"She's got brothers. She must have seen them in bed before."

"I am *not* her brother."

Poppy stepped through the doorway and stopped, her eyes popping wide open. "Oh, I'm sorry."

46

"Nah," Sykes said. "You don't have to be. Come on in. Everyone else does." He deliberately sat a little taller in the bed and let the sheet fall lower around his hips.

Poppy straightened her own shoulders. A white T-shirt and very tight jeans looked wonderful on her. The long hair that had whipped about her shoulders the night before hung down her back in a single braid and she wore no makeup. He liked her just the way she was. In fact he liked her any way she wanted to be.

"This was a stupid idea," she said. "I felt terrible last night. Like you must have thought I lied to you . . ." her voice trailed off and they stared at each other. They must both be thinking that she had lied before.

"Will Poppy be safe if I leave her with you?" Marley said, going slightly pink. "I'm not trying to be cute, but Uncle Pascal's on the warpath. I don't want him to find out there's some kind of intrigue with you two. And Nick Montrachet says there's something he doesn't believe, whatever that means. I need to get back to him."

"You're close to Nick, too?" Sykes shook his head. "Just how big is your circle of close friends?"

She pushed her chin forward. "I keep up with people I've known all my life," she said. "My circle of friends is the same as it's always been. You're the one who decided to become a loner. A bad-tempered loner. We'll talk later."

Marley put Winnie down and left with the dog at her heel.

"You don't want visitors," Poppy said, backing up. She shook her head. "You surely don't want to see me. I just felt so badly after I saw you leave last night."

"You've got something to say to me," Sykes said and didn't like his own tone. "Sit down and talk." He inclined his head to the chair Marley had vacated.

Poppy glanced at the chair but remained standing. She looked Sykes over and quickly averted her eyes.

He suppressed a smile. They surely weren't children anymore.

"Last night you asked if I knew why you'd been invited to Ward's party. You said you thought you were there as a potential financial backer and I agreed. You asked if I was, too, and I didn't deny it. I wasn't lying, I just couldn't think of anything else to say."

"It's not my business."

"No, it's not." Her chin rose. "But I'm telling you anyway. The last thing I expected was that speech about me from Ward. I'm not going to pretend I don't like him. I do, but it's not like that at all. We are friends. Nothing more."

"Really?"

"Yes, really. You always were horrible to me. When you weren't around, Ben was my best friend, but when you were there you made him just as unpleasant as you are. I made a mistake and I've apologized for it. I can't keep on apologizing."

"No. Shouldn't think so. That could get boring for both of us."

"Okay, thanks for letting me set things straight."

"You don't have a thing going on with Ward? He'd be a good catch for you."

She turned to him and her lips parted. The flash in her eyes was pure fury. "What is that supposed to mean? He'd be a good catch for me. Maybe I'd be a good catch for him, too."

"Would you mind giving me a chance to get up, Poppy?"

"Don't bother, I'm leaving. Thanks for listening."

Sheesh. "I don't like the group Ward hangs out with." He had wanted something—anything—to say, but not that.

Poppy frowned at him.

"Forget I said that. It's none of my business."

"So you keep saying, Sykes. Nothing about me is any of your business, but you've got plenty to say. Seriously, if you know something I don't, please tell me."

He finally kept his mouth shut.

Poppy took her bottom lip in her teeth and stared at Sykes as if she were trying to see inside his head.

Good luck, lady.

She started to say something but stopped herself and started toward the door. Once more she halted, turned back and pulled the chair close to the side of his bed.

He tilted his head to one side. A shower and shave would feel good. A quick look around the room and he located his tux in a heap on the floor. This was great. There was nothing like feeling you were at a major disadvantage.

"I need your help," Poppy said. She leaned close enough for him to smell her soap—something citrusy that he liked a lot. "I'm running a risk talking to you about it, but I don't have anyone else to ask."

"You've got your brothers and your friend, Marley."

"Shape up," she snapped. "Liam and Ethan would try to stop me and they'd make such a racket that Ben would come roaring back into town. I don't want that. Marley's five months pregnant and doesn't need extra stress. Now, are you going to keep on being a jerk?"

"Probably, but you've got my attention."

She gave a slight and completely disarming smile. "I bet you know how sexy you look sitting in that bed wearing nothing but a white sheet. And not very much of the sheet." Poppy cleared her throat. "That was way out of line." But she didn't look contrite—smug was closer to the truth.

"You look pretty sexy yourself. There's nothing like a pair of beautiful breasts with hard nipples filling out a T-shirt—unless the T-shirt happens to be wet."

She tried to frown but failed. "Now we've got that out of the way. Concentrate. You know I'm aura sensitive."

He shrugged. Aura sensitives were a dime a dozen.

"I knew you'd react like that. Do you realize I can read brain waves? I see their patterns and I know what they mean."

His expression changed. "Since when?"

"Always. I never discussed it because I've been working on getting things right for as long as I can remember. Don't worry, I can't read yours."

"Paranormals don't exhibit brain patterns," he said indifferently.

"That's right. To my eternal disappointment. But I've decided it's time for me to put my talent to work."

"Any change in the telepathic skills?"

She turned her mouth down. "I can still hear what any of you want me to hear but I can't send out a word."

"Bummer."

"That's putting it kindly."

He thought a moment. "You may be blocking yourself. It would be worth looking into."

"You hate me, don't you?"

He knew why she thought so, but hadn't expected her to say it. "Some mistakes take a long time to get over—if you ever can. Let's leave it at that. We're both grown-ups. Finish what you're trying to tell me."

"I didn't go looking for Ward. He and his buddies came into Fortunes. Ward seemed interested in me and kept coming back."

"He's more than interested in you."

"That makes it harder," she said. "I don't want to hurt anyone. But he can be my open door to the kinds of people I don't usually deal with. We're all—the Millets, the Montrachets, the dePalmas and others—we aren't part of the social scene. Some people think we are but we keep our distance and our own counsel. Everywhere the Embran have shown up has been where the money and pedigrees are in New Orleans."

He rubbed a hand over his chest and belly. Poppy followed his hand with her eyes.

"I didn't know you were a social climber," he said.

She threw up her hands and fell against the back of the chair. "I'm not. Don't be so difficult. I'm going to crack the Embran issue wide open and I'm starting by finding ways into places I couldn't go before. Or never tried to go before. Sooner or later I'll get a lead that will take me to whatever the Embran come up with next. Marley's talked a lot about it and they are going to come back. These past weeks when they haven't done anything are only to make us all think they've given up."

Speechless, Sykes could only wait to hear what else she had to say.

"I wish I'd had a chance to be around some of them already. I'm going to talk to that Nat Archer. You know, the homicide detective, and ask if he can get me into the jail to interview an Embran. If I can find common brain patterns in them, I could be able to start picking them out when they pop up."

He wasn't sure which would be more effective. To shake her or hug her until she couldn't breathe. "You will not go near an Embran," he said. "They aren't pixies with bags of fairy dust. They are vicious killers."

"I know that. We've all got to get together and bring them down."

"I'm not having this conversation with you," Sykes said. "You mean well. But if you think this is a way to redeem yourself for . . . to redeem yourself, you're wrong. You'd be in way over your head. I'm calling Liam and Ethan right now."

"If you do, I'll tell everyone you found another of those secret keys and you're not sharing it with them."

He closed his mouth. Between them, he and Ben had discovered three keys not more than an inch long apiece. He had found a fourth—this one in the fountain in the Court of Angels where he knew it could not have been before. This was another one with a carefully removed chip in the edge of the hole.

Sykes gathered himself. "How do you know that?" Denying it would be pointless since she obviously knew the truth.

"Marley saw you and told me."

He began to think of ways to make sure Marley stopped confiding in Poppy. "I am collecting them. I have no idea how many there are or what they mean. And they're nothing to do with you."

"Two of them were in a little red stone griffin in the courtyard and one showed up with Willow's dog."

He couldn't believe Marley had got so loose lipped. "Uh-huh."

"You all think they've got something to do with a legend or something? An angel? Are the keys here?" She looked around.

Sykes groaned. "This is serious stuff, not some sort of kids' game."

"Ben feels something different in the courtyard. He told me that. The stone angels' faces change sometimes. They glow green and he hears them laugh and whisper."

Oh, great, Ben has spilled just about everything. Everything he knew that was; fortunately Sykes hadn't told him much about Jude, although it didn't help that Jude had appeared to Ben. Sykes looked away. Jude had needed Ben's help otherwise he wouldn't have shown himself.

"For Ben and me, I'm asking you not to discuss any of this with strangers."

She made an irritated sound. "As if I would. Try to remember that it isn't just the Millets who could be dragged into this. If it was only you, then Jude wouldn't have talked to Gray and Ben."

"So much for a little privacy," Sykes said. "You could be right, but you could be wrong. And, in case you feel a need to go running to Ben or Nick Montrachet or anyone else right now, I haven't had a chance to tell everyone about the keys yet but I do want to be the one to do it. Not that there's any point since I don't know what they're for."

"Okay." She shrugged. "But I guess we can talk about it if it comes up?"

"I'd rather you didn't."

"And I'd rather you didn't involve Liam and Ethan in my business. I'm not the little sister anymore."

No, she wasn't. "On one condition. You don't make a move without letting me know what you're up to. Wiggle out of that one time and your brothers will know—all of them. And they'll have to line up behind me to deal with you. You're late to this party and you could make a mistake that would set us back badly. And maybe cause you a lot of pain."

She gave him a sweet smile she must have practiced for such an occasion.

"Thank you, Sykes. I'll remember everything you've said. I don't expect you to like me, but I think we can make a good team." She got up again.

Mmm, he could so easily wrap her up with him in his bed and they could both get the rest they had missed last night.

Another time.

Her cell phone rang and she looked at it. "I knew it was too good to be true that no one called for a couple of hours. I'm not answering it."

"Who is it?"

She raised her brows. "Someone for me—calling on *my* phone. Okay, it's Ward's office."

"Ah, well, you'll want to go somewhere private to talk to him."

She gritted her teeth and answered. "Hi, Ward? Joan? Yes, of course it's okay. Is there something wrong?" She was quiet for a couple of minutes before she said, "Thank you," quietly and hung up.

Sykes waited. Poppy kept her eyes on him but he didn't think she was seeing him.

"Ward's been arrested. A body was found at his place early this morning, and they've arrested him for it." He noted that she seemed more bemused than upset.

"I'm sorry." He was more than curious. "Who was it?"

"Sonia Gardner. She was the woman singing and playing the piano last night."

5

From the windows in Sykes's spartan sitting room, Poppy could see about half of the courtyard below. She also had a good view of the back of J. Clive Millet, the antique shop, and the flats closest to the Royal Street side of the property.

She had promised to wait while Sykes took a quick shower before doing anything else about Ward.

In the very left corner of the Court of Angels, bamboo and giant fatsia plants crowded together. Poppy looked hard and counted three angels in that one area—and a palm tree with the upper half of its crown too high for her to see.

The squelch of wet footsteps preceded Sykes's arrival and she started to turn away from the window. A small, bright patch of red caught her eye and she looked again, putting her nose close to the glass.

It must have been a trick of the light because there was nothing red there now.

"What's so interesting?" Sykes walked in and Poppy faced him.

"The courtyard," Poppy said. "Each time I come I see something I hadn't noticed before."

Sykes didn't comment on that. "I've been thinking," he said, slinging a towel around his bare shoulders. Water glistened all the way past his navel to the low waist of his jeans, ran down his face and dripped from his hair. "They're not going to let you anywhere near Ward while they've got him in custody. You might as well wait until they finish questioning him."

"What if they keep him there a long time?"

"I don't know. They must have some strict visiting policies. We'd have to find out."

"You said you'd see if Nat Archer could tell us anything." If Sykes would not help, she'd go alone.

He shoved the fingers of one hand into his hair. Sculpting must use a lot of muscle. Sykes's lean body redefined *defined*. Poppy concentrated on his face.

"What would be wrong with giving the cops more time before we go wading in there. This doesn't apply to you, but some members of our families aren't great favorites with the local police. Some of them think we're either the problem they've been having in the past year, or causing it."

"This doesn't have anything to do with the families," Poppy said. "As far as I'm concerned it's personal."

"Of course it is." His features tightened.

Sykes didn't like her involvement with Ward. Why he objected to a man who was no more than an acquaintance, she had no way of knowing.

"Ward is a friend," she said. "If he hadn't

thought he could turn to me he wouldn't have asked Joan to contact me."

"I'll get a shirt and shoes." Sykes pulled the towel from around his neck. "I'd better make some calls myself and make sure where they've got him. If I can get to Nat, he'll tell me that much."

"I just want to get going."

"I understand that," he said. "But there's no point until we know where to go. He could even have been released by now."

"He'd have got in touch with me if he had."

His long look made her uncomfortable.

"Hang in there, Poppy. I'll be right back."

"No." She made up her mind what she needed to do. "You don't need to bother with this. I'll deal with it."

"What does that mean—'deal with it'?"

"I'll go to Ward's place on St. Louis Street and be there when he gets back."

He bunched the towel in one fist. "The police will be all over it. You won't get anywhere near the building."

She turned away from him.

"I'll try to call Nat now," Sykes said.

He left the room and Poppy's first instinct was to get out of the flat before he came back.

"If you do, I'll be right behind you," Sykes called out.

Startled, Poppy jumped. She marched into the

59

hall and followed him into the bedroom. "You aren't supposed to do that."

He smirked just a little and pulled on a gray T-shirt. "Do what?"

"You know what you did. You're not supposed to get in someone's mind."

"Let me call Nat." Sykes took up his cell and punched in a number.

"Don't creep around in my mind," Poppy said. He made her feel vulnerable.

"How about if I try to teach you to find your way into other people's minds?"

"I've never managed it yet. You're supposed to ask permission, aren't you?"

He grinned. "Wouldn't do much good if you can't answer."

"I can answer out loud, you heel. You're messing with—"

"I can't believe you haven't dealt with this before. You're surrounded by people like us. Can't you feel when someone tries to make contact? Can't you choose to stop them if you want to?"

Poppy pressed her lips together.

"Hey," he said. "Those are straightforward questions."

"I've never discussed it with anyone. I've always said I didn't want to talk about it. End of story. If I hear someone entering my mind I think about a lot of things to shut them out."

His lips parted and he stared. She heard him

swallow. "You're kidding. And you never talked to your brothers about this?"

"I don't want to talk about it now. Some things are private."

He raised his brows. "Not anymore. You just told me, and that needs fixing."

"Please don't say anything to my brothers. They'll only—"

Sykes held up a hand. "Hey, Nat. It's Sykes." He listened for a while. "Yeah, and we can hope they stay gone. Maybe they've all died off in their Safe Place or Home Place . . . Lower Place or whatever it's called. I like to imagine them lying in big, twisted piles deep in the earth."

He listened, and smiled. "I'm starting to get lulled into boredom by all the peace. I like it. Hope it lasts. I wanted to ask you about Ward Bienville."

He sucked in a breath and held the phone away from his ear.

The noises coming from his phone were obviously a man shouting.

Slowly, Sykes replaced the phone to his ear. "Yeah, buddy, I know it's none of my G.D. business but it is the business of a . . . of someone I've known a long time. Poppy Fortune is pretty close to Ward."

He could have called her a friend without compromising his principles, Poppy thought. She swallowed. He was certainly being a whole lot nicer to her than she would have expected, but he had no intention of letting go of his anger with her so easily.

"She was," Sykes said. "So was I."

He held the phone away again and closed his eyes. Once the roaring ceased he tried again. "You can't blame me because I was at a party and someone got knocked off in the same building hours later. And it's sure as hell nothing to do with Poppy. All I'm asking is if you can help Poppy find out where they've got Ward. I don't expect you to. . . ."

More unintelligible noise came from the phone.

"Why are you thinking Embran?" Sykes said, not even trying to conceal his irritation. "This has nothing to do with them. If they were the only source of trouble in this town there wouldn't have been any need for a police force in the first place."

This time Nat apparently kept his voice down, and Sykes did a lot of nodding and grunting. His breathing calmed down visibly. "We'll take anything you can give us. I don't want to come there any more than you want me there. Yeah, why not meet at Fortunes? Bucky? Of course bring Bucky." He put his hand over the receiver. "Okay with you if Nat and Bucky Fist—he's Nat's partner—okay if they stop by your place in about thirty for a cup of coffee?"

She just wanted to know what was happening to Ward but she nodded, yes.

Sykes's face took on an expression of surprise

that only increased by the second. "Yeah? I more or less met her once. I think we got to wave from a distance. I kind of thought that was in the past." He flinched. "Okay, okay. Not everyone talks a lot about their personal life. I get it. You'll have Wazoo with you, not Bucky. Anything I should know about you two?"

Again he winced. "Like you're getting married or something. I just don't want to make any mistakes."

The response must have been short.

"See you there," Sykes said and dropped the phone in his pocket. He shoved his feet into scuffed loafers. "He shouldn't be that mad."

"The detective?" Poppy asked.

"Yeah. It was like he expected to hear from me and he'd been waiting to use me as a punching bag. Doesn't make any sense. People get killed in this city. It's no Boy Scout camp. We've been tied up with some ugly stuff, but this is different. Nope, don't get it."

"He's bringing a friend?"

"His girlfriend. Lady friend. Hell, I don't know what to call her. She comes from Toussaint and they've known each other at least five years. I've only seen her a couple of times. Maybe just once. He's very private about her. I've never seen him look at another woman since they met but nothing happens."

She smiled slightly. "How do you know that?"

63

"Touché," he said, but he looked thoughtful.

"You don't have to come," Poppy said. "You shouldn't have to put up with nastiness because of me."

He took her by the elbow and shunted her ahead of him to the front door and outside. "I know I don't have to come, but Ben is my best friend. I'd want him to look after my sister in the same situation, so you're stuck with me."

In other words, *Nothing personal, ma'am.*

Okay, he could keep that up but she had seen chinks in his armor and she didn't think he was as unaware of her as a woman as he wanted her to believe.

"Besides," he said. "I'm not missing the first time Nat's willingly let anyone meet his Wazoo."

"What kind of name is that?" Poppy said.

Sykes shrugged.

"Did Nat say where they've got Ward?"

"He's at the precinct house on Royal Street. I thought he would be."

They went down flights of green-painted metal steps to the courtyard itself. Redbrick walls and more steps leading to other flats surrounded the area with J. Clive Millet, Antiques taking up most of the side that faced Royal Street. Sykes's uncle Pascal lived above the shop. Poppy had never seen that apartment, but was sure it would be crammed with interesting things. Pascal

Millet was said to be an avid personal collector.

"How many flats are there altogether?" She must have known once, but she had forgotten.

"Nine plus Pascal's," Sykes said shortly.

An oversized marmalade cat sunned itself on the warm earth at the edge of a bed crammed with flowering shrubs and semi-screened by a stand of bamboo. "Whose cat?" Poppy said. The cat's eyes were as orange as its fur.

"No idea."

This was turning into an uphill conversation.

Poppy looked at the fountain angel, at her sweet face, and turned around to seek out some of the other angels that were mostly hidden in the shrubbery.

"Looking for anything in particular?" Sykes said, but although his face was remote, it wasn't hostile. His blue eyes never failed to quicken her pulse.

Her smile was involuntary. "Smiling angels," she said. "Smiling just at me. And I'd like to hear them whispering to me, too. It would be okay if they turned pretty colors as well."

"Marley really does tell you things," he said. "How come I didn't even know you were back in town? You must have been hiding out. I thought you were away all these months."

Avoiding the question, she turned to the planting bed where the cat stretched out and tentatively scratched her tummy. There were more angels in there and, barely visible, a small griffin made of some kind of reddish stone. If it weren't for the gargoyles on lintels and glowering down from the roof, the griffin would look completely out of place.

In the next bed of plants over, she parted a cascade of philodendron draped over a figure with wings folded and eyes lowered. "I'm not proud of what I did before y'know. It was only by chance that Ben and Willow got back together."

"Not entirely," Sykes said. "It was kind of a joint effort."

"I'm sure it was and I'm glad you intervened. I was an idiot. I knew I wasn't welcome here afterward so I stayed away. Marley wanted me to get everything out in the open with you and try to get past it, but I . . . well, I didn't is all."

"No laughing angels today," Sykes said. He turned away from her and after making sure the angel she had found remained revealed, Poppy caught up with him.

They left the property through tall, wrought-iron gates at the side of the shop. Poppy noticed for the first time that there was a griffin in the center of those gates. Someone must have liked them a lot.

Fortunes was only blocks away on St. Ann Street. They walked fast through a midday hot enough to raise waves of trembling vapor from the pavement. Flecks of mica sparkled through a thin layer of dust.

A small boy in a stroller cried while a black Lab licked ice cream off the toddler's face. The mom was too busy trying on sunglasses from a vendor's cart parked at the curb to notice.

"Hope that's not chocolate ice cream," Sykes said to the woman, who spun around. He pointed at the dog and baby. "Chocolate is really bad for dogs."

He reached for Poppy's hand and pulled her along with him as his strides lengthened.

"You're mean," she told him, laughing.

"Got her to look after her kid, didn't I?" He pointed ahead. "I see someone we both know."

Poppy saw her brother, Liam, pacing outside Fortunes, a phone pressed to his ear. He saw them coming and raised both arms in the air. He wasn't waving. Liam radiated anger.

"He's going ballistic," Poppy said unnecessarily. "Liam doesn't lose it like that." She broke into a run.

Sykes was faster and loped ahead fast enough to just about pull her off her feet.

"Whoa," Liam shouted. "Where's the fire?"

Sykes skidded to a halt in front of him. "You tell me. You're the one waving his arms around."

Liam turned red. He ran a hand behind his neck. "I couldn't find my sister," he said, looking from Sykes to Poppy. "No one saw you since last night when you went to that creep's place. We heard what happened to that woman and Ethan's gone over there with the band."

"The band?" Poppy frowned at Liam. "You're not serious."

"They had an early session and you couldn't keep 'em away. They're protective of you, Poppy."

Fortunes had its own regular band for backup and to play when they didn't have featured artists.

"Why didn't you call me?" Poppy said.

"I did. The number's not in use, it says."

Poppy shook her head. "You can't be using the right number." She marched past Liam to enter the club. She was grateful for the cool in the foyer.

Sykes and Liam followed her, both tall, both dark-haired, and Liam's eyes were an intense navy blue. Her brother was another heart-stopper, but he genuinely didn't seem to have any idea of the effect he had on women.

Liam taught history at Tulane. He also helped back up Poppy with the club management, mainly dealing with immediate financial issues while Ben oversaw all of the family's business interests. Their youngest brother, Ethan, was a lawyer.

The blue inside of the club enveloped them. It seemed strange not to hear live music at once. They rarely used anything canned.

"No sign of Nat Archer yet?" Sykes said. "You know Nat. He's joining us here for coffee."

Poppy half listened to Sykes. It was Liam whose expression confused her. He had relaxed and now he hovered, put his hands in his pockets, took them out again. Back in again.

He nodded and rolled from his heels to his toes. Poppy frowned at him. "You okay?" she asked.

His grin was very un-Liam-like. "Great. Just great. It just never crossed my mind, is all. I mean you never said anything one way or the other. Not either of you."

Sykes had switched on one of the fiber-optic globes that were in the center of each table. They all joked about how hokey the idea was but they had been a fixture for years.

"I'll call Ethan and tell him to get back here," Liam said. "You'll want us together. Huh! When I saw you running down the street like that, hand in hand . . . Well, it didn't come to me right off, but you know how slow I am about some things."

Poppy and Sykes frowned at each other.

"Worldly things, so they tell me." Liam chuckled. "It never crossed my mind—you two being together. Hmm. If I'd known you were with Sykes, Poppy, I wouldn't have worried. Is it too early for champagne?"

6

In the attic above J. Clive Millet, Antiques, Jude Millet passed through the curtain that separated him from the living world.

The heaviness he felt was of the mind. Of the spirit . . . he laughed silently at the thought. Physically he had no weight. At last he was des-

perate to finish what had started three centuries earlier. Yes, he had married an Embran woman without any idea what she was. But he had just lost the only woman he had ever really loved and he wanted peace, a quiet home, children.

He had gotten chaos, whispered suggestions that Mrs. Jude Millet was a witch, that she and her family were conspiring to bring down the booming merchant town of Bruges in Brussels for their own gain.

The flight to London had been cruel on the Millets. Mrs. Jude Millet wasn't with them, she had disappeared. But that didn't stop the persecution that eventually chased the family to New Orleans where other paranormal families had helped them settle and establish themselves with the considerable possessions they had been fortunate enough to rescue.

What they had not rescued was what they thought was almost within their grasp before the disastrous marriage: the angel who would lead them to the Ultimate Power, and the secret to why they had a wide spectrum of paranormal talents and even on occasion passed from life into a quiet place of contemplation that was not death, either. This had happened to Jude. He was certain he could not be the only one to experience this seemingly endless existence yet, so far, he had not been contacted by any others.

The Embran woman had been called Astrid,

or so he knew her. Somewhere, even now, she existed although he believed she was deteriorating, rotting around whatever held her shape-shifting body together. And she was blamed for bringing slow disintegration to the rest of her kind.

That was the past, the present was for finishing at least this one task. He would do whatever he must to help his progeny find the sweet angel, the Book of the Way, which contained the master rules for their kind, and eventually the Harmony and the precious Ultimate Power it contained.

As yet Sykes—and it was Sykes who mattered most—knew little about the Ultimate Power or the Harmony that held it.

The greatest obstacle, those without conscience and with their own immortality at stake, were to be stopped: the Embran.

And he, Jude, would become more involved as the Mentor. Changes were already in motion.

An opportunity had arrived in the Quarter, a stranger to him. He had decided on a daring path because he had needed a fresh slant on the problem they faced in New Orleans. He had decided to play a dangerous, possibly disastrous game; to give a practitioner of talents foreign to him a chance to intermingle with the paranormal powers he was familiar with.

Desperation has pushed him to take the chance. If it was as he had always believed and these other elements were no more than myth, then there would be no benefit, but also no harm done.

He hoped.

But this new candidate was unique, and he had begun to take it more seriously that a combination of highly developed intuition, magical practices and the manipulation of minds through suggestion—voodoo in this case—might complicate the fight against the Embran. He had no way of knowing this until the two came in contact.

On the other hand, if these magical skills were real and they could complement the paranormal powers present in such advanced forms in this city, among the Millets, the Fortunes, the Montrachets and others, then the answer to winning might be moving much closer.

Once more he had lost—at least temporarily— his intermediary, a small and unusual intermediary it was true, but also an efficient one. Jude was in the process of giving another subject a trial although this one showed far too many signs of an unpredictable and selfish spirit.

But he would persevere—there must be a way for him to directly achieve small tasks involving the family and their friends. Although he found it simple to approach them as an apparition and prod the more evolved of his progeny onward, there were some things he could not do. He could not dig around where the results of his movements, if not his person, would be seen while he searched for more of the keys that were part of that damnable mechanism in the Harmony that must be dealt with.

And he had to hope that Sykes would discover the message he had sent him within the green and gold stone. If and when—if—the real angel was found, Sykes must remember that stone and realize what he was really looking for: the Harmony and the Ultimate Power.

He was bored with his one view from the dormer window in the attic. Although he would rather not admit it, even to himself, he was . . . well, not exactly tired of his descendants, but impatient with their slow progress.

That was wrong. They couldn't move faster than the information revealed to them. Unfortunately he was coming to believe that parts of their history might have been lost, hidden or destroyed.

Almost worse, what if they had been robbed?

Driven by an unfamiliar agitation, Jude passed through the door that led into the attic room. He had not been at the top of the staircase leading down in front of him for centuries.

He descended very slowly, using one of his many extraordinary gifts: he could hear at great distances and clearly. Jude was, however, a gentleman in all things and did not take unnecessary liberties with his advantages.

Pascal was in the shop, in his office behind the mahogany desk to be precise. He sat at his *elegant desk staring, without seeing, through the windows that gave him a vantage point on every area in the showrooms.*

Jude engaged his other sight for just a moment to delight in a glance at some of the most beautiful pieces from his own day and even before. The new things, the stock from the Regency, the Victorian and the periods that became progressively uglier, did not interest him.

He cut off the sight and concentrated on Pascal again.

The man's intense agitation surprised him. Pascal was given to histrionics but usually his spirit was calm, calculating even—although he never failed to put his surrogate family first.

Jude curled his lip at the thought of that disappointment, Antoine and his weak wife leaving Antoine's unmarried brother to bring up their brood of five and shoulder the responsibilities of the family.

What was this with Pascal now?

It could not be so. Pascal was unshakable, a man to be relied on regardless of his dramatic outbursts declaring that he was tired of the burdens he had never sought.

Jude drifted back a little. He was mistaken. What he was picking up merely reflected Pascal's deep worry as he anticipated the return of the Embran and worried about where they would strike.

The instant before he passed into the attic

again, Jude paused. He gazed downward and brought Pascal's face into focus. The man had shaved his fine head of thick, dark red hair in protest of its helping make him eligible to take the place that should eventually have belonged to Sykes. Fine, jade green eyes stared ahead just as they had since Jude started to look into the showroom. Those eyes were deeply worried.

Jude raised his chin and attempted to follow the muddle of thoughts in Pascal's mind.

Something was coming? That much Jude knew. Pascal was afraid of it. That was not like the Pascal Jude knew.

Perhaps this was the reassurance he needed that the experiment he was encouraging had been a wise decision.

Paranormal powers, magic and voodoo.

They would all see.

7

Liam beamed at Poppy and gave her a hug. He didn't seem to notice that throwing his arms around a sticker bush might be more comfortable.

Laughing this off would be the best thing, Sykes decided, only he didn't feel like laughing.

"Ben and Ethan and I have always thought you two would make a great couple," Liam said. "There's that old thing about love and hate being real close together. Or feeding off each other or whatever. You two have argued forever, but we knew there was a spark there, somewhere."

Sykes looked at Poppy and the shadow of sadness he saw in her eyes gave him a jolt of guilt—and confusion. She was probably just sorry the two of them couldn't seem to get along, and that she had made things hard for Ben and Willow when they had never wanted anything but good for her.

Or . . . no, Poppy didn't wish the two of them were together the way Liam thought they were.

Did she?

Did he want her to want him? An urge to touch her caught him off guard, not that it was the first time he had felt physically drawn to her.

"Sykes has been very kind to me," Poppy said.

"I guess we just had to give the pair of you time," Liam said, smiling. He rocked from his heels up on to the balls of his sneakers. "Ethan will be back shortly."

"Oh, for . . ." Poppy threw herself into a blue leather chair. "Just stop it, Liam. You of all people. Dr. Cold when it comes to women. Why would you jump to such a stupid, embarrassing conclusion?"

Now Sykes felt embarrassed for Liam. "Poppy's uptight," he said. "Hearing the terrible news when she and Ward are so close—"

"*Shut up,*" Poppy said, pressing her palms to her cheeks. "Both of you, please be quiet. You don't know what you're talking about, either of you. We don't know exactly what's supposed to have gone down at Ward's."

"Nothing good," Liam said quietly. "Sorry if I said the wrong thing. It was just that you looked so . . . together. Um, how come you were together this morning?" He clasped his hands behind his back and glanced around at patrons sitting in groups or alone. None of them looked in their direction.

Sykes held the peace a moment and Poppy jumped in. "I went looking for Sykes," she said flatly. "And I found him."

"Tell us what you've heard, Liam," Sykes said.

"Not a lot, except that a woman died and it sounds like she had help doing it."

"You mean she was murdered," Poppy said coldly. "If it was Sonia Gardner. She performed at the party last night. She's so—was so alive. It's unbelievable. This has got to be a mistake."

They were quiet a few moments before Liam said, "You sure you don't want a drink? By the way, nice of you to bring Poppy over, Sykes."

"Nothing for me," Sykes said. "I'm glad to be with Poppy." Oh, hell, nothing came out right.

Poppy spread her arms along the flared back of the seat. "He's trying to help me out with Ward."

"Okay," Liam said. "But I want you to stay away from Ward, Poppy."

"Liam's right," Sykes said and rolled his eyes. *Dumb comment.*

"What have you got against Ward? Either of you. You don't know him."

"It could be moot anyway," Liam said. "The police are moving fast and if they've got their man, Ward won't be a problem anymore."

"Liam!" Poppy leaned forward abruptly.

"It's okay," Sykes said. "We're all off balance. Nat Archer should be here any moment."

"Is it his case?" Liam said.

Sykes sat down close to Poppy. "I don't know. But he'll try to help us out if he can."

"Why is it our business?" Liam said. He didn't take his eyes off his sister. "Let it go, Poppy. It was a bad idea to contact Nat Archer in the first place. It only draws attention to you—to all of us. You know they're just looking for reasons to breathe down our necks again."

"Ward is my friend." Poppy's fingertips dug into the leather chair.

"He's a customer who wants you as a friend," Liam said. "He wants you as more than a friend. I've been worried about him and so has Ethan. He's big time and he's not your kind."

Sykes winced, waiting for Poppy's comeback.

It didn't take long.

"What does that mean? The only people who should be interested in me are nobodies going nowhere? C'mon, Liam, explain." She opened her eyes wider at Sykes. "Is that what Sykes is? Nobody? You were happy when you were jumping to conclusions about us."

"You're being difficult," Liam said. "There's a certain type of operator and Ward's one of them. You've always liked real people."

"I like Ward," Poppy said. "He is not what you call an *operator.* He's kind and he's passionate about making important changes for Louisiana. When did that make him some sort of monster? Anyway, this will all shake down as a mistake. Wait and see."

Nat Archer walked into the club, his fedora in one hand, the jacket of his suit slung over the opposite shoulder. In front of him came the woman Sykes had kind of met in passing once, Wazoo from Toussaint, the apparent love of Nat's life.

Sykes heard little bells tinkling somewhere, but couldn't look away from Wazoo to find out where the noise was coming from.

"Hey," Nat said. "Sorry we're a bit late. Wazoo . . . we wanted to get something on the way."

The "something" was a huge bunch of orange lilies, which Wazoo walked straight to Poppy to hand over. "They go real good with a day like this," she said. Her voice, husky with the promise of a chuckle at any moment, riveted Sykes. So did the way she concentrated on Poppy.

"Thank you," Poppy said. "I love them."

"I just knew you would," Wazoo said, bouncing on her toes. "Nat told me about you, and I could see you with day lilies. Bright flowers help when things aren't so easy."

"Put them on the table," Liam said. "I'll get one of the staff to bring a vase."

Sykes realized the faint tinkle of bells was coming from somewhere on Wazoo's person, although the source wasn't obvious.

The two women looked at each other with perfect understanding. They were instantly comfortable together. Sykes let his consciousness sink away a little and opened another layer of his senses.

Just as he thought, Wazoo was no ordinary pet psychologist from Toussaint or whatever she was supposed to be. She was psychic, but tightly controlled. She was open to whatever might come her way. At the moment Wazoo seemed to be analyzing Poppy.

A small, very slim woman, Wazoo's blue-black hair sprang past her shoulders in unruly curls that suited her exotic appearance. Very pale skin, thick-lashed eyes about as black as her hair, pointed features and a deft hand with dramatic makeup—the whole package was, Sykes supposed, appealing in a fragile and unlikely way. A high-necked, long-sleeved black lace blouse fitted a very nice body. Since her full skirt, with a hint of red showing at the bottom, reached her ankles he had no idea what the rest of her might look like, other than slight. She fascinated him.

What fascinated him even more was that this woman was the object of Nat's affection, the center of all his female interest. And Nat, well over six feet tall, broad-shouldered, athletic and with a face any camera would have a ball with, couldn't be less of an obvious match for Wazoo.

He felt eyes on him and turned to look into Nat's face. The other man raised his brows. Nat had seen Sykes looking at Wazoo, for a long time.

Sykes grinned and nodded. He moved a step closer and said, "You are an interesting man, bro. Be careful you don't break her."

Nat showed his very white teeth in a soundless laugh. He sobered. "Ward Bienville's still at the station," he said. "It's not my case but it could be if I want it."

"Why would you?" Sykes stared into the other man's eyes.

"If it meant enough to all of you. I might prefer to be the one keeping a close eye on things."

"What's that?" Poppy said. "Nat? What are you and Sykes talking about?"

"How many times have I warned you not to whisper, Nat," Wazoo said. "We women can just sense it when you whisper and it always means you're bein' secretive."

They all laughed.

"I can't get away with a thing," Nat said. "Sykes

and I are going to talk boring stuff. If you ladies want to—"

"Listen to your boring stuff, we can?" Poppy said for him. She indicated a group of seating around a brass table with the currently dark globe in the center. "Let's sit down. What will everyone have? Are you hungry? I'm told our lunch menu is worth considering. The kitchen's open."

"A cup of coffee would do it for me," Nat said.

"Not a crawfish omelet? Just a little one? Or a roast beef po' boy?"

Sykes grinned at Nat's expression. He deliberately waited for Poppy to sit so he could be beside her.

"Is there lots of mayo on that po' boy?" Wazoo said.

"Uh-huh."

"Gravy made from the bones?" Wazoo seemed in a semi-trance. "Of course there is. I'll have one of those, please. If you're eatin', too. And Nat never passed up a crawfish omelet in his life."

Poppy called a waiter over and gave him their order. She ordered Sykes a muffuletta and he opened his mouth to ask how she knew he wanted one.

She gave him a tight little smile. "I must be mind reading, right? Or don't you eat them for lunch most days anymore?"

"Thanks," he said. "I still do."

His thigh brushed hers and they looked at each

82

other sharply. Static electricity, it had to be. The charge suffused his leg and his belly. Poppy moved an inch away and Sykes didn't know if he was glad.

Her cheeks were pink and she looked at her own knees, pressed tightly together now.

Liam came back and picked up the lilies. "Okay if we put these on the bar? You'll want to see each other while you talk."

He was letting them know he wouldn't stick around.

Sykes decided he would fill Liam in later if there was anything to say.

"So you can take the case Poppy and Sykes are interested in, Nat?" Wazoo said. "If they want you to?"

The lady had good ears.

"We can get to that after lunch," Sykes said, certain Nat wouldn't want to talk police business in front of . . . He might not want to discuss it at all.

"It's okay," Nat said. He touched a single forefinger to the back of Wazoo's hand and rubbed slowly back and forth. "You all will let me know what's on your mind. If I can help, I will. Ward Bienville was brought in around six this morning. Word is he's a reasonable guy."

"Reasonable?" Sykes said. "What the hell does that mean here?"

"Woken up from a sound sleep by a screaming housekeeper. Dead woman in the foyer. Hauled down to headquarters for questioning and he's still being polite."

Sykes looked sideways at Poppy and caught her frowning. "You're surprised he's polite, Poppy?" he said.

She shook her head. "Just worried about him, is all. How did Sonia Gardner die?"

"I'm sure that'll get around soon enough," Nat said. "It's a bit early for word from Dr. Blades."

Blades was the Medical Examiner. And in other words, they could discuss anything as long as it had no substance.

"Lots of blood," Wazoo said, mostly to herself. "But the worst wounds don't show."

Silence followed, which Wazoo ignored while she drank the coffee she had been brought.

It surprised Sykes that Nat would discuss police business with his girlfriend. Another moment of intense concentration on the woman startled Sykes. In the most fleeting impression, he thought he saw what she saw: a woman in a silver dress sprawled on the ground—with a lot of blood on her legs. The pianist from last night had worn a silver dress.

Then the image was gone. Nat hadn't necessarily told Wazoo anything.

"I'd be obliged if you didn't repeat what you just heard," Nat said.

Poppy pinched the bridge of her nose. "Just between the four of us," she said. "Wazoo has great instincts, don't you?" The next look she gave Wazoo seemed unfocused, as if her eyes concentrated around, rather than on the other woman.

"Some people say they're amazin'," Wazoo said. "But they're no better than yours, Ms. Poppy Fortune. You and me got to get together and compare some things."

"God help us," Nat muttered.

Was "Ms. Poppy Fortune" getting a similar insight into Wazoo as Sykes had? Or was she reading auras and brain patterns?

"Lunch is here," Poppy said at the top of her voice.

The waiter moved the low table closer to them but when he set down the po' boy, oozing thick beef gravy at the seams, Wazoo plopped to sit on the floor close to the table and dissected the huge sandwich into portions with the skill of long practice.

She ate tidily but with gusto, chewing steadily and efficiently through a meal a lot of men might not finish.

Nat, absorbed with his omelet, took no notice but Poppy and Sykes grinned at each other.

Sykes felt his own expression fade to serious, but he didn't look away from Poppy. He frowned at her but she only stared. Then he knew what she was doing. Poppy had chosen this moment to work on her telepathic skills. He opened his mind wide and listened.

I want to talk to you, she said.

Without looking away from her, he sipped coffee.

Wazoo is psychic.

He heard so clearly he coughed.

But she also has different skills from . . . ours.

Yes! he told her, but she had lowered her gaze. She had unwittingly shielded her mind again. He saw her disappointment. She didn't think she had made contact with him. He would have to wait to put that idea right.

"Did you know Bienville and Sonia were lovers?" Nat said, offhand.

No one answered.

"Supposedly some months ago now, but she didn't want it to be over."

"How do you know that?" Poppy said.

Curious, Sykes watched her reaction carefully but she was good at covering what she felt if she wanted to be.

"One of his friends told us," Nat said to her.

Poppy snorted. "What *friend?*"

"It's not important. We check everything out. Nothing is taken at face value."

"I'm sure it's not." Poppy didn't look convinced.

"The autopsy is being done now," Nat said, popping a crawfish tail into his mouth and squeezing out a fragment of shell. "The housekeeper said the front door wasn't locked. Was that a habit of his, Poppy?"

Sykes started to speak, but Poppy gave her head a single shake. "Last night was the first time I've been to Ward's home. I don't know his personal habits."

"You were both there?" Nat said, disposing of more unwanted pieces of crawfish. "You and Sykes. Did you leave together?"

"Almost," Sykes said, flinching inwardly at his own thin attempt to cover for Poppy.

"Sykes left before I did," Poppy said. "I wasn't much later."

"Does that mean Ward took you home?"

"No. It means I walked, on my own. It wasn't that late and it isn't far."

"That's not a good idea, Poppy, and you know it," Nat said.

"No, it damn well is not," Sykes said. "I can't believe Bienville let you do that."

"He didn't know. He was busy with all those people when I slipped out."

"Right after he just about told them all that he wanted you at his side, as his wife?" Sykes said, furious.

Poppy scowled at him. "He didn't mean it that way," she said. "Drop it."

"Ward asked you to marry him?" Nat said as if he were asking about the weather. "But you've never even been inside his home—not until last night?"

"He didn't ask me to marry him," Poppy said.

Sykes was angry but he took pity on her. "He implied that he wished she was interested in him. A lot of champagne had gone in. You know how those things go."

"I hope we'll learn something useful when we find out what killed Sonia," Nat said.

Sykes gave himself a moment to switch topics.

"A blow to the head," Poppy said. "Isn't that what they said?"

Nat looked away. "I want to know *exactly* what killed her."

Poppy shot to her feet. "I'm going down to ask to see Ward. I don't like the sound of any of this."

The slightly smug expression on Nat's face puzzled Sykes. "Let's wait," he said to Poppy.

Then Sykes got it. Nat wanted to get a definite reaction out of Poppy, something to show him how she felt about Ward, and he had it.

"No," Poppy said. "I'm going down there to wait and take him home. He's being ganged up on because . . . well, probably because of jealousy of some sort. Or he's being framed by people who don't want him to succeed."

Poppy signaled to Liam that she was going out and set off for the door.

Ready to go after her, Sykes wiped his hands on a napkin.

"They're just friends?" Nat said. "This only gets more interesting."

Sykes made certain he chose his moment well, then took pleasure in Nat's expression when he turned back from watching Poppy leave to find no sign of Sykes—or none that Nat was able to see.

8

At first Poppy didn't think Ward was going to answer his phone. It rang and rang and she prepared to click off.

"Yes?"

She heard his voice just in time and slammed her own cell phone back to her ear. "Ward? Where are you? I went to the police and they said you just left."

"Poppy? Honey, I thought . . . I'm so sorry you had to get dragged into something like this. I never in my life expected to see something so horrible in my own house. I don't know what happened. Poppy—"

"Are you okay?" She cut him off.

"I'd be more fine if you were with me. I'm goin' home now. I'll send a car for you?"

She stood outside the black railings that surrounded the forecourt at the police precinct. The afternoon had turned gray, as gray as she felt. "You don't need to do that," she said, trying to think what to do next. A breeze turned into a sudden hard gust and flattened her T-shirt to her back. She didn't feel sure what she wanted anymore.

"I'm going to have dinner brought in," Ward said. "You feel like lobster? I could eat . . . you don't want to know what I could eat. I don't do old coffee and stale donuts. That's what the cops live on down there."

"Ward, are you allowed back in your house, yet?"

He took a moment, then said, "If I want into my house, I get into my house. Seriously, oh, hell, this is god-awful. No, I can't go back there. I'm not thinking straight. I want you with me. It's important."

It's important? Poppy wasn't sure she understood what that meant. Maybe she didn't want to.

A heavy hand on her shoulder almost buckled her knees with shock. She looked up at Sykes whose black, curly hair blew away from his intense face. He stared at her as if he saw into her mind. She felt hot at the thought that he probably could.

"Where are you going?" Poppy asked Ward when she got her breath back.

"Sheesh. There's a carriage house next to the big house on St. Louis. I'll go there. It's mostly for guests but very comfortable."

He hadn't mentioned Sonia by name. That didn't feel right to Poppy.

What did she know about the shock of waking up to a dead body in your house? "I'll come and find you."

"Let me send a car."

"No, Ward, I—"

"Dammit, Poppy, don't be difficult. This has been a rotten day and I could use some TLC."

She felt unsure of herself, of what she wanted, or ought to want. "Of course you could." Poppy looked at Sykes and knew, without his saying a word, that he was aware of every word she had exchanged with Ward. "Go and get settled," she said.

"Just get over here, darling."

She had to say it. "Poor Sonia. She had a lot of talent—"

"And round heels," Ward said shortly. "She played around too much and it caught up with her."

Poppy held her breath. Ward was shocked, and shocked people didn't react normally. "I'm sorry it happened to her," she said.

"Would you just get yourself here?"

"As soon as I can. I've got some things to get through." She hung up and looked everywhere but at Sykes. But she felt him as if he had wrapped her up with him inside his clothes, next to his skin, in some kind of incredibly sexy cocoon. Or should that be, restraint?

Her face tingled. So did most of the rest of her.

"Poppy," he said. "I've got to be friend and brother to you. I've got to stand in for Ben."

"I've got plenty of brothers." She raised her

chin. "I don't have so many friends—apart from Marley and she's a rock."

"Sounds as if you could have a new soul mate in Nat's Wazoo," Sykes said with a one-sided smile. "I think our detective is trying to lure his woman to New Orleans, what do you think?"

"I think you're insightful," she said. "He loves her—a lot."

They stared into each other's eyes. Poppy tightened her spine, her legs. Awareness rippled through her muscles. She couldn't look away. While she watched him the angles of his face became more exaggerated, his upswept brows seemed darker, his eyes flared like blue gas flame and his cheekbones shone white and stark.

Sykes's complete absorption in her overpowered Poppy. He took a single step closer until his face was all she saw. The rest of him, his shoulders and arms, the way he tensed his core and held his belly tight, were a physical reality she felt.

She didn't move.

Sykes did.

He stroked the side of her face with the backs of his fingers so slowly time must surely have stopped, and he brought his mouth down on hers. She saw his eyes close the instant before she shut her own.

Poppy sucked in her tummy against the shock that traveled the length of her.

They didn't embrace.

Sykes moved them with their mouths, reached deep inside, nibbled her lips, ran his tongue along the soft skin just inside and over the sharp edges of her teeth.

Breathing got more difficult. She pressed her cheek into his hand and started to urge herself against him. Still her hands hung at her sides but she stood on tiptoe and kissed him as if the kiss had waited for years just for this moment.

I think it has. She heard Sykes speak in her mind.

Her eyes shot open. His lashes moved, thick and dark against his skin. He looked . . . in pain.

Poppy stepped back.

"Will you promise me something?" Sykes asked.

She couldn't speak.

"Don't go to Ward Bienville. Not now. Not until we know what happened to the woman who died at his place last night."

She felt her eyes fill with tears. "Is that why you kissed me, to make me do what you want?"

"Is that really what you think?" He watched her mouth.

"I don't know."

"Could you try believing I kissed you because I wanted to? I've wanted to for a long time."

"I thought you hated me," Poppy said.

"I don't. I didn't like what you did to Ben and Willow but I understood it—in a way."

"I loathed myself. Still do. But I'll get over it.

93

You can't tell me what to do, Sykes. Just because you're the lord high witchery-do, or whatever."

He laughed, transforming his expression into boyish delight. "I think I might not mind being *your* lord high witchery-do. Only I'm not a witch, or a warlock, and neither are you."

"I wasn't being funny." She spread her fingers. "You're just so much more of everything than any of the rest of us—except Ben, perhaps, or even Liam or Ethan. You overwhelm everyone, Sykes.

"But we are all pretty special. People gossip about us. It's all very woo-woo but not real to them. But it's real to us, isn't it?"

"It's real, period." He brushed back her hair. His eyes traveled from her mouth to her breasts. "We are so real," he said. "I think we're soon going to have to prove just how real we are—in addition to having the kind of talents that must never be wasted. I want you to work with me, Poppy. No trying to take on a world you don't know on your own."

"Are you telling me you're taking my idea about cracking our Embran problem seriously? By seeking them out instead of waiting for them to come for us."

"Maybe. I think you're serious about wanting to take this on, Poppy. But I hope it isn't only because you're trying to make amends for something that's over."

"What is this? Are you reading my mind or

something?" He just had or so it seemed but that could have been a fluke.

He laughed. "Would that surprise you? Which brings me to something else I want to talk to you about. Telepathy. The real thing, not skirting around the edges. Learning the rules, knowing when to put the block in place—and when to be wide open. Who to be open with."

"I don't believe you can learn any of that. Either you have it or you don't."

He inclined his head. "You communicated with me at the club. You told me Wazoo is psychic."

"You heard?" Goose bumps blanketed her arms. "You're serious. Of course you did. How else would you know?"

His grin made her smile back. "It could be that you've found a sympathetic channel."

She frowned.

"Me. It wouldn't be surprising if we had a special attachment, would it?" He lifted her left hand to his mouth and brushed his lips across the backs of her fingers.

Transfixed by the tingling rush under her skin, she stared at him, left her hand in his until she noticed it was there and pulled it back.

This was coming at her too fast. "I should check in on Ward. I owe him that much."

Sykes held her chin until she raised her eyes to his. "You don't owe him anything. But I think you're on to something about the kind of circles the Embran are attracted to. And Ward has them. But that's just one shot in the dark, Poppy. We don't know where they'll show up next. Or if they will at all. They've been quiet for months now."

"I want to make sure they stay that way," she said, wishing she felt as determined as she sounded. "I'm not backing off."

"Stay away from Ward. At least until you know he's not a murderer. Please, Poppy."

She turned icy. "I don't frighten easily, remember. I'm one of the superpeople."

"There are a few of us," he said. "And if we aren't nervous it isn't healthy. I don't mean scared out of our heads—just really, really careful. We need to know when to rely on each other."

"I'm going to be careful." She smiled at him, hoping he couldn't see she was tearing up again at the same time. "Thanks for caring but I'd better get going."

He stood very straight, so tall she had to look way up at him. "All right. Go. But make sure your buddy finds out Nat Archer knows where you are—and so do I. What are you going to do if he gets friendly?"

She blushed. "He won't. He's a gentleman."

"I'll be in my studio," Sykes said. "You can get me on my cell. Do you think you could commit to doing that—calling me?"

She couldn't trust this change in Sykes.

"Please?"

"We'll talk," she said, and started looking for a cab.

Sykes stood where he was, watching her. He took out his phone and talked for a short while.

She stepped into the street and looked for a ride.

"Poppy," Sykes called. "Just a minute."

He came to her side and guided her back onto the sidewalk. "That was Nat. He's hoping you spend some time with Wazoo. Evidently he's having trouble persuading her not to go right back to Toussaint."

"She didn't give any hint of that," Poppy said at once.

"People change their minds fast sometimes."

"Do they?" Watching his face, the absolute attention he gave her, quieted her. "Can we ever stop people from doing what they want to do?"

"Sometimes," he said. He put his fingertips to her temple and rubbed lightly. "When the world feels quiet just because you're with someone who means a lot to you. Think about it, Poppy. All the confusion and the fear can slip away when you feel safe, and calm."

She nodded, unable to look away. The sensation of his touch at her temple lulled her.

"We all need those times to find some perspective. Quiet time to think. Quiet time with someone we trust."

Poppy sighed. She felt so tired.

His arm slipped around her shoulders and she rested her head against his shoulder. She heard him talking softly but it didn't matter what he said anymore. She just wanted to be with him.

9

Marley came out of the bedroom in her flat.

The look she gave Sykes made him more uncomfortable than he already was.

She closed the door quietly behind her and pointed to the sitting room.

Without a sound, he did as he was instructed and got another accusing stare, this one from Winnie, who lay on the couch with her head on a fat cushion and her disgusting plastic bone just in front of her nose. The dog's shiny black eyes skewered Sykes, or so it felt.

Marley came in behind him and closed that door, too. "We don't need to pretend with each other," she said. "We both know. Are you supposed to use that, ever?"

"There wouldn't be much point in having it if I never used it—if the need arose."

"Except for situations of life or death, I meant," Marley said. "Are you going to bring her out of it right now? What will you tell her?"

"Please, can Poppy rest here?" Sykes said, drawing himself up straight—unnecessary since he had about a foot on Marley. "This is a matter of life or death. Or it may be. Trust me."

"The two most dangerous words in the language," Marley said, her beautiful green eyes narrowed to slits. "You're going to have to do better than that."

"Have you met Nat's Wazoo?" Boy, he was desperate.

"Yes."

"I think she'd be glad to come over and sit with you. She needs friends really badly. Nat's trying to persuade her to move to New Orleans from Toussaint."

"Can't you ever be appropriate?" Marley said. "I like Wazoo and I'll see what I can do to make her feel at home here. But will you deal with this disaster you've just dropped on me."

"You're exaggerating. Look, Marley, Poppy was going to Ward Bienville's place. On her own. She wouldn't listen to me."

Marley raised her eyebrows. "The man who is running for the senate?"

"Thinking about it. A woman was murdered at his place last night. He's been downtown being questioned all day. And Poppy thought she ought to go and hold his hand."

He saw Marley swallow. "They think Ward killed this woman."

"I don't know what they think, but I'm not taking chances with Poppy."

Her eyebrows climbed higher.

Sykes puffed up his cheeks. "Look at you jumping to conclusions. You always make so much out of nothing. Ben's my friend. Poppy's his sister. I feel responsible."

"How about letting Liam and Ethan be responsible for her?"

He crossed his arms. "They weren't there when I needed them."

"So you put Poppy into a trance. Useful little trick when a man wants a woman to do his bidding."

"I would never use my skills irresponsibly," he exploded.

"Of course not. It's a good thing you're here, by the way. Uncle Pascal is on a tear."

"What else is new."

"Sykes, there's something up and I think it's really big. I should have said he's on a subdued tear. He looks awful. Really tense. Anthony's worried out of his mind."

Anthony was Pascal's trainer. "And the famous green concoction isn't working to calm him down?" Whenever Pascal got excited, Anthony produced a cure-all concoction of some green "health" drink.

"Take something seriously, will you."

He rounded on his sister. "You'll never know how seriously I'm taking a bunch of things right now. I'm sorry." Her small frame, overwhelmed by her almost six-month pregnant belly reminded him he was being inappropriate. "Pascal's looking for me right now?"

"Yes. Then he said he'll want to see Gray and me."

"Okay, I'm on my way over there."

"Sykes, Nick Montrachet was by again."

"Yeah? He's a pretty rare visitor."

"I like him," Marley said. The Montrachets were a low-profile paranormal family. "Do you know anything about a pact the families made? Probably several generations ago?"

Nick was a potter of repute. Sykes admired his work. "I remember him saying something about it," he said.

"Nick knows something about a pact. He says his grandfather mentioned it but he won't say anything now. But Nick wants to know what you know." She paused. "So do I."

"Sounds like Nick's problem to me. But I'll talk to him when I can, okay?"

She smiled at him, and he felt a little better. "I'll get over to Pascal." He opened the door but turned back. "You and Gray are coming over to join us? I don't want Poppy on her own."

"You could fix that."

"I can't just bring her out of the trance until I can try to explain what I did and why."

Marley smirked. "She's going to rip you into little strips." Her expression softened. "I'll see if I can call Nat's Wazoo to keep watch. She's not a woman who finds anything strange as far as I can tell. If I can get her here, I will."

"You're sure that's a good idea?"

"You haven't sensed anything about Wazoo?"

He nodded slowly. "Yeah. Poor Nat. I hope he isn't in over his head."

10

The last thing Sykes expected to see in Pascal's apartment was the big marmalade cat he and Poppy had noticed in the courtyard earlier.

Pascal held the cat, its big head and front legs draped over his shoulder, the rest of its weight more or less supported on one forearm.

"Animals are calming," Pascal said vaguely and set his new friend on one of his green suede chairs. "Coffee?"

Sykes sucked in his bottom lip. Marley had been right, Pascal wasn't himself. If something serious troubled him, he was too calm—so calm he seemed remote, as if he was going through motions but thinking about something else.

"Coffee?" Pascal repeated.

"No thanks. When did you get the cat? Where did she come from?"

Pascal made an airy gesture with his free hand. "She needed a home."

That explanation made Sykes suspicious, but he left the subject alone. "Are you okay?"

Pascal looked up, giving Sykes the full benefit of another pair of green Millet eyes. Pascal had kept his head shaved since Sykes had been a teenager. The loose shirt and jeans he wore were out of character.

"I'm not okay," Pascal said at last. "Without your help I may never be okay again. It could be that everything we've tried to do for this family is about to be blown apart. This time you're just going to have to do as I ask and control that hard head of yours. You've seen Jude, haven't you?"

Sykes tapped his mouth with two fingers and began pacing. He should have expected Pascal to know about Jude's "passing through" on occasion.

"I take it that's a yes," Pascal said. "Now I've seen him, too. He came with a warning."

"He usually does," Sykes mumbled.

Pascal's head snapped up. "How many times has he come to you?"

"Not many."

"Who else has seen him?"

"Marley. Gray. Willow—and Ben, I think."

"I'm not offended he took so long to come to me—that's because I'm not the one who should be here, not doing what I'm doing." Pascal's mouth became a thin line that suggested he certainly was offended. He looked around his apartment. "It's all part of putting things right," he said vaguely. "I shouldn't have waited so long. I should have insisted you listen to me,

Sykes Millet." He pointed a forefinger at Sykes. "And from now on you will listen—unless you want disaster to come down on our heads again."

"Don't tell me you've come up with more dark-haired, blue-eyed Millet males," Sykes said, and regretted being flippant.

"That's crap," Pascal snapped. "Or I think it must be. It's potentially true that this family has a mystery in its past. Yes, in fact, there's something we've got to work out and we both know it. Those teeny-weeny keys have to unlock something, and if we weren't meant to use them I don't believe we would suddenly have started finding them. So that's something else you have to put your mind to. No more floating around as if you have no responsibilities. Do you understand?"

Sykes nodded, yes, with a straight face.

"However," Pascal sniffed with disdain, "I refuse to believe this bosh about dark hair." He considered. "But I don't know for sure that we won't be confronted with another dark-haired Millet, do I? Tell me that. Do I?"

Sykes shook his head slowly. "You sure don't."

"A great deal is happening and most of it may be unpleasant," Pascal said in an ominous tone. "There is definitely something we're intended to find."

"Find?"

"You haven't figured out there's something missing only we don't know what it is? Those three keys. What are they for?"

Sykes frowned. "To unlock something?"

"Oh, good, there's hope for you yet," Pascal said sarcastically. "I see your brain is actually firing."

Sykes sat on a couch and the cat launched herself onto his diaphragm with enough force to wind him. "Ouch." He doubled over. "This cat has claws like nut picks."

"You be nice to Marigold. She arrived when I needed her most which is more than I can say for you."

"Marigold?"

"Suits her. Right color."

"Mario and Marigold. Cute." Ben and Willow's dog was Mario. "That won't be confusing when the wanderers get back from Kauai, will it?"

"Don't change the subject," Pascal said. "That dog's coming back for a visit, by the way. Ben and Willow want him to have his well-dog checks here—with his regular vet."

Sykes closed one eye. "Sometimes I feel as if I'm in Never Never Land. I've heard of well-baby checks but since when did Mario have a regular vet?"

"Since Willow made him an appointment with one for tomorrow. He's being flown home. Anthony will pick him up at the airport so you don't have to worry about him."

There were times when Sykes knew better than to try to keep Pascal on track; this was one of those times.

"Try not to interrupt me, will you?" Pascal said. "I've got some difficult information to get across to you and I don't know how long I've got to do it. Of course, for all I know I could have weeks, or months—or longer. Or possibly no time at all. Or someone could be trying to take me for a ride— have a laugh at my expense. You know?"

Sykes ran his hands over the cat's satin coat and said nothing at all.

"I did get the impression the event is imminent."

Still Sykes remained silent.

"He said, tonight."

Sykes raised his brows.

"When you saw Jude, was there some sort of sound?" Pascal asked.

"Yes. Whispery—sometimes like music far away."

"Did you see . . . colors?"

"Uh-huh. Purple, green, gold, stuff like that. Like watercolor washing down over everything. Willow described it that way and it fits with what I saw."

With his hands behind his back and his head lowered so he could concentrate his gaze on Sykes's, Pascal twitched a little. "See anything else?"

"Like?"

Pascal let out a noisy breath. "A book. Think it was. Gold with gems on it. Not really a book but the ghost of a book."

Sykes cocked his head. "That's an interesting way of putting it. I thought it was a sort of—" he waved his hands in circles "—illusion?"

"Or delusion," Pascal said darkly. "Lot of drama if you ask me."

"I thought that the first time," Sykes said. "Now I think it's real. Or there is a real one somewhere and Jude whips up a copy, an image of it when he wants to show us a page or two. I'm used to it now."

"Are you?" Pascal seemed annoyed. "The Jude you see, is he tall? Dark-haired fella—long hair with white in it. Bright blue eyes. Clothes out of some other century."

"That's him all right," Sykes said. "Did he show you anything in the book?"

Pascal shifted uncomfortably. "Yes, but it didn't make much sense. It was an outline, a shape. There was an angel in it and something that looked like . . . I don't know . . . a flying cow. Small. My eyes aren't as good as they used to be." He looked cross. "Whatever I saw had something wrong with it, is all. The colors were like those others you said, purple, green, gold—lots of green. Red. I think the cow was sitting on a gold ball."

Sykes thought about that. "Did Jude explain what he showed you?"

"He said, 'Court of Angels,' and seemed to assume I knew what he meant. But I didn't make any connection then and I don't now."

Immediately Sykes thought of Ben Fortune, Willow's Bonded partner. Ben insisted there was something extraordinary about the courtyard.

Pascal said, "Jude told me I'd better get all the confusion around here sorted out and fast. He said there's a war on its way and it will be much bigger than anything we've seen before."

"That could mean a lot of things," Sykes said, although he had a strong hunch where this conversation was leading.

"No, it couldn't. Jude thinks—and I say *thinks* because I'm not sure he's got the whole picture himself—but he thinks all hell's about to break loose. He said we'd better make sure everyone knows what their position is, and their job and to be ready to cover each other's backs."

Sykes didn't like the sound of it but a sense of resolution came over him. He would be ready for whatever came.

"No more messing around with the order of things, that's what Jude said. You know what that means."

Sykes knew very well. "What's done is done," he said. "My father chose to pass me over in favor of having you run the family. He did it with the best of intentions. I'm fine with it and you do a good job."

He looked away. He wasn't fine with it, dammit, but it couldn't be changed now.

"Yes, it can be changed," Pascal said. "And I'm

not at all sure his intentions were the best. I think there's a secret he knows and we don't. He enjoyed running things too much to walk away like that."

"You are ruffled," Sykes told him. "We're the only two here and you just went poking around in my head without an invitation."

"And I'm not sorry," Pascal said. "I'm going to use any advantage I have. I'm not as strong a talent as you but I've got my own interests to cover. You've got to take over this family."

Wasn't that what he really wanted, deep down, to take the place his father should still be occupying but which, without Antoine Millet, should have gone to Sykes?

But Pascal had done the job well for twenty years. Who could even guess what upheaval would follow such a monumental change at the helm?

"I don't think so," Sykes said. "No, not going to happen."

"No choice." Pascal ran a hand over his shaved scalp. "I've got to share something with you. Then you've got to help me work out how to deal with everyone else finding out. Oh, damn, this news of Jude's can't be true. It's a trick."

He flopped into a chair, rested his head back and closed his eyes.

Sykes placed Marigold carefully on the rug and leaned toward his uncle.

He jumped when Pascal's eyes popped open. "My entire life is going to change and I'm mad as hell," Pascal said. "This is a conspiracy of some sort and I want to know what's at the bottom of it."

Sykes sat back again. "As far as I'm concerned, nothing has to change," he said. He wouldn't hurt Pascal for anything.

"Yes, it does," Pascal thundered. "If it doesn't we could find ourselves in more of a mess than we've ever faced. We will sort out the power you should have inherited from that feckless father of yours and you'll take over. It doesn't mean I'll ride off into the sunset. I will deal with all the things you won't want to do."

"That's everything, so we might as well stay as we are."

"Have respect for your elders," Pascal snapped. "You will become the face of J. Clive Millet. The front of the house. Of course you have your sculpture and I won't allow interference with that, but I must deal with my own responsibilities—especially if there are new ones I never expected."

Sykes drummed his fingers on the arm of the couch.

Pascal's eyes blazed. "It can't be so, I tell you. It's ridiculous."

"Why not explain?" Sykes said gently. "Maybe you've misunderstood something."

"I do not misunderstand things. If Antoine had not behaved so reprehensibly, this would not be a crisis. I could deal with it, dispel it, and send it on its way. I would be completely footloose and no one else's future would depend on me."

Sykes was thinking about the futures of others and having responsibility for them.

"Don't do anything hasty," he said.

A deep, deep silence fell while Pascal held his head in his hands and stared at the rug between his feet.

These rooms were amazing. Filled with rare pieces, they glowed like Aladdin's cave, but organized—or perhaps artfully arranged would be closer to the truth.

"Look," Pascal said, turning an unlikely shade of bright red. "There's something I need to tell you."

Sykes held his breath, dreading what might come next.

"I'm gay," Pascal said.

Sykes took several calming breaths to slow his racing heart. He had expected to learn his beloved uncle had a dread disease. Seconds ticked away and he realized how important it was to be serious about this announcement but he doubted there was anyone in New Orleans who didn't know Pascal was gay, or who cared.

Finally he opted for simply saying, "Yes."

Pascal eyed him suspiciously. "That's all you've got to say? You've been brought up by a gay surrogate father and all you can say is, yes? You must be so shocked."

"I'm not, Uncle. Sorry. We all know and it doesn't mean a thing to us. You are our uncle. End of story. Is that really all you were worried about?" He hoped it was because that would make things easy.

"No, it's not." Pascal frowned. "I've always led such a quiet life. I had no idea you'd realized."

"We don't care," Sykes said. "We're glad you're gay. It makes you who you are. Now, would you like me to get out of here so you can get on with your day?"

"Anthony is my significant other," Pascal said, jutting his chin, all combative invitation to say a negative word about Anthony.

Sykes started to laugh. He couldn't help it. "What did you think we all thought?"

Pascal sputtered. "Well, he doesn't live here."

"He might as well," Sykes said. "And if that would make the two of you happy, I suggest you make the change. Why wait?"

Pascal glared.

"Are you upset because you haven't managed to shock me?" Sykes asked.

The question was ignored. "What time is it?"

Sykes checked his watch. "About seven. The nights are getting longer."

"Have you met anyone you're interested in yet —and I'm not talking about casual bed partners."

"No," he said automatically. But was that completely true anymore?

"Probably just as well. God knows what we'll do about the succession. I'll have to look into one of your sisters' offspring being in line."

"This is all pretty medieval, y'know."

"We are not an ordinary family. *Jude* intimated we're up against some trials. He said there were things that would soon come clear through the book."

"The Book of the Way."

Pascal shrugged. "What he showed me was something. The cover anyway. Inside wasn't much, just some pictures that came and went. That sort of chart or whatever. Sketch of a wall. He showed me a separate picture of an angel—a bit like our angels. And a ball, but I told you that. Then he got agitated over that and brought his hand down on the picture. It disappeared. And he said it was time to prepare the Harmony in case we need it."

"Harmony?" Sykes was thoughtful. "Sounds like you had quite the chat."

"We needed to. He had to make sure I was ready. I didn't want to say I didn't know anything about the Harmony. What is it?"

Sykes shrugged. "Beats me."

A very old clock shaped like a pagoda made a muted sound, and Pascal stared at its gilt and enamel face. Sykes saw him swallow several times.

"Can I help with something?" he asked. "What are we expecting?"

113

Pascal got up and stood over Sykes. "All I need from you is a promise that you'll take over for me if I decide it's necessary."

"Just like that? I can't agree to that without having any idea what could make it happen."

"It—might—not—happen." Pascal accentuated each word. "Just take my word for it that I won't ask you for a thing if it doesn't happen. Trust me."

Sykes heard Marley telling him, *The two most dangerous words in the language.*

"Surely you can do that after all these years," Pascal went on. "I'll give you a signal to let you know."

"Thanks," Sykes said. "But I'm not agreeing to anything yet."

Sykes heard footsteps on the stairs and watched for his uncle's reaction when he noticed.

The sound reached the flight leading to the apartment door and Pascal spun around. "A trick," he muttered. "But why would he do that?"

The door flew open. No knock, it just slammed inward and almost hit the wall.

"Are you Pascal Millet?" A gangly teenager in black Goth gear took two steps into the room. Sunglasses with reflective lenses hid his eyes. His head was shaved, his ears were lined with steel rings, some dangling crosses and he had a silver ball piercing beneath his bottom lip and a gold ring through one nostril.

Pascal settled his hands on his hips. "Who wants to know?"

The cat leaped on top of Sykes again, the fur on its back and tail standing up in a feline mohawk.

"David Millet, old man. My mom said I'm your son."

11

Another set of footsteps, these slow, climbed the stairs toward Pascal's apartment.

Prickling skimmed up Sykes's spine, reminding him to breathe. He disengaged the cat's claws from his thighs and moved to get up.

More feet hit the stairs lower down, these pounding the treads a lot faster, drumming upward, in fact.

The boy stood there, unmoving, his black canvas duster almost scraping the floor. Sykes thought he was watchful but without seeing the kid's eyes, who knew?

The next kick in the gut for Sykes was Poppy, walking in slowly and making straight for him. She looked at him as if she didn't see anyone else.

"Hey," he said, meeting her before she was far inside the room. "You came to find me." Sheesh, this would teach him the dangers of acting rashly. He had never put a friend or family member in a trance until today—he was only supposed to use that ability under extreme conditions. But they *had* been extreme. She was insisting on going to visit a murderer on her own.

"Poppy?"

Okay, so he didn't know if Ward was a murderer, but the man had spent the day with the police talking about a murder.

Tentatively, he took her hands in his. Her eyes weren't tracking.

You would have done just about anything to stop her going to Ward. Admit it.

"What's wrong with Poppy?" Pascal said.

"She's had a really difficult time," Sykes said. How had she found him up here?

"Sit down, David," Pascal said in a surprisingly firm tone. "I can only deal with one disaster at a time."

Even more surprising, the boy surveyed the available seating and chose a couch to drape himself on. Sykes tried to see his face more clearly. He had very defined features. His eyebrows winged out above his sunglasses, his nose—Sykes tried not to dwell on the gold ring which didn't look as if the hole had been made quite right for it—his nose was straight and he had a good, firm mouth and chin.

"What's wrong with Poppy?" Pascal said again, keeping his voice low and even. He walked smoothly to stand where he could see her face.

The long breath he expelled sounded gusty, and angry.

"We are already in a whole lot of trouble and you have to add this?" he muttered. "When will you learn not to ignore the rules?"

Marley puffed into view. Leaning on the doorjamb and panting, she took in the scene, barely changing her expression when she saw David. She crept up behind Poppy. *I couldn't stop her.*

Telepathy could be invaluable when you wanted to keep communication under the radar. *Did you tell her where I was?* Sykes said.

What do you think? Of course I didn't. This is all your fault—behaving like a kid with no control. She walked out before I saw her go. I only found her by accident after I figured she was probably looking for you. You've attached her to you, you creep. Fix it. And don't expect any sympathy from me when she rips your head off.

A glance at Pascal's smirk confirmed Sykes's hunch that he had been included in the conversation.

I'll deal with it, Sykes told them. *Marley, stay here with Pascal until I get back. The kid on the couch says he's Pascal's son. Just help keep him here and keep everything calm—as calm as possible.*

Marley blinked rapidly, then stared from Pascal to David. *But how—I mean. You know what I mean.*

Thank you, Sykes, Pascal cut in. *You're such a help. Now go. We'll discuss this infraction later.*

So much for being the one Pascal thought should become head of the family, Sykes thought. He glanced at the boy again and realized what he should have thought of the moment he saw him: this was unlikely to be Pascal's son but if he was, he could well decide he was next in line as Millet-in-chief.

Hell.

That sounds appropriate, Marley whispered into his mind.

Watch for that signal I mentioned, Sykes, Pascal put in. *Now, go. And be very careful.*

12

Sykes had no choice but to take Poppy where he could hope they wouldn't be interrupted. The flat at the Court of Angels wasn't that place. He should have developed Ben's ability to move people across distances without anyone noticing —until the one who got moved realized what had happened.

It was getting darker.

Misty rain blurred everything and the leaden sky sat on the rooftops. Gardenias loaded the air and he could hear water smattering in the fountain behind him.

Noises from Royal Street warned him there would be a lot of humanity out there.

He put an arm around Poppy's shoulders and

walked her to the street. What choice did he have?

His cell phone vibrated in his pocket and he looked at the caller ID to see if he had to answer.

He had to answer.

"Yeah, Nat?"

"You're whisperin'."

"Yeah."

"You going to explain?" Nat said.

"Not now."

"If you need me, I'll come right now."

"*No!*" A glance at Poppy's serene face still didn't stop the thud of his heart. "No," he repeated softly.

"Okay. I just wanted to make sure you knew we decided to ask Ward Bienville back to the station a while ago. He's not being so polite this time."

Sykes grinned. "Why is he there?" He was due a lucky break. At least he could tell Poppy her buddy wasn't pining for her in St. Louis Street.

"Routine stuff. I can't talk about it. Just thought you ought to know." He was quiet a moment. "Poppy wasn't with him."

"She's with me."

"Talk to you later, then," Nat said. "It's my case now." He hung up.

Traffic had already been closed out of Royal for the night. Hunched over Poppy who had yet to say a word, Sykes walked her through the early evening wanderers to the corner.

The crowd grew thicker on Conti Street. Neon

119

flashed rainbow squiggles over the shiny surface of the damp pavement and pulsed around the doorways of clubs and bars.

They stood at the curb until a cab showed up. The trip to St. Peter Street was very short, but Sykes didn't want to risk having her slip out of the trance in the middle of a busy sidewalk.

The big question was why had Nat been put in charge of the Sonia Gardner case? Nat had become the go-to guy for unusual killings in the Quarter, and that meant unusual as in inexplicable in human terms.

Did this mean they suspected something Sykes didn't want to even consider? Were the Embran back? Or had Nat taken this on for the Millets' sake?

They got out of the cab at the little hotel on the corner of the lane leading to Sykes's house and he had to force himself not to hurry.

Once inside the house with the door locked he took her into the living room with its eighteenth-century French furnishings and put her in a straight-backed chair. The way her eyes followed his every move reminded him he had better give himself a quick refresher on his advanced hypnosis skills, the ones he hadn't used for years and then only sparingly.

Putting her into the trance had been easy. He'd gone straight into the appropriate routine without so much as a thought.

That was his problem here—not enough thought.

Not trying might be the way to go. *Just follow your instincts.* He crouched in front of her and smiled.

She smiled back, and he almost hugged her. He saw absolute faith in her face. He took her hands in his and rubbed them. Her fingers were icy. "Poppy, I'm glad you've had a rest. Remember how I told you it's important to have quiet times with people you trust, so you can feel calm again."

That smile didn't shift.

"You rested because you've been through too much. We wanted you to have that chance. But now we're going to start bringing you back to exactly the place you were before."

His need to pull her into his arms almost overcame him. The heavy beat of his heart had his attention, so did the sharp, needling little pains shooting between their hands.

Sykes almost leaped to his feet.

He tried moving his fingers up her forearms.

Little muscles beside her mouth and eyes contracted and there was the slightest jump in the muscles he touched.

His gut contracted, then his belly. Then . . . *Holy cow.* Were they Bonding?

The insignificant pains in his hands spread rapidly to engulf him entirely. The farther they went, the less insignificant they became. He held still by the power of his will. His diaphragm, his gut . . . he wasn't just aroused, he felt that if he bent in just the wrong way he would break something.

Cautious not to make any sudden moves, he made small, soft circles on her temple, hoping he had reversed direction from when he put her under. "Come back to me now, Poppy, love." He kept rubbing and she blinked.

That was a good start.

He rose to one knee and kissed her lips. As soon as their skin met, it stung, but in the most intoxicating way Sykes had ever experienced.

The kiss got more heated. He pulled her against him, massaging her back and shoulders. Poppy put her arms around his neck. She slid to kneel on the floor in front of him and urged their bodies so close together; they couldn't get any closer.

Through their shirts, he felt her nipples harden.

And he felt the changes in his own body with a kind of shock. He teetered between the greatest pleasure imaginable and an awareness that every scorched muscle and nerve seared his brain.

His own breath came heavy and fast, but Poppy matched him.

Control was slipping. This wasn't the time for that. He tore his mouth away and looked at her. Poppy stared back, her eyes clearer now, her features taut.

"Should we back off a little, slow down?" Sykes said.

"No." She reached up and sucked his bottom lip between hers.

Relief poured like a molten river through him. He didn't want to stop, not ever.

But Poppy was coming out of a trance. This probably wasn't how she would react if she was completely herself.

He couldn't take advantage of her.

"We can't stop now," she said, her voice so husky he could barely make out the words. "I've waited a long time. Too long. I'm doing this my way."

Oh, God.

"Stand up," she said.

"Poppy, I—"

Her mouth shut him up. She kissed him so thoroughly his head spun. When she looked at his face again, her eyes were huge, luminous and just about black. "Please stand up, Sykes," she told him softly.

For a man with strong legs, his felt decidedly wobbly but he did as she asked.

And Poppy sat back on her heels to look him over from head to foot. Her smile was pure delight.

The button on his jeans parted, and the zipper opened with what sounded like enough noise to wake the neighbors—if he had any.

Poppy rested her cheek against the parts of him over which he had least control, and slipped her hands under his boxers so she could cup his rock-hard rear.

Shock ripped through him.

The stroking of her long fingers sucked all the air from his lungs.

Responsibility warred with need. He had messed with her mind which had possibly unhinged her, but he needed every collision with her skin, her body.

Poppy eased his boxers down over his thighs, taking the jeans with them.

Things like this didn't happen except in early morning dreams.

With her mouth open wide on his belly, Poppy spread her fingers over his ribs and dragged her fingernails through the hair on his chest. She pinched his flat nipples and he almost choked and moved in until he felt her breasts flattening to his thighs.

A duck of her head and small, hard kisses rained where they felt best and did their worst to his tenuous restraint. He flexed his hands in and out of fists at his sides.

He didn't trust himself to reach for her.

If he did he would tear off her clothes and this might end up as a day when he had even more apologizing to do.

And Ben might kill him if word got back somehow.

Ben *would* kill him.

Just stop her. You're so much bigger and stronger, you loon. Stop her and make sure she's out of the trance.

"Do you think I'm a slut?" she said, and sucked in as much of him as her mouth would take.

He heard himself keen before he controlled it. "Of course not," he panted. "You're the sweetest woman I ever met. You're magical. You're amazing. Oh, hell."

She nipped him gently, over and over and weighted his balls, squeezing, pulling . . . and kissing.

"Poppy," he said, insisting she look at him, "are you sure this is what you want? You've had a rocky day—"

"Could you stop sounding as if you want to talk me out of making love with you?" she said.

Sykes ran his hands from her elbows to her underarms and started to lift her.

Poppy stopped him. She pulled his hands over her breasts and went back to what she had been doing.

It was happening. Sykes locked his legs and fought against his own reactions. . . .

Sykes climaxed and felt like a pent-up storm breaking free: unstoppable. Rather than let him pull away, Poppy hooked her feet behind his ankles, keeping him in her mouth until the spasms faded. He slid to his knees and leaned on her.

Poppy stared at a very old picture on the wall, a nude of robust proportions. A muzziness clouded her head, but it passed and she leaned her cheek against Sykes's.

"You can seduce me anytime," he said. "I didn't know what I was missing."

She smiled to herself, a secret smile and rested her chin on his shoulder. So he thought she had seduced him, well, they each had to use their special powers, didn't they? He was sleepy now, she could feel it in his weight. But she needed more from him.

"Kiss me," she murmured and shifted to see his face.

The lion awoke as if she had pinched him, and he made sure the kiss was everything it needed to be. He would want to talk about the way it felt for them to be together like this, but she wasn't in the mood for talk. She frowned. The magic of the moment was in the way he made her feel. Almost as if she were in a trance, suspended and completely new.

They were at the beginning of what was meant to be.

"Poppy," he whispered against her lips, "do you feel it?"

Men did have a problem with having to ask the obvious. "I surely do."

"What do you feel—exactly?"

"Like I'm losing my mind and loving it," she

told him honestly. "And I don't know what took us so long to find this together."

She shucked his shirt over his head and sighed. Confronted with the wide expanse of his chest, she ached inside, and outside, and she was wet. And it was wonderful.

Sykes was meant to be with her. Why hadn't she known that with such certainty until now?

He took his time with her T-shirt, skinned it up her ribs, rubbing her body from front to back with each fresh inch revealed.

"You're like silk," he murmured. "Do you know how sexy you are?"

She held his face still and kissed him soundly. "Yes."

His thumbs met the undersides of her breasts. Poppy shuddered. The hidden parts of her clenched, but they felt incomplete. She wanted him inside her.

Under her shirt, he stroked her breasts, used the backs of his fingers to press up and weight them, made circles around each one. When he lifted the shirt over her head, the rapt concentration on his face stunned her.

He set her away from him where he could watch her and the longing in his eyes seemed tinged with uncertainty.

She would get him past that.

Power drove Poppy to her feet. She stood with her hands on her hips, watching him watching her.

The trail he followed with his tongue started at her navel and slid up close to one nipple. He held her by the waist and teased her, coming close and closer, but never quite touching what she wanted him to touch.

She let her head fall back, and he gave her the dream move she had waited for, flicked first one, then the other nipple with the tip of his strong, talented tongue until she sagged.

Holding her against him where the hair on his chest teased every raw nerve for her, he worked on her jeans, but Poppy pushed his hands out of the way and finished the job herself.

Naked, they layered together and Poppy grabbed for everything she needed. And she needed everything now.

Sykes laughed deep in his throat and gripped her wrists, put her hands behind her back and walked with her until she stood against a wall. Helpless, she tried to cross her legs, to stop the climax that bore down on her. He saw the movement and grinned, his eyes so bright and blue, they hurt to look at.

Everywhere they touched felt singed. She loved it.

A knee between her thighs parted her legs and in one smooth move Sykes was back on his knees, burying his face in her soft, wet hair and seeking with his tongue.

He released her hands to hold her hips, and Poppy

drove her fingers into his unyielding shoulders.

The scream she tried to make didn't happen. Collapsing over him, her body jerked with every spasm. She felt herself falling, but Sykes was too fast. Her bottom landed on the edge of a table.

"Now," Sykes said, and it wasn't a question.

His first thrust was slow, slick, and it destroyed her. The second made her wonder if she could take a third.

His body was too damp for her to get a good hold on any part of him. Then it didn't matter. They shunted together across the top of the table, their breath mingling, and their cries.

"Why didn't we know before now?" Sykes said. "It's real. God, so real."

They convulsed together. The room spun for Poppy and the meager light turned to formless bursts. Sykes stood. She wrapped her legs around his waist and they rolled, shuddering, to the carpet.

"Don't leave me," she told him.

"We've got to talk," he said.

"No," she said, clamping his face against her neck, "we don't."

13

Jude felt time and space shift around him.

He concentrated on a sound, the whispering he knew so well. No words formed and he frowned. Agitation—yes, there was plenty of that. And fear. A scrambling to be heard, to be understood.

These were the ones called the Ushers and they mostly kept to themselves unless Marley needed them when she traveled out of her body. She would not risk leaving while she was pregnant, so these frantic ones had another reason for their babbling.

The Ushers had existed much longer and in more forms than anyone but Jude realized. They were the guides and the guards, the last defense for the paranormal families of New Orleans.

In a decision made even before Jude's time, the Millets had become hosts to the Ushers, whose French Quarter waiting place was in the Court of Angels.

A scene gradually formed in Jude's mind, a crowd of people dressed for celebration. They interacted and he could see them laughing, but he couldn't hear them. That of itself was unusual, in fact it had never happened before.

He made himself study one person after another. Women in shiny dresses with diamonds sparkling at their ears and throats. Men in the evening wear of present time. But not all of them talked or laughed. Some of them were watchful and hung back on the edge of the throng.

Small clusters pressed together, often taking surreptitious glances at one person or another. They all appeared intense.

One man drew his special attention. Brown hair,

pleasant to look at. But unremarkable, he stood apart from the rest and, for their part, they showed no interest in him.

The man's arms hung motionless at his sides. He shifted his eyes only occasionally.

Until a tall, light-haired man separated from the rest and made his way toward a corridor. He checked the contents of one pocket and then another, looked at his car keys and slipped them away again. And on his way he passed the motionless man who showed no sign of noticing.

The man with the keys disappeared.

Within seconds, the watching man turned and strolled after the other one, around a bend in the corridor.

Only the elevation of the Ushers' whispers penetrated Jude's focus. They touched him with their sounds, brushed at him, exhorted him.

He concentrated on the curved corridor and relaxed a little when the tall person came into sight again and returned to the group he had left. Silent, rapt, he listened to his companions.

The other one, the watcher, did not come back and, Jude decided, he must have gone home.

A woman moved apart from everyone, a glass raised in her right hand. The rest faced her. Whatever she said caused them to raise their glasses, too. Jude gauged the mood as serious. She spoke for a while and bowed her head. Someone handed her a handkerchief and she dabbed her eyes. Then she raised her chin and the silent message was one of resolve.

"It's time." The two words jumped from the whispering jumble buffeting Jude. "Time. Time. Be ready."

Under other circumstances he would reproach the Ushers for their unruly behavior; they were disorganized and highly emotional. Best let them find a way to settle and make more sense.

He saw two men make for the curved corridor, absorbed in their conversation. They had come from the same group and gestured in an agitated manner. But they went around the corner, and he no longer saw them.

Two more men approached, from opposite directions. They didn't look at each other and one walked slightly ahead of the other until they were both gone.

Minutes went by while Jude was tempted to put his hands over his ears to shut out his almost manic companions' prattle.

Eventually the first two men came back and settled into their group. They listened, apparently with nothing to add to the conversation anymore.

Time no longer had meaning to Jude, but he knew an hour or more must have passed by the time he counted at least a dozen people, men and women, who went along that corridor, presumably to the bathroom.

Each time they were followed.

Each time the first ones came back but the followers did not.

Each time those who returned were attentively silent and remained so.

Jude paced. He pointed at the veil across the attic and when it had parted, marched to the dormer window and looked far down to the street. It was late. If what he saw was happening now, surely it would soon be over.

"Use your power." This time it was a clear instruction.

"Hush. Be calm. What are you afraid of?" he said.

The gathering in an elegant room became clear once more. The woman had started talking to all the others again, pleading with them. And she pointed to a pile of small black boxes that covered a weathered Dutch table that seemed out of place. A pretty piece, probably from a farm and hand-carved, but incongruous nevertheless.

He took another look around, checking on those who had left the room and returned. Those he identified continued to add nothing to any conversation.

The woman filled her arms with the boxes and went into the crowd, smiling as each guest took and opened one. They all seemed pleased. They seemed like a movement bent on a single goal and whatever was in the box had something to do with that.

Jude used his extra sight to watch a man take a gold pin from one of the boxes and attach it to his lapel. Then he moved even closer and read, "WWW."

He frowned. There was much to learn and his little friends behaved as if time was short.

Another man caught his attention.

Jude knew a Fortune when he saw one, but he didn't recognize this one. Ben, of course, he had recently seen with Willow but they were in Kauai, not here. This man looked quite like Ben. Another one too good-looking for his own good. Jude smiled a little. For some reason they had all been endowed with startling looks. Perhaps that had been to ease their way when they needed to enter any group, but it also made them obvious.

This young member of the Fortune family slid his box into his pocket without donning the pin. He turned in Jude's direction and, although surely it was an illusion, this one behaved as if a shiver had climbed his spine. He turned on his heel, searching in all directions and when his back was to Jude, the man passed a hand behind his neck as if some sensation disturbed him.

Liam Fortune. Jude remembered the name. This was the brother of Ben, Ethan and Poppy, the one who was a history teacher.

The vision began to fade. The purples, golds and greens Jude was so accustomed to seeing as *he exited such an experience washed smoothly down, dulling the figures.*

The Ushers were so loud, Jude gave up and said, "Quiet, all of you. Go, and let me think."

"No time. No time," came the reply.

"He doesn't believe us."

The air grew still.

Jude also stood still, ready for whatever might come next, and something would come.

A gush of brilliance rose from the floor and before his eyes a ball of brightness shimmered. It revolved slowly while the Ushers made a humming noise.

"It's time."

Staring, Jude tried to get closer, but the ball moved farther away.

It had to be an image conjured by the Ushers. It could not be the actual thing, which he had never seen.

"You must find the real Harmony," a female voice told him. "Now you need the power it hides, and so will the others. Look carefully and remember what you seek."

Jude made a grab, but the ball leaped higher in the air. For an instant he saw the faint tracings he knew were on the real thing. The size of a large grapefruit, there were seven marks circling what made up the Harmony. Seven keyholes. And so far they had only four keys. Inside the Harmony was the Ultimate power designed by the families hundreds of years ago, but it had disappeared a very long time ago.

This gold orb contained what the wise ones had assembled to intensify their descendants' gifts, but only if there was no other answer to protecting themselves from destruction.

"You have made a start," a husky voice said. "Now, through the others, you must finish. Help them open their eyes. You saw what is happening. Do not delay."

He saw what was happening?

Jude wrapped his cloak tightly about him and walked away toward the shadows. The illusion of the richly glimmering ball hovered but he ignored it. This was a reminder without substance.

The shadows swallowed him.

14

Sykes liked having Poppy in his bed. She felt right beside him.

While she slept, he followed the paths of his intuition. Premonitions had hovered since he learned Nat was to take over the Sonia Gardner case. Holding Poppy as the early hours passed, he had opened himself to any message that might come. The only answer had been clear, and it prevented him from sleeping. It was not quite time to act but he must be ready.

He was ready.

For the rest, his inner sight repeatedly returned to a vision of a wall where it met the ground. An old wall, cracked in places, and at the bottom an insignificant hole. Nothing more. It meant nothing to him.

He had overstepped his authority by checking on the safety of his family members. Blessedly, each of them was alive and in no immediate danger. Their minds were mostly quiet but in the manner of sleep, not death. Sykes contained a shudder. Pascal was as on edge as he was and had probably already performed the same exercise before sleeping himself.

His father, mother and older sisters, Riley and Alex, in London had showed no particular tension.

In Kauai, Willow felt excited, but he could think of a good reason for that. He had not compounded his sins by reading any thoughts.

His muscles twitched from holding still when he wanted, so badly, to move. He needed to know that he had not made any of the mistakes he feared he might have with Poppy.

He knew using the trance for his own ends in the first place had been pushing it, but he could justify that as protecting her. What he didn't know was whether she had been as clearly focused as she had appeared when she made love to him—and he made love to her.

Despite his concerns, he smiled a little. He had been seduced, by a bombshell of a woman who had fascinated him for years. She had seemed off-limits because she was Ben's sister. But Ben had married Sykes's sister and that felt absolutely right.

Poppy rolled toward him and burrowed her face into his neck. She curled her warm, naked body across his and hooked a hand over his shoulder.

Her breasts were an erotic pressure against his chest. The hair at the apex of her legs rubbed against his hip. Her upper leg settled on his pelvis and he gritted his teeth to keep his mind elsewhere.

"I want to take a bath," she said, so clearly he jumped. "With you."

Sykes swallowed. "Whatever the lady wants, the lady gets. There's only one tub in the house and it isn't that huge."

"We'll make a sandwich," she said, sounding a little more sleepy again. "We'll take a double-decker bath."

His body sprang to attention. "Stay here, and I'll run the water." She might fall asleep again, but there would be other baths—he hoped.

Gently, he disentangled himself from her and slipped from the bed and into the bathroom where the freestanding tub sat on claw feet. He had searched for just the right one to please him and this was it.

He pushed the door almost shut to let Poppy rest, and he went over what they had done only an hour or so earlier. Unbelievable. He would never be the same as he had been and never wanted to be. She was entirely his, her every thought and action for him. He was no longer interested in anything else.

Fleetingly, he thought of his studio and the beautiful piece of marble in which he had yet to find the promised hidden shape. After the upward-pointing hand and loose sleeve had appeared, he had worked with fresh zeal, following what he knew must be an arm. It appeared under his touch, rounded, young. Then a shoulder, a neck and the arch beneath the chin.

But his concentration had become exhausted and he had to leave the piece and walk around. And before long events had unfolded that kept him from returning to the studio.

He must get back, and soon.

The bathroom door slowly swung open and Poppy stood there smiling at him, her black hair tumbling over her shoulders, her smooth, olive skin shining as if polished.

Her naked body was incredible. He'd like to sculpt her one day.

"Hi," Poppy said. She bent over the counter searching for something.

Beautiful ass, were the words that came to Sykes's mind. In fact it was perfect.

"See something you like?" she asked.

Startled, he met her eyes in the sheet of mirror

above the sinks. "Since you want to know—yes. I see something I like very much—you."

She picked up a bar of soap, eyed it on all sides and gave it the sniff test. Her wrinkled nose didn't suggest approval.

"Where do you keep your new soap?" she asked.

"Cupboard." He pointed at double, floor-to-ceiling doors.

She sauntered over to open them and stood back. Piles of towels faced her. And the promised soaps, together with toothpaste and toothbrushes and cleaning agents.

Poppy whipped out a couple of large towels and a toothbrush. Then she examined the soaps as if they were volumes in a library. "Hmm," she said. "I suppose I shouldn't have hoped for plumeria. Lime it'll be. We'll just have to be really fresh."

He gave her a sideways look, turned off the water and climbed into the bath. He crossed his hands on his chest, slipped deeper into the water and closed his eyes.

Her bare feet smacked the white tile floor. Sykes made his eyes remain shut, even though he felt her somewhere close beside him.

Soft lips settled on the corner of his mouth. She kissed him several times and whispered, "You look cute. I'd say *vulnerable* if I didn't know better."

His eyes shot open.

To reach his face while she knelt on the floor,

she leaned over, her breasts on top of the bath rim in a fascinating, even paralyzing, manner.

"I'm glad you wear your hair long," she said. "It's sexy."

"You should know what's sexy," he said, giving up on the pretense that he wasn't fixated on her rose-colored nipples. "What's happening to us, Poppy? Forgive the cliché, but this is so sudden."

She looked away. "Did we get here completely because of me? You didn't want us to be together like this?"

"What do you think?"

Poppy treated him to a dark look from her velvet eyes. "I think I'm as surprised as you are. I'm not going to lie. I've wanted you for a long time, but I didn't think you were interested. I really did think I'd ruined any chance I might have had with you."

"And I never thought you were interested in me at all. Shows how we can sink ourselves by not coming right out and saying what we're thinking. I guess fear of rejection runs deep, hmm?"

"To the bone." She laughed, squeezing her eyes shut, and he could have watched her forever— or at least until he got her into this bathtub.

"You can't go around telling people you've fallen for them when they don't seem to know you're alive," she said.

He caught her hand and rubbed it up and down his chest. "I've always known you were alive. And for a number of years just looking at you has driven me to various stages of crazy."

With her other hand she got the big bar of pale green soap wet and slid it from his neck all the way to the fold between his torso and his thigh.

Sykes's knees jackknifed. He howled and grabbed for her hand, but missed.

Poppy used a single finger to push him back to his former position—not that he didn't help. The scent of lime blossomed. She lathered his chest and belly, then massaged every inch, working lower until he gritted his teeth.

He assumed the teeth did it, because she covered his face with soap instead and laughed at the noises he made when he got the stuff in his mouth.

Once his face was sluiced, he wiped water from his eyes and blinked at her. "I thought *we* were taking this bath."

She put a finger on his lips to silence him and proceeded to wash all the way to his feet. Unfortunately she knew better than to lather up anything too sensitive because the outcome would have been beyond her control.

Without warning, Poppy hopped into the tub and layered herself on top of him, her back to his front.

"It's a good thing I'm a big man," he said. "Otherwise you'd either drown me or crush my ribs."

"You want me to get out again?"

He snaked his arms around her, held a breast in each hand and murmured in her ear, "Try it. Go on, just try."

"What would you do if I did?"

He tweaked her nipples until she squealed and slid a hand down between her legs. "Incapacitate and take advantage of you."

She squirmed. "Like you already are?" Her voice rose and she swung her hips from side to side, grappling with his hand. "You rat. You're taking advantage. Oh!"

"Taking advantage? Let me point out whose on the bottom of the tub with a gorgeous woman on top of him, trapping him."

He bit her neck.

He did not stop sliding his fingers firmly over the stiff nub of flesh he'd found so easily. Very quickly, Poppy turned her face into his neck and panted. He felt the tension gradually leave her, and felt the pulsing beneath his hand.

For a while they lay there in the deep water, almost floating. Sykes let peace take him. He shut out any doubts and absorbed her.

Until she reached, without warning, to pull his penis up between her legs.

He didn't trust himself to say anything. Her well-soaped hands slid up and down his shaft. She popped up to sit on his ribs and leaned to bury him in her cleavage, sweeping her fingers upward along his length. She kissed the very tip, and he couldn't even hold on to her. He slapped the water, sending it over the bathroom like a tidal wave.

Clamping her waist was the best way to stop himself from slipping beneath the water altogether.

"Poppy Fortune, listen to me," he said, pushing himself closer to a sitting position. "You're really into this control thing. I think it's my turn." Somewhat clumsily, he raised her a few inches in the air and spun her to face him.

Again she laughed, but not for long. Her expression grew serious and she stared into his face. "Sykes, this doesn't feel real. Wonderful, but not real. I'm going to hang on to all this until you suddenly regain your senses and send me packing."

He swallowed, settling her on his chest. "Not going to happen," he told her. "Ever."

With a hand on the back of her head, he kissed her deeply. There wasn't a millimeter of his skin that didn't hum with edgy sensation. Poppy framed his face and concentrated on exploring every possibility a kiss might have.

She was as soapy as he was now and their bodies slipped together.

He turned his head to nip her ear, and she used his instant of preoccupation to plant a knee on either side of him. Once more she sat on his stomach, but this time he could see her face, the way her shiny lips parted to show her teeth, her lowered eyelids and the feverish light in her eyes.

Sykes stroked as much of her as he could reach and she gasped with each fresh touch.

Cupping her bottom, he pushed her up and over him until her breasts were above his face. Poppy braced herself on her hands, lowered herself slowly to receive his kisses.

Sykes could not have separated his own sighs from hers.

"I can't wait any longer," Poppy said. She pressed the middle of his chest and knelt up. She wriggled backward until she was poised over him.

"Neither can I."

He clamped her to him, found his place inside her, and couldn't tell the order of things, or when reason fled altogether.

When they were finally still, Sykes supported himself on his elbows or he was sure he would have drowned her.

She sighed and let her eyes close. "We're animals," she said.

"True."

"I don't know if I'm burning up or freezing."

"Probably both," he said helpfully. "We've got about an inch of water left in this tub."

Her arm snaked around his neck and she kissed him, yet again. "That means the rest of it is on the floor."

"Uh-huh. The floor will be really clean."

"And slippery," she commented.

He sensed her growing sleepy.

"We are going very carefully to bed," he said. "In fact, I'm going to do a little trial."

That got her attention. "What?"

The towel he grabbed and dropped on the floor squelched around his foot as he climbed from the tub. "Up, sweetheart," he said, helping her until they clung together, eyeing the thin sheet of water that surrounded them.

Sykes calculated the best and the worst result of what he planned. "Either way, no one dies," he said.

"Sykes!"

He made sure she couldn't see by clamping her face to his chest. For the rest, he did what came naturally, choosing the easier course, complete invisibility rather than the illusion of himself he sometimes created, and shifted to the carpet in the bedroom.

When he knew he had taken Poppy with him, he almost yelled with triumph. Ben wouldn't think much of a clumsy effort that only involved a few feet, but it was a first for Sykes. But then, he had never seen the need to move anyone but himself before and in that, Ben could eat his dust.

Poppy wasn't moving.

"Hey, tiger," he said, moving her face so that he could see her.

"I didn't notice," she said, and he didn't think she was talking about a fast trip to the bedroom. "It's all wrong."

15

"I don't know how I missed it," Poppy said. "I wasn't looking for it, I suppose."

The staccato beat of rain on the window snapped her back to the present moment, to Sykes and herself, arms entwined and naked.

"We're in the bedroom," she said. "You moved us, didn't you?"

"Yes." He looked . . . relieved? Pleased with himself?

"Ben does that stuff. I didn't think you did."

"I haven't before. But there was never anyone I wanted to fly with before. Kept you from landing on your . . . rear, didn't I?"

She frowned at him. He didn't sound at all like himself. "We've got work to do. Or I do. Can I borrow a shirt?"

"Aw—do you have to?"

"Yes, I do," she told him firmly. "And you need pants, if I'm going to concentrate."

He glanced back into the bathroom, awash with soapy water.

"We'll clean that up later," she told him. "This is really important."

The grumbling sound he made only caused Poppy to giggle. "I don't feel sorry for you."

"Well, you should. You're messing with some really good loving time, lady."

"I think I've just discovered something that'll be invaluable to us."

"Like what?" He took out a white shirt and tossed it to her.

Poppy located her thong, put it on and slipped into the huge shirt. Once it was buttoned and the sleeves rolled back five or six times, the thing was still way too big, but at least she could use her hands—and keep his eyes off her breasts for long enough to get some concentration out of him.

The shorts Sykes donned did nothing to deaden the imagination.

He peered through the slatted blinds over the window. "It's raining hard now. I can see steam coming off the roofs. We've got some hours of darkness left before we can get going."

"Going where?"

He looked at her. "I have some family stuff to deal with. As soon as I get the go-ahead, I'll explain."

Which meant he was the one with a time limit and the *we* had been a slip of the tongue.

"It was the brain patterns," she said, too aware of how good it would be to curl up with him in the bed. "I just realized something was different. In the four superalphas I saw at Ward's campaign kickoff."

Beard shadow already darkened Sykes's jaw. In the glow that seeped into the bedroom from the bathroom, he was a tall, lithe series of shadows. She shuddered, but not with fear.

"I don't know what you're talking about," he said. He climbed on top of the mattress to sit cross-legged and patted a space in front of him for Poppy. "Come and explain."

She joined him, wrapping the tail of her borrowed shirt around her shins. "I told you I see brain clusters."

"Yeah, and auras."

"The clusters or patterns fall into specific categories. There are some crossovers, but I know those, too. And depending on the way the patterns behave, I get an indication of what motivates the subject."

Sykes's eyes had narrowed. She had his full attention.

"At Ward's I saw something I never expected to see, not ever—four superalpha brain clusters in one room. That's four subjects with the most evolved brains that have been typed so far."

His chest expanded with his next breath. "And you could see—or figure out—what motivates each of them?"

Her heart beat harder. "That's the kicker. I see everything—love, hate, avarice, fear—those are all common. But all four of these people had the exact same pattern and the same emotional trigger."

"Hold my hand," he told her. "And calm down. You aren't on your own with this."

"There are always some things we're alone with, Sykes. You know that."

Their hands felt welded together.

"So what did these four want?"

"Revenge and power."

His grip tightened. "Could you tell if it was all for the same reason?"

"It was," she said without hesitation. "Fear. The room hummed with all the stimulation in it. The brain clusters for superalphas are a chartreuse circle pulsing in the middle of tightly packed clumps of violet spheres no bigger than fine dots. But there was something else and it only just came to me. I don't even know why it has now. Something different is happening to me."

He kissed her hand, but didn't answer.

"You said you wanted to work with me to try to stop the Embran. Do you still mean that? I don't think I want to do this alone after all."

"You won't get rid of me, Poppy. Even if you want to. I don't trust you." He laughed.

"Meaning?"

"Meaning I don't want to have to rescue you when you get into trouble with something out of your league."

"I—" He was trying to goad her and she wouldn't let him. "Concentrate on what I'm going to tell you. Of course, it'll be a piece of cake for you to understand, but listen anyway."

Goose bumps shooting up her spine surprised

her. She wasn't cold or scared. A careful look into Sykes's shadowed blue eyes didn't show anything particularly unusual.

He was guarded.

Well, hoo mama, there was something going on here.

"Poppy?"

"Yes. Those four superalphas I recognized . . . there was a solid, darker green line around the chartreuse. I don't think I noticed it at the time, but just now, thinking about what they looked like and what it meant, I did see them. That's not normal."

He waited for her to go on.

"They were mutations."

"You'll have to explain where you're going with this," Sykes said.

"I've never seen them before."

He leaned closer. "I think you already said that, more or less."

"No—" she had to think about this some more "—I'm not ready to make a determination about them."

"You've already made it," he said, his voice dark and silky. It was more of a demand than a statement.

She raised her eyes, effortlessly re-creating what she had seen at Ward's. "I don't think they were human," she said quietly.

Absolute silence fell between them. He massaged her fingers, but she doubted if he knew what

151

he was doing. The pressure increased, but she didn't complain.

"Ward." The name burst from her. Agitation scrambled her senses. "I was going to Ward's. He'd been at the police station with Nat and they let him go home. I said I'd go and keep him company for a while."

The grip was so tight now she couldn't have pulled away if she had wanted to.

"Do you love Ward Bienville?" Sykes asked.

That made her angry. "How dare you ask that. Do you think we would have had sex if I loved someone else?"

He shook his head.

Impressions came and went—the black railings outside the Police District house. They had come from Fortunes before that, hadn't they? "Nat was at Fortunes," she said. "With Wazoo. He couldn't have been questioning Ward at the same time."

"It wasn't his case. . . . Other officers were with Ward."

"Oh, my gosh. I'm losing my mind. I spoke to Ward and said I'd go to St. Louis Street."

"Yes, but it wouldn't have made much difference because they took him back in for more questioning. As far as I know he's still there. It is Nat's case now."

"How do you know all this?"

"Nat called when we were on our way here."

She couldn't concentrate. "But . . ."

"Poppy, listen to me. I caught up with you at the police station. You talked to Ward on the phone and said you were going over there. I hypnotized you to stop you from going because we don't know whether or not the man's a murderer and—"

"Hypnotized me? Sykes, that's awful. That's like, like, kidnapping."

"I wasn't prepared to risk your safety. Do what you like about it. Report me to someone."

"Like the police?" She didn't like him making fun of her, not now. "You did something really wrong. Of course I can't go to the police but it was still wrong."

"I know."

"I don't remember coming here."

"You were still in a trance." He sounded miserable. "I had to get you away somewhere private until you came out of it."

A lot of other memories, most of them a great deal clearer, poured back for Poppy. "When exactly did I come out of the trance? Can you explain what we were doing, where we were and why you didn't tell me right off what you'd done?"

With his fingers, he rubbed up and down on his forehead.

"Sykes?"

"This is more awful than you think it is. Do you remember us making love?"

"Of course I do. Don't be ridiculous. There's still water all over the bathroom."

He groaned.

"What's the matter with you? Having regrets? You ran the bath and we made love."

His groan was more agonized this time.

"What? Tell me what's wrong—other than the obvious."

"You think I put you in a trance and took advantage of you."

Poppy thought about that. "I'm not sure. I liked making love with you—a lot."

"You said you wanted to," Sykes told her. "You, you—it was fabulous, like nothing I've ever experienced before. You're amazing."

She shrank inside. "You're pretty amazing yourself." But there was something she was missing here.

"Thank you. You liked being in control. Boy, I liked you being in control. I thought we'd kill ourselves falling off that table."

Cold didn't come close to describing the state of her skin, before it started to boil. "Which table would that be, Sykes?"

"Oh, hellfire. The one in the living room with the marble top we made love on."

"And that was my idea?"

"How do I know anymore," he said, his voice rising. "I'm dying here. I was afraid you weren't fully out of the trance but you kept insisting you wanted exactly what we did."

"What else did we do . . . exactly?"

He blew up his cheeks. "Oh, this and that. It'll come to you."

"Jog my memory."

"Poppy!"

"Do it."

He brought his hands down on her shoulders and held on. "You liked it, honestly. More than liked it. It was your idea." His mouth snapped shut.

"Yeah. Did you like it?"

"Oh, lordy, I never liked anything more than everything we did. When you took me out of my pants and made me come, I thought I'd passed into another world."

Very faintly she got a memory. She tasted him.

"You made me stand in front of you while—"

"Stop!" Poppy shook her head, no. "Okay, I get the picture."

"And then we changed places and—"

"If you say another word, I'll—"

"Not another word," Sykes said. "But you were wonderful."

"Sykes."

"Honestly, if you think about it, if the trance was hanging around you were only doing what came to you naturally. It was what you would have done if you weren't inhibited by—"

"Sykes, I warn you."

"Not another word. I'm sorry. I thought—at least,

I hoped everything was your conscious idea. When you first showed me your breasts I thought—"

Poppy scrambled past him, shot inside the bed and pulled the sheet over her head.

16

I've got to talk to you. Pascal's voice came to Sykes as strongly as if the other man were in the same room.

Lying on his back, Sykes had been listening to the relentless rain on the bedroom window but he leaned to see Poppy's face. Her eyes were closed and he hoped she really was sleeping. *I know I left at a difficult time. It couldn't be helped,* he told Pascal. *My fault but we can't go into that now.*

You mean you'd rather avoid the topic of illegal use of hypnosis?

Sykes ground his teeth. *Hardly illegal, Pascal.*

As you say, we'll go into that and other bent rules later. The boy is here, sleeping in my guest bedroom. He's exhausted. I couldn't push him too far when he seems sick or something.

Sykes foresaw considerable problems over his unwise practice of hypnosis. *He is probably scared. Had to have taken everything he had to show up on your doorstep like that.* At least Pascal had the skills to repel any straightforward human attack. Sykes pulled his lips back from his teeth. He really should not have left Pascal—and

Marley—alone with a boy who walked in off the street.

Did Gray come for Marley?

Yes. And they both stayed until the boy was in bed and asleep. Or at least in the room with the door shut. We have nothing to fear from him.

Unless he's some sort of renegade extreme talent.

You believe he is who he says he is, Sykes?

Damn, that's what this early morning mind chatter was about—Pascal was panicked and Sykes didn't blame him. *You're the one to answer that question.* He eased off the bed, grabbed a pair of jeans in passing and carefully left the room.

This is damned embarrassing. Anthony thinks it's cute. Cute, mind you. He's talking about what good parents we'll make for a troubled kid because we're not judgmental. Says the Goth shows how sensitive the boy is.

Sykes was glad that, unlike himself, Pascal couldn't summon up an image of a psychic he contacted long distance. If he could, he would not appreciate Sykes's grin. In fact, without Sykes's help, his uncle could not track other psychics who were out of his range. They had set up an emergency channel for Pascal to make contact with Sykes, and Pascal was using that now. Fair enough, Sykes decided.

What are you thinking? Pascal said.

Sykes crept downstairs. *That Anthony's a nice guy. He has to be to put up with you.*

He is more than nice, Pascal said. He didn't sound amused. *If the boy is what—who—he says he is, what am I supposed to do about it?*

Sykes grinned again. *So you admit this David could be your son?*

Pascal's silence lasted so long that Sykes had time to hop into his jeans and make it to the studio where he turned on the lights and shut himself in. What, he wondered, would Pascal think of the inscrutable piece of marble?

We have all gone through our wild younger days, Pascal said at last. *I just don't remember anything that wild.*

Being with a woman, you mean?

All these things are a matter of perspective, young man. This was Pascal at his haughty best once more.

Not all things, Uncle, but many. Where were you when David was, er?

Another heavy and angry gap in conversation began.

He's eighteen? Sykes said. If Pascal wanted help with this he would have to be open.

I don't want to discuss this, Pascal snapped. *What I want from you is an agreement to take over as head of the family. That way I don't have to worry about some young punk showing up and saying he has a claim to what belongs to the rest of you.*

158

It sounded to me as if the only claim he's making is to you. It's not uncommon for a young person —or anyone, in fact—to want to find a parent.

He imagined Pascal's shudder and was tempted to take a look at him, but decency prevailed. They did subscribe to the rules of decent privacy supposedly found in the Book of the Way.

Please, Sykes. I haven't asked you for many things but this is for the entire family. Please say you will shoulder the burden with me while I work out a way to pass the mantle entirely to you.

I don't want the entire bloody mantle. Sykes puffed hair out of his eyes.

I meant—um—on paper, of course. I promise I will be your partner. It's just that we can't risk some newcomer complicating matters.

Pascal, where were you—

Not now, Pascal said loudly. Then he lowered his voice. *If you give me your word that you'll work with me, I won't kick him out in the street.*

That left Sykes without an easy comeback. Finally he said, *That would not be my responsibility.*

You don't feel any responsibility for a boy who may be your cousin?

The stone glistened under the overhead white lights, beckoning. Sykes grew impatient. *First things first. We find out if this boy was conceived while you were in a moment of confusion.*

How dare you.

Be cordial. Listen to anything he has to say. When I can get there, I will. It won't be in the morning.

Pascal made a grumbling noise. *That damnable Mario has gone to ground. Anthony picked him up at the airport and brought him here. He took off somewhere around the courtyard and we haven't found him yet.*

It took Sykes only moments to remember Ben and Willow's dog who had been sent home to New Orleans for a vet's appointment. Craziness. *Willow loves that dog more than she loves you,* he said, deliberately unkind. *You'd better hope he surfaces again. Goodbye.*

He let his guard drop firmly and instantly into place and locked Pascal out, at least until he felt he had the strength to deal with him again.

The stone with its amazing shapes and textures magnetized him. With his hands extended, he approached and let his fingers run over the surface. In places it was silky, in other spots the finish was rough. Most of the gold veins had a porous quality, much of the green, especially where it was a brighter shade, felt as if it had been polished.

He checked his watch. This room was soundproofed so he could work without fear of Poppy hearing him, but he didn't want her to wake up and be confused. He winced. Not more confused than she was already.

160

She had not insisted on rushing away from the house, although he thought she might have left at once if it were daylight. He wasn't even sure if she was deeply angry with him for exerting power over her, but was she embarrassed at learning she was anything but an unwilling partner in their . . . encounters?

Muscles tightened and a shiver went through him. Being with her was unbelievable—but he was willing to try making it real, again and again.

He took up a pointed chisel and a small mallet to refine the line of the arm he had revealed, but he was drawn to the neck. It was young and inclined to one side. As he worked, the lobe of an ear followed naturally and the start of hair, full and flowing away from the jaw.

An image came to him. A woman with a joyful face, but then, he had known this would be a woman. The questions were, who was she and why was she here in his studio?

The hair was fuller than he expected, with windswept smooth lines. What he had done was very crude, but he could see where he was being guided.

Then it was all a little jumble, lumpy and almost formless. He hesitated.

He must get back to the bedroom before Poppy woke up.

The overhead lights grew dimmer. Sykes glanced up at them and watched the beams pale to yellow, flicker off, then on, only the shade had turned purple and hovered above his head, a glowing purple cloud.

Sykes prepared himself. He breathed deeply and opened his senses wide, ready for whatever was to come.

Purple turned violet and intense, a fog that shrouded the studio. And he heard whispering. He knew from Marley and Willow that they also heard similar sounds, particularly Marley when she was traveling. And Ben spoke of faint laughter and light voices in the Court of Angels. Ben also insisted the faces of the angels there changed, but Sykes had never seen it happen.

It is time to discuss the Harmony and what it holds. This was the voice of Jude. Sykes would know it anywhere.

Welcome, he told the newcomer. *I wasn't expecting you.*

I am never expected, Jude said. *Those who went before me hoped it would never be necessary to seek out the Harmony but I begin to be sure the time has come. I have seen things changing.*

Through the violet film, fading to mauve in places and drifting into green, Sykes saw Jude. As autocratically handsome as ever, the white streaks in his black hair seemed no more or less than when he had last appeared. His clothing, from another time and place, fitted him perfectly. His image was not clear and although he wasn't in the semi-invisible state Sykes liked to play with himself, neither was he substantial.

I've never heard of the Harmony, Sykes said, and he didn't think he wanted to.

It is explained in the preamble to the Book of the Way. It was written by one of our ancestors with help from several unrelated paranormals of his time, members of other families. Families you are aware of.

The Fortunes? Sykes asked at once. *Perhaps the Montrachets?*

Perhaps.

With respect, Sykes said, aware that he had better be respectful but he was on overload. The past couple of days had come at him like rockets. *With respect, sir, I'd like to see this preamble. If it's so important at this time, I need to be aware of it. If you want me to do something about it, that is.*

You will have to find the angel, Jude said. *I had hoped you would do so by now, but . . .* He made a disappointed gesture.

How are we supposed to know which angel we're looking for? Sykes said. *There are so many of them.*

If you had found her, we would know, Jude said. *The ones who want this city are acting differently. Expect more of them to come, perhaps many more.*

Sykes rotated his shoulders. *Is it to be some sort of invasion, then?*

I cannot say with certainty. My concern is for the family and those closest to them. The Harmony was created in case a great power was ever needed. It is well-guarded and beyond price. It is with the angel.

Frustration overwhelmed Sykes. He pointed to the foot-high piece of marble on its plinth. *You sent that to me, you must have. Is it part of the answer?*

Hurry, was all Jude said. *I don't know how long we have so you must hurry. You need the preamble. It will show you who our closest allies are, the ones we can call on if the worst comes.*

Gliding, Jude approached. The book appeared in his hands, large with a heavy gold cover studded with gems.

He turned it to face Sykes and opened the front cover to the flyleaf. This was the Book of the Way, the Millet family rules.

This is our book, Sykes pointed out. *Why would others have anything to do with what was written in it?*

Because we were entrusted with what was written. We were to keep it safe and make sure it was acted upon if it became necessary—for the good of all our kind.

Sykes ran his eyes over the yellowing parchment. *Show me.*

Jude turned the flyleaf and smoothed it flat. He put the book closer to Sykes who leaned over it.

He wanted to touch the paper, not that he would be allowed to make contact even if he did try.

Close to the spine he saw the ragged edges of a number of pages that had been torn out. He glanced quickly up at Jude. *This preamble you talk about. Is this where it's supposed to be? Is it gone?*

Stolen, Jude said simply. *And unfortunately I never saw it, so you must find it.*

You said you knew all about it.

I know its message but not the details and that is why I cannot tell you more. He turned several more pages and there, in deep yellow, was a circle divided into segments from its center, like a wheel. *I believe this is the Harmony with its seven partitions. Count them.*

Sykes did so and nodded.

There are seven keys needed to open the sections and get to the Ultimate Power inside.

But we don't have all of them, Sykes pointed out.

Jude closed the book and began to distance himself. *Liam Fortune may know something,* he said and faded from sight.

17

No way would Sykes allow Poppy to return to Fortunes alone. He wasn't sure he would be able to let her go anywhere alone until he had answers to the questions coming at them like bullets fired at close quarters.

They went into the building by a side door and Sykes set aside the umbrella they had used. The streets were hot and steamy—and breathless.

"I don't need a bodyguard," Poppy said. "You've got other things to do."

He took hold of her arm and made her look at him. "You matter a lot to me. More than a lot. I'm not leaving until I make sure you're in a safe place."

Her lips parted and he saw her struggle with her emotions. She pulled away. "I am in a safe place. This is where I live and work."

She marched along a deserted passageway past storage closets, freezer compartments and eventually the kitchens. Sykes prepared himself for another confrontation with Liam or Ethan who had every right to disbelieve any arguments Poppy and Sykes came up with about not being involved with each other.

When it came to Liam, finding a way to ask Jude's question was uppermost in Sykes's mind.

"Um, Sykes." Poppy skidded to a halt and faced him.

Their eyes met for long enough to make him reach for her, but Poppy held up her palms. "We've got to get our acts together. This can't be all about sex."

"Is that what it is for you? All about sex?"

She made an ugly face. "Tricks and traps. What else should I expect from a man who gets me from the bathroom to the bedroom without my seeing anything happen."

Inspiration hit Sykes and he ran with it. He leaned against a wall, crossed one foot over the other and assumed partial invisibility.

Poppy's eyes enlarged in a very satisfying way. "What are you doing?" she whispered, looking around. "What if someone comes?"

"I choose who sees me like this. At the moment, you're the only one who knows I'm here at all. Now, could I get your attention, please?"

She gaped.

"That'll do," he said. "Good reaction." And to increase the effect, he rose a foot from the floor while keeping his position against the wall.

"Sykes," she squeaked.

"Just listen. I know your brothers are going to look at us as if we just got out of the same bed."

"We did." She did another quick visual of the area.

"We can deal with it in one of two ways. Let them think that or try to keep denying the obvious."

She turned pink and moaned. Sykes grimaced. "Am I so awful you don't want anyone to think you'd sleep with me?"

"Keep your voice down," Poppy said. "I *don't* go around sleeping with just anyone."

Sykes inclined his head. "How am I supposed to take that remark?"

"Don't take it at all. I'm not making sense because I'm rattled and it's all your fault." She wiggled a forefinger at him. "You hypnotized me without permission and that was a creepy thing to do. You invaded my privacy, took over my body and mind."

"I know, and then I forced you to make love with me."

She looked away quickly. "No, you didn't. You were right when you said the trance must have gotten rid of my inhibitions. I did what I wanted to do."

"So did I. But it wasn't just about sex. I really like you, Poppy. I care about you. I don't know where we're going, but that doesn't seem like such a bad start."

He thought her eyes filled with tears. Then she looked up at him and he knew they had. "What is it, Poppy?"

"Have you forgiven me for being a selfish pig?"

"It isn't for me to forgive and I don't think you're a selfish anything. But let's save the topic. I've got to be certain Liam and Ethan know to keep an eye on you if I'm not around. It's possible we need to have a chat with Nat about police surveillance."

"Please don't do that." She sounded desperate. "We have no proof that anything's really wrong yet."

"One woman is dead? At Ward's you saw four

people you think weren't human? Nothing wrong?"

"I could have made a mistake about those people."

"And you could be right. We're not taking the risk. There are enough of us to look out for each other and that's what we're going to do." Jude had made the point and Sykes agreed with him.

"I'm not helpless, Sykes. I won't take any stupid risks."

"If Ward Bienville is released, will you spend time with him alone?"

She peered into the kitchen, obviously buying time.

"Poppy?"

"If it looks like that could happen, I'll let someone know. Okay?"

It wasn't, but he had no right to push too far. "Be very careful."

The door from the club banged open.

Ethan Fortune stopped in the act of hurrying into the passageway. "Poppy! What the hell is the matter with you? Are you going to keep scaring the hell out of us?"

Sykes backed up until he could reappear and join the two of them without Ethan seeing what he was up to. "Calm down, Counselor," Sykes said, hoping his own easy smile would defuse the other man's anger.

Ethan, the youngest of the Fortune brothers,

169

glared at Sykes. They were all blue-eyed and dark-haired, these male Fortunes. Too bad the Millets couldn't get over their aversion to the same coloring in their own family. Poppy's were the only dark eyes among her siblings.

Every time she looked his way, Sykes got sucked in by Poppy's eyes.

"Okay, you two," Ethan said. There was not the faintest crack in his anger. "Liam told me he met you coming back here together yesterday. Today it's me who has the honor. Both times neither of us saw you for hours, Poppy. You're a big girl. What you do is your—"

"Business," she finished for him. "That's right. Why are you so doggone edgy?"

Ethan looked here, there and everywhere but at Poppy.

"Look at me," Poppy told him.

She got the brilliant-blue Fortune stare. "We love you. Is that okay? We're worried about you. Is that okay?" He threw up his hands. "For cryin' out loud. If we know you're with Sykes and not a maybe murderer, we won't be eating our nails up to the knuckles."

"Ward isn't a murderer," Poppy said.

"You don't know that for sure," Sykes said quietly.

"Okay. Would you mind coming through the club to the office?" Ethan said. "I don't think we should be doing this out here. It'll get busy soon enough."

"It's only seven-thirty in the morning," Poppy pointed out. "It isn't going to be busy for hours. But it's fine with me to use my office."

The inference was clear. She didn't appreciate what appeared to be a general takeover of her life—and her office—by her brothers.

"Follow me," Ethan said, his face set. He pushed open a padded door into the very blue Fortunes club. "Things aren't quite as quiet as you seem to think. We've already got visitors and they're looking for you, Sis."

Liam met them in the middle of the club floor. He didn't take his attention off Poppy. "What are you trying to do to us?" he said, turning a little red.

Then he did look at Sykes. "Don't worry, I'm not going to make the mistake of jumping to any conclusions again—not out loud. But I know what I think and I don't understand what the pair of you are playing at."

"Really?" Sykes said, all innocence.

Poppy elbowed him. "When everyone's calmed down, Sykes and I will explain what's happened."

That should be interesting.

"Where's your cell phone?" Liam said to Poppy.

She pulled it out of her jeans' pocket. "Right where it usually is. On me."

With finger and thumb, Liam took it from her. "It helps if you turn it on." He did so himself and handed it back. "Your buddy Ward called here three times before I told him I'd let him know when I saw you. Ethan's tried to get you, and so have I."

"I'm sorry, okay?" Poppy looked furious. "I'm not ten. I don't have to tell anyone where I am."

"You sure as hell don't have to tell me," Liam said, poking his face into hers. "Just as long as I'm pretty sure you're alive."

A few employees were busy cleaning in the bar or polishing the brass tables but they still managed to send interested glances at the Fortunes.

"Nat's in the office with Bucky Fist," Liam said. "They just got here. I was coming to see if Ethan had found you."

"Where did Ward call from?" Poppy asked.

"How should I know?"

Sykes began to feel sorry for Poppy's brothers. He knew how it felt to worry about someone who meant a lot to you.

The door to Poppy's office opened and Bucky Fist, Nat Archer's partner, came out. As always he wore a baseball cap back to front on his sandy hair and twirled a toothpick between wide-spaced front teeth.

"Later," he said, passing them. "Nat wants to talk to you first, Sykes, and Liam. Poppy, hang around, please."

"How did you know we were here?" Poppy said.

"Wazoo was keeping watch," Bucky said and sauntered out of the club.

18

Wazoo waved from a corner booth.

"Has Nat managed to persuade her to stay in New Orleans?" Sykes asked. "I wouldn't have expected him to take her to work with him."

"That's mean," Poppy said promptly and meant it. "She could be here to see me. Did you think of that?"

Sykes rubbed her arm and smiled. "Sorry. I'm surprised to see her is all."

Her arm tingled and just looking at his smile made sure everything else tingled, too. "You'd better get in there to Nat," she said, softening her voice. "Although I can't think why he wants to see either of you."

From Liam's frown, Poppy figured her brother didn't know, either.

Both men left and Poppy went to greet Wazoo. "Is Nat's plan to keep you here working?" She knew what she had just said was not so different from Sykes's suggestion. And she did not feel guilty.

"Sit with me and I might just tell you somethin' about it," Wazoo said. The mug of coffee wrapped in her hands smelled too good. "You want coffee? Hah, I guess you're the one to see about that."

Poppy gave the bartender a high sign and pointed to Wazoo's mug, signaling for a second serving. She slid in beside the other woman who was as darkly dramatic today as yesterday.

Wazoo looked into Poppy's face. "You are gorgeous, girl. But you know that."

Poppy started to return the compliment but Wazoo cut her off. "I'm gorgeous, too, I know. We gorgeous girls got to make the best of ourselves —and the best use of ourselves, if you know what I mean." She winked.

Laughing, Poppy nodded to the barman, Otis, who delivered a second mug and topped up Wazoo's.

"They're making beignets in the kitchen," Otis said. "You tempted?"

Before Poppy could comment, Wazoo said, "Hoo mama, I could eat a hundred of those babies for a starter."

Otis left with a big smile on his face, and Poppy caught a flash of light from Wazoo's lap. She took a better look and jumped. "You've got a dog there!" What she had seen were bright eyes staring at her.

"I'm watching him for Nat," Wazoo said.

Poppy said, "Oh," and decided a dog was just fine in the club if it was with a cop—maybe.

"I don't know if I'm going to tell Nat this, but the poor little thing has far too much on his mind."

Not a single word of response came to Poppy.

"He's a master at covering up his feelings." Wazoo stroked the dog's wiry fur, and Poppy heard him sigh. "He looks so relaxed, but inside he's like a jumble of overstretched rubber bands. I just don't know how much more he can take."

Still nothing came to Poppy.

"Oh." Wazoo patted Poppy's shoulder. "You are lookin' at me like I've got horns." She laughed. "I probably do only you can't see them. I'm an animal psychologist, among other things. I feel what they feel and see what they see—and I know when they are distressed. This is one distressed dog."

Poppy found her voice. "And you don't think Nat ought to know this?" She had forgotten the animal-psychologist bit.

Wazoo stretched the dog up until he stood with his back feet on her lap and his front feet on her neck. "We will make sure he gets whatever he needs. Are you gettin' what you need, Poppy?"

She had another jaw-dropping instant.

"With Nat and me it's interesting. Who would have thought he'd ever take a second look at me?" The dog curled up on her lap again.

"It doesn't surprise me," Poppy said. "As you've already admitted, you're gorgeous."

"Surely, but I am not, well, I'm not the woman a man waits for because she's the right one to take home to his mama."

Poppy had coffee in her mouth and she burned her throat when she swallowed and laughed at the same time.

"I haven't met Nat's mama," Wazoo said, looking pleased with Poppy's reaction. "I'm not sure he has a mama. But if he does she has got to be some good-looking woman. One look at that man and all those important parts of me do the two-step—fast."

Getting the rhythm of this conversation, Poppy said, "Sounds to me like you've made up your mind where you belong. Must be time to stop torturing Nat and tell him you're his."

Beignets arrived on an oval platter big enough for the Thanksgiving turkey—for twenty-four people—and Wazoo promptly took a large, sugary bite out of the closest one before tearing off a piece for the dog.

"I see things," she said when she could speak again. "That worries some folks. They don't like it."

"What kind of things?" Poppy turned sideways on the seat to look directly at Wazoo.

She got just as straight a return stare. "Things. I don't talk about them unless I think I ought to. Usually because I like someone. I don't know you well but Nat says you're good people, so that makes you okay with me."

Poppy ran a forefinger through powdered sugar on the edge of the platter and put the finger in her mouth.

"Sometimes we women keep things private," Wazoo said. "You know what I mean?"

"I'm not sure."

"Men are special. I'm real glad we've got them around, but they don't think the same as we do."

"Mmm." Poppy screwed up her eyes. "I'll give you that."

"I'll give it to you straight. If Nat finds out I talked to you about things I'm not about to discuss with him, I may never meet his mama—if he's got one."

Poppy gave a little smile. "We can talk between the two of us. As long as you haven't robbed a bank or something."

When Wazoo smiled she looked like a teenager—a beautiful teenager. "Not yet, ma'am. It's you I need to say somethin' about. You and the men in your life. I thought a long time before I came with Nat today. And I had to do some persuading to get him to let me come at all. You and I hit it off yesterday, that's what I reminded him. And he thought it was a good idea for the two of us to get together again."

"Nat's crazy about you," Poppy said. Why not toss some of her own reserve to the winds? "I think he'd forgive you anything, if he thought there was anything to forgive."

Wazoo's smile was secretive. Coy wasn't something she could ever be. "I'd say that's the way your sexy Sykes feels about you."

Sometimes Poppy thought she needed help speeding up the way she thought. Almost everything that came out of Wazoo's mouth didn't have an obvious response.

"He is drop-dead fabulous," Wazoo said. "He's the kind of man makes a woman want to turn herself inside out for him. I bet he's some kind of wonderful in bed. Probably leaves you feelin' he's stripped off your skin and you'd give him your flesh and bones to go with it."

"Um." Poppy looked around. She had done that a lot this morning.

"I'm not asking you to give away any details. I can't help it when I see a man and a woman made to get joined up together as often as possible. It makes me happy." She lowered her voice. "Makes me feel sexy, too. But don't you ever tell Nat that."

"No."

"You need to work hard to snap up that man of yours. Don't let anything get in your way. Do it fast. There's trouble coming and if you—" she paused and looked into the distance, absently stroking the dog. "If you don't keep your eyes wide open and stay close to Sykes, you could be in deep shit."

Poppy cleared her throat. The way the hairs on her spine rose was more than nasty. It would be easier on her to write Wazoo off as weird, but Nat Archer wouldn't be so close to someone who was weird.

"Nat looks like a movie star," Poppy said but her heart wasn't in it. "Denzel Washington move over."

"He doesn't look anything like Denzel Washington. Not that Denzel isn't a peach. No one looks like Nat. The first time I saw him in Toussaint, I said to myself, 'That is the sexiest man you ever saw, Wazoo. Maybe you got to do something about that.' So I did. The problem is . . ." She frowned. "We're talking about you and the blue-eyed raven. How is it to have his arms wrapped around you and that luscious mouth doin' some of the things it can do to you?"

Poppy felt almost weak. She was grateful when Otis came by to fill their coffee mugs.

"You can tell me all about that later," Wazoo said, tucking into another beignet. "Let's get to the other one. I don't have anything on him yet, or not much, but from what Nat said, I'm not inclined to approve of him."

"Other one?"

"The man who wants to run Louisiana."

"You mean Ward?" Poppy said. She drank more coffee. "Ward is a nice man. He's probably going to run for the senate—if they don't stick him with a murder rap."

"Murder?" Wazoo whispered, her eyes huge. "Huh, that wouldn't be so good, would it? I mean if he wanted to be a senator."

Poppy wrinkled her nose. "You'd think. Could be it wouldn't matter at all."

"You listen to me, Poppy Fortune. Is this other man real interested in you like I think he is?"

"Who told you that?"

Wazoo looked blank. She cleared her throat and said, "Nat."

"He thinks he is. He started coming here and decided I was something special, probably because I didn't show any interest in him."

Wazoo's fist came down on the table and she laughed, showing all of her perfect teeth. "Isn't that the way with them. They want most what they think they might not get. Good, 'cause you belong with Sykes."

Do I? Poppy wondered.

"There's been a lot of parties for this—what's his name?"

"Ward Bienville."

"Sounds like a money name," Wazoo remarked. "Parties to raise interest and money? Is that right?"

"Absolutely."

Wazoo got her distant look again. "What else are those parties for?"

"I don't know. Nothing, I suppose."

"We'll see," Wazoo said. She held the dog close and it didn't seem to mind being squeezed. "We'll have lunch today."

"That would be great," Poppy said without thinking about it.

"It won't be till after, though."

"After what?" Poppy asked.

Wazoo shrugged and signaled to Otis.

19

Waiting for Nat's attention had started to grate on Sykes. He wanted to get to Royal Street, but not until he had made sure Liam or Ethan understood the importance of keeping tabs on Poppy.

Nat had been on the phone ever since they had joined him in Poppy's office and since he might as well have been talking in code, even that didn't ease the irritation.

Poppy's office didn't contain anything blue that Sykes could see. The room was as spare as he liked to keep his own spaces. Nat sat at her glass-topped desk. Liam and Sykes used two cube-shaped gray leather armchairs a shade or two lighter than the wall-to-wall carpet. The walls were an even paler shade of gray.

Nat got up and turned his back on them. "Rotary?" he said. "Corkscrew? What the hell does that mean?"

Sykes leaned closer to Liam. "Poppy must not be allowed to go off on her own. And she can't be with Ward Bienville unless we keep an eye on them." He raised his brows at Liam. "I'm sure you know what I mean."

"We're going to spy on my sister if she's alone with him. No problem. I'm with you all the way." Liam studied Nat's broad back to make sure the policeman was still engrossed in his conversation. "Anything else on your mind?" he asked, when he was satisfied they wouldn't be overheard.

"A suggestion was made that I should ask you a question."

Liam cocked his head. "Ask."

"What do you know about changes in the situation with the Embran?"

This time Liam wasn't so quick to answer. He raised his shoulders. "Nothing. At least, I don't think I do. All the information I get comes from you and your family. We're ready to be of assistance when you give us the word."

"You can't think of anything you've heard or seen that might be a clue to what they're planning?"

"No."

Sykes changed the subject. "Did Ben say anything to you about finding some really small gold keys?"

"When?"

"Right before he Bonded with Willow and they took off for Kauai."

Liam shook his head slowly. "No, he didn't. Are you going to fill me in?"

"Probably," Sykes told him, "but . . ." He didn't finish because Nat cut off his cell phone connection and turned toward them.

"Is Poppy out there, I hope?" he said.

"Uh-huh," Sykes said. "What's this about . . . separating us for questioning?"

Nat gave his charming white smile. "Well now, am I separating you from Poppy, or Liam from Poppy? Or Poppy from both of you?"

"Things have been tense around here," Liam told him. "Not much is amusing me right now."

Liam said aloud what Sykes was thinking. And Sykes was grateful.

"Poppy could just as well have been in here. I wanted to give her some time with Wazoo. Wazoo likes her and I can use all the persuasion I can get to convince that woman she needs to move from Toussaint to New Orleans."

The argument didn't convince Sykes, but he let it go.

"You and Poppy arrived together this morning?" Nat asked Sykes. "Her brothers hadn't seen her since yesterday. Was she with you all that time?"

"Am I providing Poppy with an alibi?"

"What the hell are you talking about?" Liam sputtered.

"Just pulling his chain," Sykes said. "Yes, Poppy was with me. All except for when she took a little nap at my sister Marley's place. Marley was there. So I can account for her every minute of the time."

"All night long?" Nat said. He returned to the black leather chair behind Poppy's heavy glass desk and jotted on a notepad. "Until you got here?"

Sykes peered sideways at Liam. "Yes." He would rather Poppy had been there to speak for herself.

Liam drummed his fingers on his thighs.

"How about you?" Nat asked Liam. "Anyone who'll admit to spending the night with you?"

Liam smiled. "Unfortunately not. I slept in my cold little bed alone."

"But you didn't get there until pretty late, hmm?"

Sykes glanced at Liam who frowned and wrinkled his nose.

"I'll take that as a yes. Just trying to put everyone somewhere last night. Someone was pretty busy. We've got another body. Male this time, but there are some similarities to Sonia Gardner's death."

"What kind of similarities?" Sykes asked bluntly. "Was this guy wearing a silver dress, too?"

"Ha, ha, ha." Nat leaned forward and rested his elbows. "You were at some sort of high-price-ticket event last night, Liam?"

"It could be as high priced as you wanted it to be, depending on whether you felt like giving a lot of money away. I didn't. I was there because I'm a curious man. It was possible I could learn something that would be interesting to a member of my family, so I went."

"But you were invited?"

"Yeah. I imagine everyone will be eventually. It was here in the Quarter. A fundraiser for Ward Bienville's potential senate run. I guess you'd call it a name-gathering event to draw in would-be contributors. I went because Ward has a thing for Poppy and I'd like to know more about him."

"You didn't mention any invitation when I was here yesterday," Nat pointed out.

"I would have preferred it if no one knew I went. It wasn't my kind of thing. And Poppy would be furious if she knew. She considers Ward a friend."

"Was the new body found wherever the party was?" Sykes said.

"That's not public information." Nat looked at Sykes. "But, yes, the body was found at the party."

He got the stunned silence he must have expected.

"That makes two nights, two fundraisers or whatever and one person from each event murdered. You and Poppy both attended the first event, Sykes. Liam was at the second one."

"Lucky us," Sykes said, meeting Liam's eyes.

"I don't know how long I can keep the powers that be from turning all their attention on you and the rest of the . . . the rest of your close friends," Nat said. "Bad news follows you around."

"You've seen enough to know what we've been up against," Sykes said, and stood up. "You were there the last time. You saw those *things* at work trying to kill us—or kidnap us, if they could. We're the good guys, remember?"

Nat nodded. He breathed deeply and let his head hang back. "Liam, did you see or hear anything unusual last night? Nothing is too insignificant to repeat."

"He's got that right," Sykes muttered. "Why did they have the party without the party boy?"

"A woman and three men who said they were Ward's advisors did the honors. And they didn't say Ward had been taken in by the police, if that's what you're looking for. They just kept repeating that he'd gotten held up by someone very influential."

"I guess I just got more important," Nat said. He didn't smile. "Nothing else you can tell me?"

Liam shifted in his chair. "Just the weirdo in the bathroom."

He crossed his arms and met Nat's eyes.

"And?" Nat said.

"Followed me in as if he didn't know it was a one-customer-at-a-time variety, and shut the door."

That got Sykes's full attention, too. "You're kidding."

"Stood there staring at me as if I ought to know him. Kind of a smile on his face. When he moved I thought he was leaving. I expected him to apologize. When he didn't, I made kind of, 'after you' motions and started to get out of there. Only he blocked my way."

Nat threw down his pen and gave Liam his full attention.

"Look," Liam said, "this is going to sound off

the wall. He walked straight at me until he slammed into me." Turning his face, he pointed to a red mark on his jaw.

"Right into you?" Sykes said. "Deliberately?"

"The real kicker was that he looked more puzzled about it than I did. He kept looking into my eyes like he was trying to see inside my head. His eyes were too big or something. Then he backed up a couple of steps and did it again. Wham."

Nat squinched up his eyes. "Had to be drunk or something."

"I don't think so," Liam said. "He turned away and left, shut the door hard enough to make the thing rattle."

"You didn't go after—"

"Sure I went after him. The bathroom was in a kind of curved corridor. I must have chosen the wrong direction. I ran back toward the party and he hadn't gone that way. By the time I went the other way there was no sign of him."

20

Every few seconds Poppy glanced at her office, expecting to see the men coming out.

"They won't be much longer," Wazoo said.

"Good." Poppy looked quickly at her companion. "How do you know?"

"Just a wild guess." She reached into a skirt pocket and pulled out something, which she pressed into Poppy's hand. "This is nothing, just a little thing because I like you so much."

In her hand Poppy held a dark green velvet bag embroidered with even darker green beads. It hung on a silk cord. "It's cute," she said.

Wazoo folded Poppy's hand over the bag. "It's also special. I think you know what I mean. Please, for my sake, keep it with you at all times. You can easily wear it under your clothes."

Slipping the cord around her neck, Poppy put the soft bag with it's slightly lumpy filling under her T-shirt. She wasn't sure what she thought about fetishes, amulets, but things were strange all over so why not hedge her bets?

"Thank you," she said. "You made it, didn't you?"

"It would be worthless if I hadn't." She leaned to see around Poppy in the other direction. "And here comes more interesting company looking for you."

The interesting company was Ward this time. He strode into the club in that way he had of seeming to take up all the space around him. And he didn't look as if he'd spent harrowing hours under police questioning.

"There you are, honey," he said, spotting Poppy and switching paths. "I finally decided I would come here and wait until you showed up. To be blunt, I kind of thought you'd be here anyway. Did your brothers tell you I've been trying to get you for hours?"

"They did," Poppy said, overwhelmed as she usually was by his larger-than-life presence. He seemed to pull a whirl of air with him and anyone in earshot stopped to watch.

His cream silk shirt was open at the neck to show a V of tanned skin and his pants, light brown and also silk, hit the well-toned muscle in his thighs with every step.

He slid in beside Poppy and tipped her face up to his. She didn't react quite fast enough to evade the kiss he dropped on her lips. "You have no idea what those goons put me through," he said, holding the sides of her head as if she were made of fine china.

"Couldn't have been that bad," Wazoo said from the corner recesses of the booth. "You look pretty fresh and feisty to me."

Ward looked at her as if he hadn't noticed she was there before.

"This is my friend, Wazoo," Poppy said. "And her friend's dog."

"Yeah" was the most reaction that got. "Best news in the world, sweetheart. It's all over. The monster who did that to poor Sonia showed up on the surveillance tapes from my place. But she didn't die for nothing. No, sir, not for nothing. I'm going full steam ahead now, because I believe Sonia died so someone could use her to stop me doing what I set out to do. Well, it's not going to work."

Wazoo sang, "How Come My Dog Doesn't Bark When You Come Around?" Not quite under her breath.

Poppy didn't know where to look or who to talk to, but she did see the door to her office open and Nat emerge with Sykes and Liam.

They came toward the booth but paused when Ethan appeared from the back, briefcase in hand. The four of them exchanged a few words before Ethan walked out of the club.

"That must be another of your brothers," Wazoo said. "My, oh, my, such delectable men there are in the French Quarter. There's something irresistible about a really dark man."

If Ward wasn't so self-confident he might notice the comment, but he knew he was good-looking, dark or not.

"Having a good time, ladies?" Liam said. The moment he stood beside the table he took a beignet and a napkin and managed to eat the now-cold dough without dropping a speck of sugar.

"We were," Wazoo said with a glance in Ward's direction.

"Hey, Archer," Ward said. "You still following me?"

"No," Nat said shortly. "Have you met Liam Fortune and Sykes Millet?"

Ward gave the two men a sunny inspection. "Hey, Liam, it feels good to be back here. Where have I seen you, Sykes?"

"A lot of people seem familiar," Sykes said flatly. He obviously wasn't happy to see Ward.

Poppy caught his eye and recoiled from his deadpan expression.

The deadpan disappeared fast and dramatically. "Mario," he said, pointing at the dog Wazoo held. "My sister Willow's dog. Where did you find him?"

"He followed Nat in here, and Nat said for me to look after him. Now I understand the poor little boy's confusion." She hugged him close. "You got lost, but you'll be just fine now. Relax and let all the tension out."

Poppy actually heard the dog sigh.

"Sheesh, I'd better call Pascal," Sykes said. "Ben and Willow shipped the dog home from Kauai yesterday for a vet's visit. Pascal said they'd lost him and they were worried sick."

"He walked right up to me outside," Nat said. "Good boy, aren't you?" He reached across the table to scratch Mario between his ears.

"Must have come here looking for Ben and Willow," Liam said. "Must be a bloodhound in disguise."

"I was just telling Poppy my good news," Ward said and sounded unusually strained.

"That Sonia Gardner apparently wasn't murdered by you, but by someone else?" Nat said.

"Exactly. Not that anyone could seriously have thought I was capable of something like that.

Wow, I'm going to celebrate. We're going to celebrate, aren't we, sweetheart?"

Poppy could feel Sykes's reaction without looking at him. He went stiff. When she did look at him his face was devoid of expression.

"Too bad Sonia can't be around for the celebration," Nat said, dropping his face and looking up at Ward from beneath well-defined brows.

"Poor, poor girl," Wazoo said. "Do you have the killer in custody, Nat?"

He frowned at her.

"Sorry." She hunched her shoulders. "I forgot I'm not supposed to ask questions like that."

"Who did you say this was?" Ward said, looking pointedly at Wazoo now.

"My very good friend," Nat said. "My best friend."

All eyes were on Wazoo who swallowed visibly. She held Mario close but only had eyes for Nat.

This was not, Poppy decided, a one-way love.

"I'm taking my girl to Bayona for lunch," Ward said leaning over Poppy. He lowered his voice but not enough to stop everyone from hearing what he said. "I didn't waste my time this morning. I got you a little something to say sorry for putting you through so much. Sweetheart, you know I would never deliberately worry you."

"Whoops," Wazoo said and fanned herself with one hand. "Is it getting hot in here or is it just me? This isn't your day after all, Mr. er . . . Poppy and Sykes are all tied up already. Spa for couples. Oh, my. Let me tell you *that* is some experience. Although, I guess, it's what you make it. What is that place called?"

"Hands On," Liam supplied helpfully.

Poppy wanted to laugh until Sykes said, "It wasn't that easy to get a reservation but I suppose . . ." He let the rest trail off but he had already showed Poppy just how much he did *not* want her with Ward.

"Don't be silly," Wazoo said. "Poppy's been looking forward to it all morning."

"I'll need you with me, Wazoo," Nat said gruffly. "We'll get Mario back to Royal Street for Sykes. I need a few words with Gray anyway. He may be there."

"Poppy?" Ward said.

"I'm sorry to spoil your plans." She smiled apologetically at him and when he didn't move, Wazoo hastily left the booth to let Poppy slide out.

"I guess that leaves you and me, Ward," Liam said. He sat down beside the other man. "I went to one of your fundraisers last night. Maybe you can fill me in more on your plans—since you weren't there. We can have an early lunch right here. I'll have our chef come out and talk to us. He's very accommodating. He does magical things with a pheasant. Not as magical as what gets whipped up at Hands On, I'm sure, but . . ." He shrugged eloquently.

21

Sykes expected one of them to laugh.

They stood on the sidewalk outside Fortunes. Wazoo's hand was tucked under Nat's arm and he held Mario. Poppy looked at the ground.

"We'll be off then," Nat said.

"Where's your car?" Sykes asked, glancing around.

"Bucky took it back," Nat said. "See you later."

"Why are you looking for Gray?" Sykes said. He couldn't contain his curiosity.

"I'd be grateful if you didn't mention it unless he does, but Gray may fill in for Bucky Fist. Bucky's got to go off on compassionate leave. Illness in the family."

"Fill in for Bucky?" Sykes's voice got louder with each word until he realized he was shouting and dropped his voice. "As your homicide partner? Does Marley know, for God's sake?"

"I wish I hadn't said anything," Nat said. "Maybe we'll decide against it but I really need him and he's the only one who can slip into Bucky's shoes without needing any training. Plus, he knows the cases we're dealing with."

"Marley's pregnant," Sykes said.

"I think that's sweet," Wazoo said, looking distant. "I'm looking forward to meeting her."

"This will all be over long before the baby's

born," Nat said, but he did have the grace to look uncomfortable. "You'll be late for your appointment if you don't go now."

Sykes squinted at him. It wasn't raining anymore and the sun had awoken ferociously. "What appointment?"

"Hands On," Nat said weakly. "Isn't that what you told me?" he asked Wazoo.

With no warning, Mario wriggled and fell from Nat's arms. The dog jumped at Sykes, who automatically caught him.

"He wants to be with you," Wazoo said, wrinkling her brow. "Look at him."

Mario settled comfortably.

"Forgive me but I'm going to have to duck out fast on this party and get some work done," Poppy said. She sounded angry, and looked angry. "The last thing I want is to have Ward rushing out here and finding us before I can get to my apartment."

"Why don't you tell Mr. Smooth to get lost?" Wazoo said.

Poppy smiled at her and tapped her chest, like a sign between the two of them. "He'll lose interest."

"You don't like him," Nat said. "So why are you encouraging him?"

"She's not encouraging him," Sykes said through his teeth. "In case you didn't notice, he's hooked." And he didn't blame the man even if he did instinctively wish he'd leave town for good.

"I've got to go." Hurrying, looking over her shoulder at the entrance to Fortunes, Poppy slipped up the alley beside the club and disappeared inside the door she and Sykes had used earlier.

"Excuse me." A tap on his shoulder interrupted Sykes's plotting. He wanted to get to Poppy again and very soon.

"Yes?" He glanced behind him and started. David, the teenager who said he was Pascal's son, stood there, sunglasses still firmly in place, heavy black duster zipped from hem to neck despite the warmth.

"I was out for a walk and I saw you here."

Sykes didn't think so but he'd figure out the truth when they did not have an audience. "Hey, David. Be with you in a minute."

He turned to Nat and Wazoo again. "I'd appreciate it if you'd tell Pascal I'll be there shortly. He's not going to be pleased about Gray, either. This is a bad time to drag him into the middle of everything." He remembered the boy. "This is David—" What else was he supposed to say?

"David Millet," David filled in for him. "Who are you?" He stared at Wazoo with open fascination.

"Detective Nat Archer," Nat said. "Homicide. This is—"

"I'm Wazoo. I come from Toussaint but Nat's my good friend." She glanced at him, smiled and added, "My best friend. That's why I'm in New Orleans."

With satisfaction showing, Nat pulled her away but Sykes didn't miss the significant once-over he gave David. He would ask Pascal about the boy. Sykes was almost sorry he'd miss witnessing that.

"Okay," Sykes said when the other two had left. "Who told you where to look for me?"

"No one."

Sykes stood quite still and concentrated. With his own guard up, he sent out receptors for any signals from David's mind.

"Pascal didn't tell you I could be over here?"

The boy's mouth tightened. He leveled the big lenses of his cheap wraparound sunglasses at Sykes. "I said I was going for a walk. He told me to be careful."

The kid's Adam's apple bobbled and something in Sykes responded, softened. "Pascal is a very good man," he said, not sure why he felt he had to say as much.

David nodded, yes. "I'm an inconvenience. Bound to be."

"Are you hungry?" Sykes asked.

This time he got the head shake, no, but he did not believe it. This boy could use a whole lot of eating.

Sykes considered the best way to make sure the Fortune brothers were on the case with Poppy being upstairs at the club, alone.

And he felt a distinct if faint series of attempts to join his wavelength. Small, almost imperceptible probes.

Finding out where they came from was easy for him but he identified the locators with some trepidation.

David. Just as he had expected. Millet or not, this was a paranormal and unless Sykes was very mistaken, there were considerable powers here.

"Let's start walking," he said, hiking Mario under his arm. "There's a little place I like on Chartres Street. It won't take us too far from the shop. Do you mind if I make a call?"

The glasses turned toward Sykes again. "Sure."

David was almost as tall as Sykes. Whatever else he might not have done today, he had given his scalp a fresh shave. His duster had large pockets that snapped and they bulged—with the things David held most dear, Sykes imagined. But he had felt he could leave his backpack at Pascal's place.

Sykes pulled out his phone and called Ethan. He told him Poppy was at home and Ethan's reaction revealed that he understood the message.

They walked down Dauphine Street to Chartres where Sykes stepped through the open doors to Arlo's Diner and led the way to a booth near the windows.

The good old smell of fried everything permeated the place and unintelligible shouts through a pass-through behind the counter sent two wait-resses trotting back and forth with steaming plates.

When they sat down facing each other with Mario stashed quickly under the table, Sykes said, "Aren't you hot in your coat?" Just looking at it made Sykes overheat.

"No."

Okay.

"I don't know what to do, or I didn't." David swallowed audibly. "I think I do now."

Sykes waited, afraid to turn off this sudden flow of words.

"Something's going on here, isn't it? It's really bad. I never felt anything like it before but I've been a long way from anywhere most of my life. I'm used to things being real quiet."

That prodded Sykes into a response. "Let's take all that, but one at a time. Start with where you come from."

David smiled a little. "I must have shocked all of you. It shocked me that I came here at all, but I didn't know where else to go."

"How did that happen?"

"I turned eighteen. They couldn't keep me there anymore."

Sykes gave him time, but David didn't volunteer more information. "Will you tell me about *they* and *there?*"

"My mom and stepdad. We moved around all

the time—small towns. My stepdad's a good mechanic but he doesn't stay sober, and we had to move on each time things got bad."

"Will you let them know where you are?" Sykes figured that would tell him all he needed to know about family love.

"I don't reckon so, not as long as he's around. I'll keep tabs on my mom."

"How?"

"I've got my ways."

"Was your stepfather mean to you?"

"Hey, handsome." Joannie who was seventy on a good day ran her fingers through Sykes's hair and sighed. "Do you know how many girls would give it up to have those curls?"

Sykes smiled into her bright blue and slightly watery eyes. "You flatterer, Joannie," he said. "What's good?"

"Gumbo," she said without taking a breath. She always said that. "Sweet corn bake. Lots of eggs and shrimp. It's all good."

Arlo's didn't run on menus apart from the chalkboard on one wall where smartass comments were as plentiful as the food items written there.

"You want coffee?" Sykes asked David.

"Green tea," David said, and Joannie's mouth dropped open until he took a bag from one of his deep pockets and put it on the table. "Just bring me boiling water, please."

Joannie's thin eyebrows rose high enough to

show all the creases in her turquoise eye shadow. "Got it."

"I'll have toast and a boiled egg," the boy continued. "Any fresh fruit?"

"I think we got some raisins."

Sykes put a fist over his mouth. "I'll have coffee and make it two boiled eggs with toast for me. Hold the raisins."

Joannie left in a hurry to share the news of the strange orders with her cronies.

David laughed softly. "He would have said raisins were fresh fruit," he said, apparently referring to his stepfather. "Probably maraschino cherries and olives, too—not that he bothered with refinements."

It was impossible not to smile with him.

"Have you graduated high school?" Sykes said.

"Yeah. When I was fifteen."

"Fifteen? A brain, huh? What have you been doing since then?"

"Working wherever I could to save money so I could get away. I don't kid myself it's going to be easy, but I want to go to college."

And what, Sykes wondered, should he believe or disbelieve from this stranger? Other than the signs of paranormal talents.

"First I'm going to be needed around here, though. I can do stuff. You know what I mean?"

Sykes was afraid he did know. "You tell me."

"It's gotten me in trouble as long as I can

remember. I can move things—but that could be my age and if it stops as I get older I won't be surprised. Biggest deal is following marks. Everyone's got a different mark. If I look for them, I can see them and they lead me to people."

"So much for you taking a walk and just happening to bump into me this morning," Sykes said.

"I did tell Pascal I was taking a walk," David said. "But I wanted to find you because you're the power, man. I never felt power like yours before, although I haven't been around much of it. But I recognize big stuff when I walk into it. Pascal's strong, but I expected that from what my mother said. Not that she said much. Marley's real strong, too, and Gray's got powers. Not Anthony. I don't know what to think about him. He brought the neat red dog over." He frowned. "I like dogs."

"What is it? You look worried."

Joannie returned with a mug of coffee and one of hot water. "Better put that tea thingie in there fast before this cools off," she said. "You want milk?"

"No! No, thank you," David said. "That's kind of you, but milk doesn't go with green tea."

Joannie wagged her white-blond head. "Learn somethin' every day. Food's comin' up."

"You were going to tell me something," Sykes said, hoping to push David a bit.

David shook his head. "No, no, nothing. Wazoo's a puzzle to me but you must know about her."

202

"I thought I was asking the questions around here. Wazoo is my friend, Nat's girlfriend. I like her a lot."

David ripped open the tea and plopped the bag into his mug. "There's Antoine and Leandra, right? And Willow, Riley and Alex as well as Marley. You're the only son."

"That must have been some night," Sykes muttered, thinking of Pascal with David's mother —if he had been and it was looking more likely —spilling family stuff the way none of them ever did.

"You mean the night I was conceived?" David said, absolutely serious. "Mom liked your uncle. When she had a few drinks and we were alone, she'd talk about what he told her, that's how I know the things I do. It isn't much."

"Do you know where they met?"

"Mom wouldn't tell me. She said it didn't matter."

But it had mattered enough for David to ask. Sykes realized he was starting to warm up to the kid, which might or might not be a good idea.

"My mom's okay. I guess Sim wasn't always the way he was by the time I knew him."

Joannie delivered their plates, pulled a rack of condiments forward and fished sachets of jam from the pocket of her apron.

"I asked for one egg," David said, his face turning pink.

"Memory like a sieve," Joannie said, slapping her forehead. "The second one's on the house."

Sykes noted that David had four rounds of toast to his own two and figured Joannie's motherly instincts were in play. The woman started to leave, then looked around before pulling a scrunched napkin from the same apron pocket and giving it to Sykes without a word and walking away.

He waited a moment before checking the napkin, smiled at David and put both the napkin and the scraps of sausage it contained under the table.

He was glad of the high volume of gabble in the place to cover Mario's chomping.

"Are you going to tell me what's going on?" David said. He ate both eggs in four bites and began piling jam on the toast.

"What does that mean?"

"I already told you I've figured out you've got big trouble. And I did meet the homicide detective, remember."

"Nat's a friend."

"You said you didn't want Gray pulled into things."

Sykes studied him. "Observant, aren't you?"

Muscles worked in David's thin cheeks. The toast disappeared steadily.

"How are we supposed to know if you're really anything to do with the Millets? Just because you show up at the shop and decide to use our name doesn't have to mean we're related."

"I've got proof," David said. "But it's for Pascal first. I haven't been alone with him. As soon as he saw me this morning, he went downstairs to the shop."

"He goes to the shop every morning," Sykes said in defense of his uncle, but also to shield David's feelings for some reason.

"I like him," David said, turning red again. "He's . . . he's someone special. He knows stuff, I can feel it."

Sykes realized David wanted to like Pascal and he wanted someone he could be proud of. "That's true," he said. "Tell me one thing. How did you know to come to New Orleans?"

"I knew is all. I've got it written down. And he was easy to find once I got here. I want to stay." He looked hard at Sykes. "I can stay if I want to, I know that. But I want to know my . . . dad."

It was Sykes turn to swallow. The kid was needy, but not sorry for himself. Determined. But he also longed for family connections.

The glasses were a nuisance. Sykes was convinced that without them, when he could get a good look at the eyes, he'd know if this was a Millet—even if they weren't green.

"How long have you been into the Goth thing?" David shrugged. "My stepdad hated it."

"Does that mean you're into it because of that?"

"It made it more appealing," David said. "It's been a while now. Will you help me persuade

Pascal to give me a chance? I mean a chance to prove myself?"

Sykes considered the question. "Do I seem like a soft touch to you?"

"No! But you're fair and you're too strong to be afraid of anything. What can you do?"

The way David phrased that made Sykes smile. "Leave marks for you to follow evidently. What do they look like?"

"Black shapes."

"That's it? The shape of feet in black or what?"

"Black shapes. All kinds of them. Now it's your turn."

Sykes laughed aloud. "Fair enough. I'm telepathic. So are you, but you can't get past my guard. I could get past yours if I wanted to, but we have rules about respecting privacy. Unless we're threatened, or someone innocent needs help."

"You know I'm telepathic because you felt me trying to read you," David said, matter-of-factly. "I couldn't figure out why I wasn't getting anything. Tell me what else you can do."

"No. In time you may learn more about me, we'll see."

"Who are the Embran?"

Sykes didn't feel like laughing anymore. "Where did you get that?"

"Gray. He's worried about them. With Marley expecting a baby he's afraid the Embran will hurt her because he thinks she'll try to help stop them.

I just don't know who they are or what they're doing."

"I think we should get back to Royal Street."

"You just figured out I'm the real thing, didn't you?" David said.

Sykes took out some bills and put them on the table.

David unzipped a couple of inches at the top of his coat and contorted himself to get a hand deep in an inside pocket. He took out two tens. "How much do you think this was?" he asked, craning to see the blackboard. "I ought to pay for both eggs."

"This is on me," Sykes told him.

"I pay my own way."

"You didn't decide to come in here, I invited you. It's rude to turn down hospitality."

David stared at him. "You don't need to feel sorry for me. I'm just fine."

Just fine, and desperate to prove you can carry your own weight.

"I don't feel sorry for you," Sykes said. "But I'm buying this meal."

David tightened his hand around the money, his eyes trained hard on the table. Then he slid the tens back inside his duster.

That was when Sykes saw traces of green and yellow bruising above the baggy neck of a black cotton turtleneck.

22

"I'm going to find him," Pascal said. "And when I do, I'll kill him."

He couldn't keep still and moved from one side of his office at the back of the shop to the other.

For once Anthony didn't try to calm him down. As buff, blond and all-American-looking as ever, he watched his partner with the same kind of rage mirrored in Pascal's eyes. Anthony might spend most of his time in sweats and looking after Pascal's health, but he had also learned at the elbow of a master and knew his antiques well enough to be very useful. In many ways he was Pascal's right hand and he was certainly his number one fan.

Sykes glanced through the windows of the office toward the steps up to Pascal's flat where David had been sent to wait with Gray and Nat.

"I'm making a lot of assumptions," Sykes pointed out. "I don't think he wears all the heavy clothes because he likes being hot as hell. I think he's covering up bruises and the only kind of bruises you take that much trouble to hide are the kind you don't want anyone to ask about."

"Did it look like someone put their hands around his neck?" Anthony said.

"Could be. I can't be more exact than that. He likes you, Pascal. He's ready to idolize you."

His uncle closed his eyes tightly and in a rare show of affection, Anthony put an arm around his shoulders. "You gotta keep an open mind. Whether he's your boy or not, maybe this is a chance to do something for a youngster who would benefit. Sykes says he's got talents."

"I think he could be powerful," Sykes said. "I caught him trying to read me. Didn't get him anywhere, of course—he didn't deny it. But the way he found me at Fortunes couldn't have been an accident, and I told him so. He reads energy patterns. Says they're black and white—on the ground—and we all have different ones."

Pascal nodded slowly. "Yes. I can't recall who else has something like that, but it'll come to me. I want a doctor to look at him."

"Good luck," Sykes said, although Pascal's reaction didn't surprise him.

"He wants to please you," Anthony put in. "If he thinks it matters to you for him to see someone, he'll do it."

"I'll have my guy make a house visit." Pascal drew himself up. "Then we'll see what comes next."

"He's got things to tell you," Sykes said. "He told me a bit but I'm going to let him talk to you himself. He says he's got some sort of proof he is who he says he is."

"He is," Anthony said, fixing his eyes on a distant point.

Pascal frowned at him. "How would you know?"

"I may not be paranormal, but I've got some good instincts."

"Hogwash," Pascal said with his customary command of contemporary lingo. "I'll be the one to make my mind up about this."

"He knows about the Embran," Sykes said.

"What?" Pascal scrubbed a hand over his smooth scalp. "How can he? Who's he been talking to?"

"He hasn't been talking to anyone. It was last night. He was hooked into Gray and Gray's worried about Marley trying to help out with the current situation."

Pascal's smirk, rather like a proud parent, made Sykes smile.

"There's trouble up there, y'know," Pascal said, replacing the smile with a frown. "Gray's told Nat he'll fill in for Bucky Fist."

"Ah." Sykes drew his lips back from his teeth. "And Marley's pissed."

"It's Wazoo who's angry. She says Nat's taking advantage. As soon as Marley went to her workroom, Wazoo laid into Nat. Things were going badly when you arrived."

Sykes had sent David up to the flat and told him to ask Pascal to come down to the shop where Anthony was watching over things.

Mario sat on Pascal's desk looking from one

face to another as they spoke. Sykes couldn't imagine another animal who would get away with being on that venerable piece of furniture, but Pascal had an obvious liking for the rough-haired red critter who's little ears stood up in perky points while his whiskers stuck out in a bristling mustache.

"We're really busy," Anthony said in a hoarse whisper. "Right now. Look at this map. It's an English county map from the 1700s."

Sykes and Pascal moved as one to bend over the desk and stare at a hand-drawn map in poor condition but interesting just the same. "What's going on?" Pascal said.

"Drama on the stairs," Anthony said, offering Pascal a magnifying glass. "Love is such sweet sorrow."

"That's, 'parting is such sweet sorrow,' " Sykes said.

"Same difference," Anthony remarked. "Probably fits the situation better."

"Gawd," Pascal said. "Arguing Shakespeare, no less."

Sykes contrived to look up from beneath his brows. Nat and Wazoo were talking on the stairs but almost at once Wazoo walked the rest of the way down and headed for the door.

Nat followed and when he took her in his arms she didn't resist. Sykes cleared his throat. "Keep studying the map."

His next check showed a passionate kiss that had staying power.

Wazoo flattened her hands on Nat's chest and slowly withdrew. She looked up at him and Sykes saw the sheen of tears on her face. Then she opened the door and hurried away.

Nat stood there looking out, his hands in his pockets, before he bowed his head and sank to sit on a dark wooden stool.

"O-kay," Sykes said. "We need to get out of this carefully—unless Nat does us a favor and decides to leave, too."

Nat stood up again and scuffed his way across the floor. He had seen the three men in the office and he opened the door. "Gray's up there with David. Nice kid. Gray's going to come back on board with me for a little while. I'm going to need you, Sykes, and both Liam and Poppy later this afternoon. I'll let you know when."

"Right," Sykes said.

Nat made to leave the office but stuck his head around the door again. "In case you're interested, Wazoo's got to get back to Toussaint to see some clients. That's all I've got to say about it, so don't ask any questions."

When he had been younger, Pascal thought that if he was ever in a stable relationship it might be a good idea to adopt a kid. When he was forty he met Anthony and now they had been together for

212

eight years. The subject of a child had not come up between them.

And now, while he sat in his sitting room surrounded by the collection of beautiful things he had put together, and thought about the comfortable patterns of his life, it amazed him that the thought of having someone who was part of him, and could turn out to be a big responsibility, appealed so much.

His doctor was giving David the once-over. At first the boy demurred, but just a little harder push and he gave in.

Anthony wanted David to be Pascal's. Pascal knew his friend too well not to recognize the difference between sincerity and trying to make him happy.

Dr. Phil Cooper came into the room.

Pascal leaned to one side, expecting to see David behind him.

"He's getting dressed, and I told him to lie down and rest a bit until you went back to get him. He's worn out and undernourished. I'd like him to come to the office for some blood work. I think he's probably just exhausted, mentally and physically, and he'll bounce back fast if he's given the opportunity."

"Did you find out . . . what else do you think?"

The doc rested his bag on the arm of a chair and pushed his glasses back up his squat nose. "Someone beat the crap out of him. Probably tried to strangle him, only he fought them off. David's thin but he's strong. Whoever did it used something that allowed him to beat him without getting too close. The mess around that one eye must have slowed the boy down, too. It looks worse than it is. It'll be fine."

Pascal listened and simmered. He didn't realize he'd made fists until his fingernails dug into the skin on his palms.

"I can't work this out for you, Pascal," Phil said. "But if you want to talk, I'm there for you. Let him have a quiet twenty-four hours, then get him to me. I want to see him regardless."

"Regardless?"

"Of what you decide to do about him. He's a very bright kid and he's had a rotten time of it. The recent beating was only the latest of many. If you want my guess, I'd say he stayed wherever he was for someone else's sake."

When Phil had left, Pascal took a while to gather himself. What did he know about kids? True, this one was eighteen and as good as a man, but he wasn't a man yet. He needed guidance from someone who understood the right things to do.

He couldn't let the boy wait in there and wonder what was going on any longer.

The door to the guest bedroom was ajar. Pascal knocked once and when he heard a mumble, pushed his way in. Rather than lying on the bed, David sat in a chintz wing chair Pascal kept because it had belonged to his mother. The sunglasses were on the bedside table and there was no sign of the black duster. In a long-sleeved gray T-shirt and jeans, David looked different, and not just because the bruises around his neck were clear to see, or he had a short wound by his blackened left eye that sported a couple of fresh butterfly dressings Phil must have applied. David was, indeed, very thin.

"I'm sorry," he said. "It was stupid to come here like this. If I came at all I should have waited till—" he touched his temple "—till all this was faded. I heal fast. But once I made up my mind to find you, I felt like I had to hurry. Don't know why when I waited so long already."

Pascal sat on the edge of the bed where he could get the best look at David. "Is your hair red?" He thought he saw the start of red glints growing back.

"Yeah. I used to dye it black and wear it long to make Sim mad, but it's easier just to shave it."

The eyes that looked at him as if waiting for a death sentence were as green as Pascal's own. David's eyebrows flared and when his face filled in a little, he would look like Pascal, only it was obvious David would eventually be taller.

Pascal looked at his hands.

"We have something in common," he said. "We're both rebels. I shaved my head for a different reason but it was because I wanted to make a point, just like you."

David gave a single laugh and cleared his throat.

"We've got a problem," Pascal said. "You understand that?"

"Of course. And if you don't want to know anything else about me, I'll understand and I'll get lost."

"What did you think would happen when you came here to me?"

"I didn't know. My mom said you were a really good guy. She always told me that. She said the two of you weren't meant to be together, and she understood that. But Mom wasn't sorry to have me. She told me that a lot."

"What do you want to happen now?" Pascal said. He couldn't admit he didn't remember the boy's mother.

David spread his long fingers. "I'm embarrassed," he said. "I feel like a little kid who believed in fairy stories. Like you were going to throw your arms around me and tell me you'd been trying to find me for years, or something. I'm just being honest but I've got it together, so don't worry. I'll get a job and a place to live, and now I don't have to deal with my stepfather anymore, I'll see about getting into college."

"You're paranormal."

David smiled. "Yep."

"I've been trying to remember who else I know who can follow movement energy patterns."

"Sykes told you."

"Yeah. He says you're going to be really good."

David looked pleased. Thin white curtains billowed away from an open window, bringing the heady scents of the city into the room. Pascal noticed the appreciative flare of David's nostrils.

"You move things but you don't expect that to last as you get older," Pascal said, smiling a little. "It may, though. How much control do you have?"

With his eyes lowered, David appeared deep in thought. Pascal jumped when the wraparound sunglasses landed on his face.

Impressed, he said, "That's a permanent thing. You're a hundred percent in control. Really useful."

David took the glasses back from Pascal. "Sykes wouldn't talk about his talents—except the telepathy."

"I don't suggest you ask him again," Pascal said, amused. "And you'd better hope you don't find out because he needs to neutralize you."

"He's a killer?" David said in hushed tones.

"I didn't say that." Pascal decided it was time to move on. "Dr. Cooper wants to do some blood work on you."

David's brow furrowed. "I'm in great shape. This is nothing." He touched his eye and winced.

"I want you to get it done."

In the silence that followed, they looked at each other.

"I should get out of your hair." David laughed

and ran a hand over his own scalp. "So to speak. The Y will do until I can get a place of my own."

"Do you have a picture of your mother?"

The kid went still.

"Do you?"

"Yes. Three of them. My mom's a looker." He got up and went to pull his backpack out of the closet. He unzipped a side pocket and took out a long envelope. When he slid the photos from inside, he looked at them one at a time, his expression closed. Then he handed them to Pascal.

David's mother as she must be now: tired-looking but attractive with light brown hair falling straight and shiny from a side part. The hair turned under at the bottom. Her eyes were blue. She wore a floral sundress and had a nice figure.

It was the earliest picture of the woman, somewhere in her twenties, that made Pascal catch his breath. In baggy denim overalls, a check shirt with the sleeves rolled up and her hair tied back, this girl's wide smile smote at him. He managed not to blurt out that he knew it had been taken at a Habitat for Humanity project in Alabama, or that he wouldn't be surprised if David's mother had never had a drink before that night but that, together, they drank enough to pass out cold. He didn't tell him that he and the girl had been friends and they had really liked each other. They had gone their separate ways after that night, the last night they had been there, and never been in contact again. Gillian. He remembered her name now.

Gently, David touched a folded piece of paper to Pascal's fingers.

Their eyes met and Pascal took what he was offered, unfolded it and looked at his son's birth certificate.

23

"One instruction," Nat said. He closed the door behind them in a small, windowless room at the station. "It'll save time if I can have you all look at what we've got together. But hold any comments until I split you up afterward."

The door opened again and the Medical Examiner, Dr. Blades, stuck his familiar hollow-cheeked face into the room.

Gray Fisher had already moved into his usual negative thoughts about the man when he surprised him. "Fisher, a word. I don't have much time."

"Charming as always," Gray muttered of the man he had dubbed Dr. Death back in the days when Gray and Nat had been full-time partners.

"Nat?" Blades said.

They joined him in the corridor outside. Nat had already made the mistake of grinning.

"Something funny, Archer?" Blades said. His stooped frame was still closer to seven than six feet tall.

Nat shook his head emphatically. "Not a thing."

"Liar," Gray said. "You didn't expect my old friend here to want to speak to me. I'm back in the department, Doc. I know that'll make you happy."

Blades's high, domed head shone. Beneath the bones where his eyebrows should have been, his haggard eyes flashed a hit of humor, something rarely seen.

"We need a more in-depth discussion but it'll wait until you can get over to my place," he said.

Gray didn't have to ask what he meant by "my place." Blades just about lived at the morgue.

"Sure," Nat said.

"Something about our monster friends has been nagging at me for weeks. And something about the way they kill and what happens to the bodies afterward. The chief thinks he's keeping things under wraps, but I know the Embran gradually deteriorate and the process gets faster after close contact with humans.

"They could be allergic to us in some way, simple as that. Or complicated as that. You think about what that could mean. Chief Molyneux's story is that the reason I can't see any of the subjects you people have captured in past months is because they've been quarantined in some secret clinic. That's shit. Something weird goes on with them. I've got to get back now."

He sloped away, gray jacket hanging from his hunched shoulders, and never looked back.

When they reentered the room Gray was not surprised to find Poppy, Sykes and Liam sitting silently on their folding metal chairs.

"I'd rather not show this to you, Poppy," Nat said. "It's difficult to watch, even for some of us who deal with this sort of thing every day. If you start to—"

"I won't," she said, but Sykes scooted his chair closer to hers.

"It isn't long," Nat said, sliding in a disk.

The camera was trained on the inside of what looked like a front door. Nat had already told Gray that despite poor light the scene was distinct enough to be identified as the foyer at Ward Bienville's St. Louis Street house.

The front door opened and a male figure entered with a woman slung over his shoulder.

Gray glanced at Poppy.

What was left of the woman's dress covered little of her body. Her shoes were gone. Rivulets of dried blood showed starkly against the white skin of her legs.

Liam exclaimed, but didn't say anything clearly.

Poppy curled into herself, huddled on her chair, ignoring Sykes's attempts to hold her hand.

The man set the body carefully on the stone tiles in the foyer. The dress hung in silver rags attached to the body only by one shoulder strap. Gray was grateful her face was indistinct.

Gray recoiled from the sight of the man standing back to survey the body. He looked at it from two directions before he loosened his shirt collar, and glanced up and around, smiling.

"That's it," Nat said.

"Did you find the murder scene yet?" Sykes asked.

"Yes," Gray said. "The victim's home. She was then brought to Ward's house."

"Let's go through it again."

"Let's not," Liam said.

"D'you want some water?" Gray asked.

"I want a shower," Liam said. "We've got work to do first, though, right?"

"The lab got good stills from the surveillance tape," Nat said. He got up and went toward the door.

"We don't need stills," Liam said. "Or I don't."

"Do you know who that man is?" Poppy asked him.

"No. At least, I don't think so," Sykes said.

"I do," she said. "Not his name, but I've seen him before."

"Me, too," Liam said.

Gray saw Nat make the decision to let them talk if they wanted to.

Liam stared at Poppy and said, "He followed me into a bathroom at that fundraiser last night. I went to one for Ward. Don't get mad—I just wanted to see the kind of people who were there. I worry about you."

"You need to," Sykes said. "You're not the only one, either."

"The night before last, at Ward's." Poppy nodded toward the now-blank video screen. "He served me champagne."

24

They left Gray and Nat behind and went out to the street. Poppy felt as if she wanted to start touching people, ordinary people, and greeting them just to hear normal voices saying meaning-less things.

She wasn't sure where to go, but it couldn't be back to Fortunes.

"I feel sorry for Ward," she said.

"Save it, Sis," Liam said. "I'll feel sorry for him when I'm sure none of this craziness has any-thing to do with him."

"Go away!" Poppy said. "You're so mean. Someone left Sonia's body at his house to frame him but you're still picking on him. I'm sick of it."

"Tell me this . . ." Liam caught her by the arm and swung her to face him. "Look at me and tell me you really like the guy. Tell me you aren't trying to prop him up because you always do prop up the underdog."

"*Underdog?* Ward? He doesn't even know the meaning of the word. He knew it was nothing to do with him."

"You didn't answer my question," Liam said. "Do you really like the guy?"

She glanced at Sykes whose face was averted. He stood motionless with his hands in his pockets.

"I don't have strong feelings about Ward," she admitted at last. "He wants me to be his friend, and I'm not mean to people."

"Thanks," Liam said. "Now will you admit that he seems to have dangerous stuff going on around him."

She felt rotten about everything. "Maybe."

"I did my best," Liam said. "The more I try to persuade you to give the guy a miss, the harder you'll hold on to him, so I give up. I had lunch with him and I think he's a self-absorbed boor. I'll see you later."

He walked to the corner, turned left and headed away from the center of the Quarter.

"Now it's your turn," Poppy said to Sykes.

"You're a big girl. You get to make up your own mind."

She gave him a suspicious stare and stepped out of the way of a woman who was drunk and wearing enough gaudy beads to throw a less sturdy person off balance.

"I'm going back to my flat at Millet's," Sykes said. "Why don't you come with me? You could check in with Marley to see how she's doing and say hello to Pascal. He loves to see you and you haven't been by much recently."

"In case you've forgotten, I managed to make myself unpopular."

"The only one who knew that—until you told me—was you. And Willow. Willow doesn't hold grudges. It's time to let it go."

"You're so full of platitudes," Poppy said. She crossed her arms and felt out of control of her behavior. "Why can't you just be as nasty as you want to be sometimes?"

"I can. I don't feel nasty right now. Sad, maybe. And worried about you. But not nasty."

"Can you kill people with hypnosis?"

His expression turned guarded. "Where did that come from?"

"It's been on my mind. Everyone knows you're over-the-top talented, but what it is you do is hardly mentioned."

He took a deep breath and moved closer to her, looking down while she had to raise her head to return the stare.

"You're not yourself," he said. "I don't blame you. The tapes were horrible."

She felt tears prickle and blinked fast. "I handled it fine."

"Of course you did."

"You're not going to answer my question, are you?"

He studied her face for a while then said, "I can kill with hypnosis. The brain just stops and the subject dies. I would never use that kind of power

225

except to save an innocent life. Are you satisfied now?"

She felt her face crumple and bowed her head. The experience of watching that murderer had shocked her terribly. There was no point denying it. "I'm sorry," she said.

"There's something I'm looking for. Ben was helping before he and Willow left for Kauai. Maybe you can come along and try being an extra pair of eyes and ears for me."

Confusion scrambled her mind. "I don't need sops to make me feel needed," she said. "I want to be alone. Why don't you just get lost. Leave me alone and get lost."

She closed her eyes and covered her face. And she felt him walk away from her. At first she was going to call after him, but then she turned her back on the street and fought to calm her breathing.

"Sykes," she said when she could, turning around.

She looked up and down Royal Street, stood on the curb staring in the direction of the Millet's antique shop.

Sykes had done as she asked. He'd got lost.

It took Poppy twenty minutes of pacing up and down to admit just how ridiculous she felt but only another two to decide what to do about it.

She arrived at J. Clive Millet out of breath from running and hurried into the shop.

Pascal was there, a tray of fabulous jewelry on top of the counter while he explained each piece to a teenage boy with a black eye.

"Poppy!" Pascal saw her and his pleasure showed. "Hey, it's a long time since you came to see me. Come and look at these."

His trainer, Anthony, stood behind him looking even more cheerful than usual.

Poppy looked down on pins and lapel watches, bracelets loaded with diamonds and enamel, and unusual dress rings.

Pascal went into his office and took a ring box from the safe. When he brought it back he said, "Look at this one," and pushed it onto the middle finger of her right hand. "It's got a secret compartment for carrying your poison in." He laughed.

Poppy smiled. "It wouldn't hold much mad money."

"With a ring like that why would you need mad money?" Anthony said.

"Maybe it was for carrying hartshorn," Poppy suggested. "Isn't that what ladies sniffed if they felt faint?"

"Clever girl." Pascal beamed. "That's what I was told. But I've always thought it was for poison. Makes a better story, too, only nobody can figure out how to open it. Those are old rubies, and they're good. Hold them up to the light. Oh, sorry, this is David."

The boy beside him, who also had a shaved

head, smiled at her and held out his hand. She shook it thinking that the multiple piercings he wore looked out of place—although his clothes were all black and visibly old.

"Hi, David," she said. "I'm Poppy Fortune."

"She's a family friend," Pascal said. "David is my son, Poppy."

Her smile fixed and she glanced at Anthony, only to find him grinning like the boy's other proud parent.

"It's super to meet you," Poppy said to David. "Now I look at the two of you, I can see the likeness." Apparently Pascal had made an exception with at least one woman.

"I know," Pascal said, laughing. "He's going to be taller than me but when he's had a few weeks of eating properly, you'll see just how much he's like me."

David seemed overwhelmed.

"Are you looking for Marley?" Pascal said. "She's in her flat."

"And madder than a wet hen at Nat for luring Gray back into the department," Anthony added. "Rotten timing."

"I, um, wondered if Sykes was here," Poppy said.

Pascal and Anthony's quick look at each other wasn't quite quick enough for Poppy to miss.

"Yes, yes," Pascal said. "He came through a while ago."

"He did," Anthony echoed.

"He looked pissed," David added, and all became silent.

Poppy cleared her throat. "Thanks. I'll go find him." And she scuttled toward the French doors that led to the courtyard. "Oh, the ring," she said, turning back.

"Wear it," Pascal said, waving a hand. "It's lucky. I've always been told that. You wear it as long as you like."

Poppy hesitated, but decided she'd give it back before she left rather than refuse Pascal's kindness. "Thank you. I feel luckier already," she said.

The first thin membrane of evening had slid a grayish fuzz over the courtyard. Poppy stood still and took in the beauty of the place. In a city filled with beautiful courtyards, this was the loveliest she had seen.

She looked up toward Sykes's flat, then at Marley and Gray's. Her resolve wavered. Sykes wouldn't be unpleasant but he might be cool and she didn't think she could handle that today. And if she went to visit Marley and he heard about it, he would know she had really come looking for him.

"Would it be okay if I got found now?"

She jumped at the sound of Sykes's voice, then had to smile. "That's why I'm here," she said. "To find you and apologize for being a worm."

He emerged from a dense stand of bamboo,

the same one where she had found him on that day, months ago, when she had decided to confess how she had meddled in Ben and Willow's relationship.

Mario bopped out behind him, his whiskers covered with dirt, and Marley's Boston terrier, Winnie, followed, dragging a huge and yellowed plastic bone.

Sykes put an arm around her neck and hugged Poppy's face into his shoulder. "Have I ever told you how much I like an outstanding worm? Very tasty."

She put her arms around his waist and held on.

"Poppy, I don't go around killing people for fun." His voice was suddenly tight.

"Of course you don't." She eased away from him. "I shouldn't have asked what I did."

"It doesn't matter as long as you aren't wondering if I thought of . . . you know I would never hurt you, don't you?"

"Of course." She stared at him. "It never crossed my mind. I want to help you look for whatever it is you've lost." Her heart beat wildly.

The bluest eyes she had ever seen were very serious. Sykes was weighing the truth in her denial. "I never actually had it," he said. "But it's something we need to clear up. I'll tell you why later—if you want to listen, that is."

"I do. What are we looking for?"

He dug a tiny gold key out of his pocket and

showed it to her. "With this one we've got four of them. I want to know what they unlock."

"Four keys. For four different things, you think?"

"No. Probably one thing. It could be that we'll need whatever these unlock to help with the Embran friends."

Poppy shook her head.

"You need to know more about the Embran," Sykes said. "That's what we'll talk about later. Over a really good bottle of wine. In my flat. Where I keep my etchings."

Poppy laughed and poked him in the chest. "I know all about your etchings."

"Oh, no, you don't," he said and kissed her cheek. "You've only begun to explore my etchings."

His expression changed abruptly, the smile disappeared and he glanced to his right, then back at her.

Mario whimpered and took off in the direction Sykes had looked.

"Do you hear anything?" Sykes said.

Poppy's scalp tightened and her face felt stiff. "I don't know. What sort of thing?"

He was already concentrating again. A light wind picked up, ruffling his hair and distracting Poppy. She could look at Sykes forever, or pretty much forever.

Shushing, or what sounded like several people

shushing each other, came to Poppy on the wind and she frowned, suddenly even more edgy. "Do you hear that?" she said, catching hold of Sykes's sleeve. "Where are they?"

She could have sworn he gave her a satisfied glance.

The sound grew louder.

Scraping brought her attention to Winnie who made for a flight of stairs leading to the flats, her bone dragging on the ground. There was no sign of Mario.

"It's happening," Sykes said. "Ben used to tell me about it but I wasn't aware of anything for a long time. Do you see it changing?"

His hand folding around hers was a relief. "I'm not sure. Do you mean the colors?"

"What are they?" Sykes asked, squeezing her fingers. "The colors."

"They're mixing together. Sliding down. Green and violet. And dark purple. Like they're running over each other."

"It's something to do with the angels," he told her. "There's a particular one we're supposed to find but I can't. I keep looking at them but not one of them is right."

"How do you know what the special one should look like?"

"I'll explain," he said. "Give me time on that, okay?"

"Okay."

"Help me look at them again. I think our angel has long hair. Nothing on her head, no headdress or anything like that."

"How would you know if she has long hair?"

"Because I've started to see her." He faced Poppy. "Why didn't I know that until now? Of course I've started seeing her. That's why the stone came."

"You're being very mysterious."

"I don't mean to. Look for an angel with long hair that sweeps away from her face."

Poppy went to the first stone angel she saw. A veil completely covered her head. But there was something about her face that stopped Poppy. "She's not the one but she's lovely. She's smiling."

Sykes joined her. "Not usually," he said without inflection.

A door slammed and they both looked up. Marley waved and started down the steps.

The closer she got, the more vivid her expression seemed. "Winnie ran upstairs to hide," she said. "I figured something was going on down here. Where's Mario?"

"Digging something up," Sykes said. "How are you doing, Marley?"

"They're here," she said, her green eyes almost unfocused. "Listen. Oh, you can't hear them, can you? I always wondered where they went and they've been here in the courtyard all the time."

"You two are starting to scare me," Poppy said. "That's not easy to do."

"What do you mean?" Sykes asked Marley.

She turned bright pink. "I have some, er, friends I call my Ushers. They talk to me when I need them, usually when I travel. This is the first time I've ever heard them when I wasn't traveling." She glanced at Poppy and swallowed. "Out of body, that is."

"Yeah," Poppy said. "Some people might think we're a pretty weird lot. Imagine that. You're not getting ready to . . . to go somewhere right now, are you?"

"Oh, no." Marley rubbed her rounded belly. "Not at all, that wouldn't be a safe thing to do."

Sykes grinned at both of them. "This is a landmark occasion. There are three of us here and we're all hearing the angels communicating."

"You hear them, too?" Marley's voice rose, then she frowned. "The angels? You think the sounds are coming from the angels?"

"They are," Poppy said.

"Yep," Sykes agreed. "Ben told me about it for years but I didn't hear it so I didn't believe it. I wonder how long before we figure out the significance. Or if there is some significance at all."

Poppy wanted to ask Marley if she saw all the color but decided not to push her luck.

"We're looking for an angel with long hair but no headdress," Poppy said. "We just started."

Immediately, Marley looked in one direction after another, obviously seeking out angels where she already knew they stood, or knelt, or sat. "I don't remember one like that."

Mario snuffled his way across the gravel path, lifted his head as if listening, and streaked out of sight again.

"That dog is weird," Sykes said. "Cute, but weird."

"He's lovely," Poppy told him, watching the exit of the lovely, weird animal. "At least he moves as if he's got a purpose. Look at all of us standing here, not knowing what to do next."

"And the dog does?" Sykes sounded tolerant but amused.

Poppy started out, looking at one statue after another until she assumed the other two were also looking. Then she took off after Mario. When she could, she would have a dog of her own.

A tiled pathway ran in front of all sides of the buildings fronting the courtyard. The lowest floor housed storerooms, some with barred windows, all with very large doors painted green.

"There are some on the door and window lintels," Sykes said, catching up with her.

She frowned. "Oh, you mean angels? Those things mostly look like gargoyles to me."

"Most of them are," Marley said, appearing around the next corner.

"Why is this blocked off?" Poppy checked out a concreted-up area in one wall. It was hard to tell if there had once been a door there or if the bricks had needed repair.

"Don't know," Marley said. "It was always like that."

Scrabbling sounded and they all searched for the source.

Sykes shrugged, but more scratching and scrabbling followed.

Poppy stared at the foot of the patched wall, pointed, then got down on her knees. A gap the size of a tennis ball showed where the wall met the tiles.

"This is where the noise is coming from," she said.

Both Marley and Sykes came to take a closer look.

"Ew, mice," Marley said, leaping back.

Several animal whiskers poked through the hole. Grubby whiskers.

"Not mice," Poppy said. "Mario."

"Damn dog." Sykes went to the nearest door and slid it open on rusty tracks.

They all crowded inside only to find a high-ceilinged, empty and very dusty space. Exploration showed it didn't extend to the repaired section of wall.

Single file behind Sykes, they left the place, closed the door and headed for the one on the other side of the patch. The door into this one revealed piles of broken pieces of furniture.

"Don't laugh," Marley said. "But I store some of my stuff here."

Poppy knew Marley was a restorer, particularly of lacquer, silvering, gilt and various exotic finishes.

Sykes was already examining the exterior wall. He worked his way to the corner and threw up his hands. "I'm damned," he said. "Know what I think? There's a space between this room and the one we were just in. It looks like it was walled off years ago and I don't see any way in."

Marley looked stricken. "There has to be. Mario's in there and he didn't crawl through that little hole."

25

"Okay," Sykes said. "Stop panicking, you two. We'll get him out."

"Who's panicking?" Marley said.

He crouched beside the hole, poked a finger through and felt Mario's tongue giving it a lick. "I am," he said. "Shoot, I'm going to have to break in there and if I'm really unlucky, I'll hurt him in the process."

"Cool it," Poppy said.

"*Cool* it?" Sykes and Marley replied in unison.

"He got in there somehow, didn't he? He'll get out again when he's ready."

"If he can find the way in and out again," Marley said. "You know how that goes some-times. Sort of like a maze."

Pascal's voice thundered through the court-yard, "Where are you? What's going on?"

To Sykes it seemed as if the soft whispering sounds around them rapidly rose to hoarse bellowing. "Over here," he called back. He dropped his voice and added, "Do we have to tell him?"

"I'm not lying to Pascal," Marley said.

David accompanied Pascal, his arms behind his back and his step tentative.

"Hey, David," Sykes said. So far he hadn't found anything in the boy to dislike—other than the multiple piercings.

"Hey," David said.

"Is your dad dragging you into a family fracas already?" Poppy said.

The boy laughed politely.

So, Sykes thought, *if Pascal had told Poppy about his son then the fatherly instincts were already in full bloom.* "Have you met Marley, yet, David?"

"Yep. And Anthony and Gray."

Pascal beamed. "So what's all the racket about out here?"

Sykes looked silently at the ground and he didn't hear either Poppy or Marley rush to explain.

"Oh, you might as well know. Mario's got himself into a jam. He's in there." Sykes pointed to the small hole at the base of the wall. "We can't find where he got in and I doubt he can remember, so it looks as if I'll have to start knocking down walls."

Puffing with exasperation, Pascal headed for the door on the left.

"You won't find him in there."

Pascal halted and set off for the door on the right. This time they didn't say anything and he went inside. They heard the overhead light snap on and very soon, Pascal's exclamation.

Out he stomped, glaring at them as he went by, and back inside at the door on the left.

This time he didn't say a word but emerged after a few minutes and stood before the patched wall. "Walled off," he muttered. "This bit. It's always looked like this and I never thought anything of it. How big is it in there, d'you think?"

"Six or seven feet wide," Sykes suggested. "And probably the same depth as everything else on this side."

"Poor little Mario," Poppy said. "We'd better keep talking to him. We can push food through if we have to."

"I want Gray to get home," Marley said, sounding forlorn and not at all like herself. "It's getting dark. He'll figure out how to get him out."

Poppy elbowed Sykes in the ribs and gave him a sideways smile.

He knew when he was being told to bury his ego.

"Easy enough," Pascal said. "We'll knock the wall down."

"You could kill Mario," Marley said.

"Not if we take a pickax, stick it in that little

hole and work till it's bigger. Dogs are smart. He'll back off while we're making a lot of noise and dust."

"Hey, fella!"

They all turned to David who dropped to his knees at the edge of the nearest planting bed and gathered good old Mario into his arms.

"How did you get back out?" David said. "We're gonna change your name to Houdini."

26

"Okay, folks. Disaster averted. We can all go home." Sykes stood against the patched wall and raised a hand as if to wave the rest of them off. He settled a hand on the back of Poppy's neck.

"No, no, no," Pascal said, turning up one corner of his mouth. "Not this time, my friend. Don't forget I know all about your ego. You want to find out what's inside that space and you want to do it all on your own. Then you'll announce it to the rest of us so we can tell you how brilliant you are."

"Maligned," Sykes said and kept a straight face. "No such thing. It's getting late and we all have more important things to do. Maybe we should wait till Ben and Willow come home before we fess up to almost losing their dog."

"We didn't almost lose him," David said, still holding the happily settled Mario. "He went in there and got bored. So he came out."

Sykes avoided congratulating him on saying the obvious. "You're right," he said. "I'll take him up with me if you like."

Mario launched himself from David's arms and Sykes had to catch him. "Whoa. Welcome, I guess. You'd think he understands what we say."

Nobody was moving.

"I've got an idea," Pascal said. "You said something about a pickax, Sykes. If you know where one is, why don't you get it. There's a heavy flashlight in Willow's store at the end—if the Mean 'n Green group hasn't nicked it."

Mean 'n Green was Willow's concierge company, run in her absence by one Zinnia, and assistants Chris and Fabio. Chris and Fabio had almost been Embran casualties, together with Caroline who was now Chris's constant companion.

As soon as Pascal set off, Sykes said, "The rest of you don't need to hang around. I'll let you know if we find a stash of Rembrandts in there."

Marley leaned her back against the wall.

David widened his stance and put his hands behind his back. Without the sunglasses his eye was a mess.

Poppy smiled up at Sykes. "I wouldn't dream of leaving you here on your own to work. You must be tired after all you've been through." Her voice was sweet but the look she gave him, definitely suggestive.

"Okay, okay." He shook his head, gave Mario

to Poppy and went back into the storeroom to the left of the concreted wall where he thought he had seen a pickax. He found it too quickly and actually considered saying he hadn't found it at all. "Shape up, Millet," he told himself under his breath.

Pascal arrived outside the door as Sykes emerged with the pickax.

"We'd better go through from the inside," Sykes said. "Keep the rain from getting through the outside wall."

Leading the way, Pascal chose the storeroom on the right because it was empty and switched on a big and brilliant flashlight as he went. Bricks in the added wall looked as old as the rest but Sykes didn't comment.

"Maybe they changed their minds when they were building the place," Marley said.

"Could be the spans were too wide or something," Poppy added.

"Mmm" was all Sykes said. He wasn't sure what he thought except that the space was damn strange.

"Now," Pascal said. "I wonder where the best place would be."

The rest crowded in behind Sykes. If he swung the pickax, he'd kill someone.

"Eye-level," David said. "Doesn't make much difference but that way it'll be easier to look in there."

Sykes placed the pointed end of the pickax

against the wall and gave a significant look around to make them all back off.

"Lower," David said. "Marley wouldn't be able to see through there without a ladder."

Muffling a retort about smartass kids, Sykes moved the tool down the wall and gave an experimental tap. Dry old mortar crumbled away easily. He tapped again and broke straight through. A bump with the end of the handle sent first one, then two abutting bricks through to the other side.

"What can you see?" Marley said.

The look she got from Sykes only make her snigger.

He used the straight edge of the pickax head and pulled the next brick in his direction, stepping out of the way when it fell. Four more and there was enough room to put an arm and a head through. "Flashlight," he said without meeting Pascal's eyes.

He got the rubber-coated flashlight slapped into his palm and aimed the business end through the hole.

Carefully, he put his head into the space and gradually swept the light beam around then swept it carefully back and forth. Cobwebs draped his hair and he couldn't brush them away.

He felt hands on his back.

"What's in there?" Poppy said. "What do you see?"

Sykes worked himself forward until his head

was all the way through and looked all around. "I'm damned," he said.

"What?" It was a chorus.

Slowly, he withdrew. He made for the door and fresh air. "Stinks in there. Stale."

"Well?" Pascal demanded.

"Nothing," Sykes said. "Nada. Not a thing. It's empty. Except for rat droppings."

27

"You don't think one of the others will have the same idea?" Poppy whispered, although there was no way anyone but Sykes could hear her.

They had turned on the light in Sykes's living room, waited half an hour and now stood in the dark hall near the front door, listening for any movement outside.

He held Mario who bristled with attention. "Knowing how we are, anything's possible. Marley won't go down there without Gray. Or I don't think she will. Pascal's the one who might sneak back, but he said we'd wait till morning to take another look."

"Sneak?" Poppy said. She guessed most people justified their own actions. "What are we planning to do, if it's not to sneak back?"

He leaned across and kissed the end of her nose. "That's different," he said. "We could wait in the living room."

"No. We have to be able to look for lights in the windows without being seen."

"And we do that, how?"

"Look through the mail slot."

He grunted. "I don't even know if it still opens. It isn't used."

Tentatively, Poppy took hold of the flap and lifted. The thing creaked enough to make her wince, but it did open. She bent down and peered through. "Everything's dark."

"They could all be waiting to go back to that storeroom and investigate some more."

Poppy snorted. "So we all bump into each other down there. Then we all look stupid."

"You've got a point." Sykes was quiet for a moment. Then he said, "I think it's important for me to go on my own—with Mario."

"Why?" She crossed her arms.

"It's hard to explain but . . . Poppy, I think I'm the one who should do this. Can we leave it at that?"

"I'm coming with you. Don't talk about that anymore."

He puffed out an exasperated breath.

"Are you sure no one will see light when we open this door?" Poppy said.

"As close to no light as possible," he responded.

He looked through the mail slot himself, then turned his ear to it and listened.

Poppy almost started tapping her toe but stopped herself.

"I'm going now," Sykes said, standing up.

"Good." She wouldn't say anything argumentative but she also wouldn't miss any action.

Sykes opened the door a couple of inches and with great caution.

They waited again and then he slipped outside with Poppy behind him. He closed the door with equal care.

"The stairs can sound like gongs if you're not careful," he whispered into her ear.

Poppy nodded and they set off, single file, not stopping until they walked inside the empty storeroom to the right of the walled-off space.

Poppy put her mouth to Sykes's ear. "We've got to be careful with the flashlight. It could show under the door."

He nodded and slid the door shut painfully slowly. "If they see it, they see it. We can't pack the whole door. I'll try to keep the light away."

They looked at each other in the faint upward glow from the flashlight Sykes aimed at the wall. Then they looked at Mario who continued to be all bristling whiskers and bright black eyes.

"Put him down," Poppy said.

Sykes did so and Mario promptly sat between them, looking from one to the other.

"They don't have long memories, do they?" Sykes said. "He's probably forgotten all about what he did earlier."

"We don't know which side he got in from," Poppy said.

"David picked him up outside this one."

She wasn't convinced that proved anything.

Sykes began running a hand from brick to brick along the length of the wall, pressing as he went. Poppy followed him, taking the next row.

"Maybe he'll get bored watching us and go in there," Poppy said.

"We could have brought something he likes to eat and pushed it through the wall outside." Sykes kept moving. "If he could smell it in there he might go after it."

"Shall I go get something?"

Sykes said, "No, one thing at a time."

Poppy knew they worked there a long time. Her fingertips grew sore from the rough bricks but she kept going. "Hey." She stood still. "There's no reason we can't just knock enough of the wall out to get in there. That's what they'll do tomorrow."

"Noise." He turned and rested a hand on the back of her neck. "I wasn't kidding when I said I wanted to find anything that's in there myself. There are answers I need that would make a big difference going forward."

"Like what?"

He sighed. "Like whether or not I'm the family curse who should be shunned, or if I need to be ready to take things over around here." He repeated the old theory that because he didn't have red hair or green eyes like the rest of the Millets, he could bring catastrophe to them as the only other Millet with his coloring had supposedly done.

"That's ridiculous," Poppy said. "I bet it was nothing to do with Jude. And if anyone says there's something wrong with you, just send them to me and I'll fix their opinions."

Sykes swung her against him. "I think I got myself a champion. But for what it's worth, I agree with you. So does Pascal. He wants me to start taking over. And we have to find the angel we keep being reminded of, and the Harmony, whatever that is—and I think that if it exists, it's important. And there are some missing pages from a book of rules that might answer all my questions."

"Or not."

"Or not," Sykes agreed. "I just want a chance to find out if there really are any answers and it's not all just a big flimflam." He rubbed his lips back and forth on her brow and they clung tighter, shivering.

Poppy's eyes were just above Sykes's shoulder level and she peered into the gloomy room. "Where's Mario?"

Sykes released her and abandoned caution with the flashlight. He swept it around the room. The little red dog wasn't visible.

"He can't get out of here," Poppy said, bemused. "Mario," she whispered loudly. "Come boy."

Nothing moved and Sykes kept sweeping the light around.

They both caught their breath at the same time and headed for the farthest corner, the one between the back wall and the wall opposite the one where they had been searching.

Shadows gave a different perspective. The wall to the right sloped inward toward the back, meaning the room got narrower there.

Poppy hurried to the corner. On the ground she saw a small pile of debris and crouched to look at it.

"It doesn't really meet here. It's only an illusion that it does."

Sykes pressed his shoulder against what appeared to be a gap, turned his head sideways. Gradually and with difficulty, he disappeared.

On her feet at once, Poppy followed.

In front of them steps rose, barely wide enough for one person to climb with a lot of caution and hanging on to the walls either side. The space was minute and went almost straight up.

"Why didn't anyone find this before?" Poppy asked.

"They weren't looking." Sykes's voice came echoing down to her. "Maybe if Marley had used this storeroom instead of the other side, she would have seen it, but I don't think so. Look on the bright side, someone had a reason for going to great lengths to hide something."

She felt excited but didn't say so.

Mario's face appeared as Sykes's head cleared the top of the stairs and they stood, nose to nose, until Mario turned away again.

"He's one weird dog."

"Don't let Willow hear you say that," Poppy said. "Pascal says she's crazy about him."

Sykes crawled from the top of the steps into a tunnel, and Poppy wasn't far behind. Again, the space was claustrophobically small and went on far too long for Poppy.

"We're going over the storeroom," Sykes said. "You don't have to do this, y'know."

"Oh, yes I do. Hurry up."

Eventually they reached the top of another flight of tiny steps. Sykes turned around and started downward.

Poppy had a headache and a stomachache. Tension did those things to her. She followed Sykes's lead until they slid along another wall arranged to be an optical illusion.

They were inside the false space.

They faced each other. Sykes raised his hands and let them drop.

"We found a nifty hiding place," Poppy said. "That's something."

"It would be if we needed a place to hide."

"Yuck," Poppy said. "Now we have to go back. I don't like it in that tunnel."

"I'll be right there with you. Come on, dog."

Mario stretched out at the base of the patched wall and rested his head on his front paws.

"Come," Poppy said in her best dog command voice.

He didn't move.

"He'll be filthy from lying in all this dust," she said, hunching over to scratch his head. "Not that he cares."

"This was a window, not a door," Sykes said abruptly. "Or a patch in the wall. Someone took out a window and blocked up the hole."

Glancing up from Mario, Poppy looked straight at a very old but solid horizontal piece of wood. She touched it. "Because of this? You think this is a windowsill? The patch goes all the way down outside."

"But not inside." Sykes hunkered down beside her. "None of the other storerooms have windows."

"Neither does this one, now." Poppy smirked a little then met Sykes's eyes and straightened her face. "Do you think this was all one big room once?"

"Could have been."

Poppy used the old sill to pull herself up. She bent sideways and looked underneath. "It's solid," she said. "There should be windows in these spaces to make them lighter."

"Safer not to have them if you're storing valuables." He got up and rapped the wood.

Frowning, Poppy knocked it, too. "Does that sound solid to you?"

Sykes knocked again. "Nope. But it's probably wormy and falling apart."

"Look at it." The piece of dark wood, that was very much out of place, still held a luster.

On his knees this time, Sykes wiggled, pushed and pulled. "Maybe you could move, Mario," he suggested. "It does feel a bit loose."

Poppy took the sill in both hands and pulled it completely free of the wall.

"How did you do that?" Sykes said, taking the wood from her. "I must have knocked it free."

Her very strong hands were something she didn't usually think about. "You must have," she said. Her brothers used to make fun of her unscrewing caps their father couldn't move.

"It doesn't look rotten," Sykes said, turning the piece over and over. He held it out in front of him. "It's perfectly finished."

"Like a long box," Poppy said. She touched the bottom and pressed. Nothing happened. The ends were solid.

The side closest to her moved, started to slide open, and she yelped.

"Careful." Sykes didn't hide his excitement. He turned the sliding side upward and slipped it all the way open. "I don't believe it."

Puzzled, Poppy picked up a roll of pages from inside. She could see writing on them and noted that they appeared to be torn from a book.

About a third of the box held a round case made of leather.

"The Harmony?" Sykes took it out reverently. He made a grab at it when it fell open.

Poppy glanced at him. "What's that?"

"I'm not sure myself. I hope those pages tell me."

"It's another box," Poppy told him. Her heart thudded. She was afraid to hold the roll of paper too tightly.

"This must have been where the Harmony was, but it's gone," Sykes said, and she heard his disappointment.

Through the walls, as if they were made of muslin, traveled an unnaturally cold wind. It blew hard, swirled around them.

Poppy heard wildly agitated voices whispering.

28

The gray people.

Some walked down Poydras Street; others along Canal, heading for the Mississippi.

They didn't go that far.

Not one of them caught particular attention. Ordinary people often don't. And these men and women were ordinary. Not tall or short. Their bodies average in every way and unremarkable in their dress.

Their faces were the faces seen on any street in New Orleans—unless you looked into the eyes and then the difference was obvious. No expression. These people showed no happiness or sorrow, no anticipation, no disappointment.

Nothing.

They gradually merged with a line of people buying tickets at a movie house and went inside the building without looking at posters, or buying popcorn and soda.

Among the pairs and groups who laughed and talked, the gray people were careful to pass without touching. Into the theater itself they merged, taking scattered seats. Perhaps there were fifteen of them, or twenty. It would be hard to count because they blended into the seated crowd.

"Please be considerate of others and make sure your cell phones are turned off."

The announcements rolled, the talking French fries, the dancing hot dogs, the full screen of heads in a darkened theater where someone spoke too loudly and the rest shushed them.

Then came a brief pause before the first short for an upcoming movie.

Black and white flashes broke across the screen. The sound changed to clicking that built to a roar.

And then absolute darkness.

The rolling click continued.

Some caught the hand of a partner for comfort

—or out of a desired thrill—their chatter barely audible over the broadcast noises.

As quickly as the glitch happened, it stopped and the right pictures were shown again.

All continued as it should.

The show ended and the lights went up a little. Patrons blinked as they filed from their seats—most of them.

From the audience at the opening, the fifteen or twenty gray people were missing, not that the others noticed.

There was less chatter as they all exited.

Among the departing crowd there were pairs of eyes that registered no emotion.

Fifteen or twenty of them.

29

There had been a tense moment when Mario insisted on scuffling about among the bamboo on an evidently important mission and a light had gone on briefly in one of Pascal's windows.

Fortunately Pascal must have decided not to investigate because the light went out again and he didn't appear at the back door of the shop in the next fifteen minutes.

Sykes and Poppy made it into Sykes's flat and he led the way to the bedroom, turning off the living room light on the way. When she raised a brow at him he said, "Don't want anyone to wonder why we would stay up all night," and shut the door. He also locked it—with Mario on the outside.

He set the box in the middle of the bed and yanked the pillows against the headboard. "Might as well be comfortable," he said, hoping his smile was innocent.

Poppy climbed to sit on the nearest side and Sykes went around to the other one.

A piece of thin green ribbon, tied around the roll, kept the papers together. Sykes untied the ribbon and carefully smoothed out the sheets. They were thick, like old, handmade paper and ragged at the left edge.

Sykes tapped the papers. "If this doesn't give me anything useful, I'm not sure where to go next," he said.

Poppy worked the white coverlet over her legs and settled more comfortably.

The writing—ink and in a fine, bold hand—was still clear. Sykes realized he had no idea if this was really old or if he was just supposed to think it was. "Someone could have planted this," he said.

"Could have," Poppy agreed. "Is it likely?"

"No." He began to read. . . .

This extraordinary meeting of the Order of Bella Angelus is convened because we vow to protect our families, our fortunes and, above all, the ultimate safekeeping of the Harmony, our final source of rescue, if our powers are in danger of annihilation.

We are heads of the seven families marked by the power of the Harmony:

Millet

Fortune

Montrachet

Averill

Villiers

Savin

Vaux

As the most senior family, the Millets shall safeguard this book and the Harmony . . .

"I think this is what it's supposed to be," Sykes said aloud. "I saw the book these sheets were torn from." He didn't add that he had seen a manifestation of the book, not the actual thing.

Poppy didn't answer and he continued reading to himself:

We have been threatened several times over centuries and always we have prevailed. Our adversaries are those who want the Harmony, the source of our power, to use for their own unacceptable purposes, even though they have no way to know the exact nature of what we have.

They do not know that we need to go to the Harmony only if we are threatened with extinction and in need of its protection, or that we are the only ones for whom the Harmony holds restoration. In all other situations it is only necessary that it exists, as it will forever.

We are in dreadful danger now, otherwise you

would not be reading this explanation. Although we do not know if it will be in a week or a thousand years, we have heard of a coming threat, a great threat. There is to be a stranger in our midst whom we do not recognize as the enemy, and this one will begin our downfall if we do not protect ourselves.

Unfortunately the presence of the interloper will not be known until harm has been done. Then, as this creature's kind come for our power, and if it seems they may win, it will be up to you to turn to our source for renewal of our strength.

The round leather box stored with this book contains the Harmony. Treat it with deference, for it has its own will. With the golden Harmony in your hand, use the seven gold keys, one from each family (these to be presented when required by the current head of the Millets), to unlock the segments.

Spread them open and there it will be, the Heart of Harmony. You need not shield your eyes from its brilliance. Our eyes may safely look upon it.

Hold the Heart of Harmony in your hands and it will prepare you for whatever is to come. Those family members who cannot touch it will be strengthened by the light only they will see. Only the seven families are joined by the one Heart. We cannot tell which families may be charged with protecting the rest or if all will be involved.

Then, when it is safe to do so, it will be time to

replace our beautiful angel in her rightful place —in the Court of Angels.

Signatures of seven men bearing the last names in the body of the instructions followed.

And no mention of any curse. "None," Sykes said, filling his lungs with air. "They just decided there must be one because it was the only thing they could come up with and Jude didn't know what this said." He flapped the paper.

He rolled the pages again and tied them together carefully before putting them back in the box.

"Why are you grinning?" Poppy asked.

"Because I'm not cursed."

She looked blank. "Of course you aren't. What did you just read, or can't I ask?"

"Of course you can. And I'll tell you. You have a right to know. But we have a job to do, Poppy. We've got to find what was in the leather box." He grew serious. "And why someone found it necessary to tear out those pages and come up with such an elaborate hiding place for them."

"Now?" she said, scooting a little lower beneath the coverlet.

He looked sideways at her. "I'll need to work some things out first. Maybe the family heads changed their minds about leaving their instructions in the rule book and hid them instead. Separated them for safety."

"Could be."

Poppy read the pages. "I still don't get why the

keys were spread around. They should still be with the families."

"I'll have to contact each of them," Sykes said, unhappy with the idea.

He dialed Ben who told him the first key he had any knowledge of was the one he found in the griffin.

Next Sykes tracked down Nick Montrachet and pounded the bed with a fist when Nick said, "You've got problems and now you call me to solve them for you? Maybe you should start at the beginning."

"Thanks," Sykes said. "I'll tell you all about it later."

When he cut the conversation off, he said, "Damn. It would help if I knew where ours was."

Poppy tightened her fingers in his. "Oh, no. Pascal would have said if he had one, right?"

"Yes."

Sykes bolted upright and sat cross-legged. "Damn," he said. "Damn, damn, damn. In the papers they didn't say where their Bella Angelus is. We're no closer to finding her."

30

*S*ykes *curled his toes. Gold keys lay scattered on the beach, at the water's edge. Dozens and dozens of them. The ocean's gentle scallops of shallow surf brushed the keys closer and wet ripples ran beneath the soles of his feet.*

If he stepped back, he'd leave the moist, tickling caress on that sensitive place. He stood firm and tossed his head to the side, smiling at the tickling brushes.

The water lapped. . . .

His eyes opened in the dark bedroom. He lay on his back on top of the bed wearing his shorts, his legs spread as usual, the fan sending the lightest breeze across his naked chest.

Two firm hands held his ankles while a soft, wet tongue played with the bottoms of his feet.

Sykes barely stopped himself from leaping out of bed.

Beside him the bed was empty of Poppy, who had worn one of his shirts to sleep. They hadn't discussed making love, they simply took their sides and were quiet.

He smiled up at the fan, its blades barely visible as light through the blinds caught them. Poppy had given up on sleep and she was making sure he didn't get any more, either.

Why not wait and see what she intended to do to get his full attention—not that she didn't already have it.

She nibbled the arch of his right foot and Sykes gritted his teeth.

Would just a teensy something special be so wrong?

Not for a good cause.

He stared straight ahead and visualized her back, the way it tapered at the waist and flared over her bottom, the soft cleft that disappeared between her legs.

And he heard her intake of breath the instant before he closed his eyes and assumed a deep sleep appearance.

He could project his touch. Down her spine, lightly spanning her waist until she wriggled, spread over her bottom, cupping the cheeks, and so softly tracing the dip all the way around in to the warm moisture between her legs, the vibrant hair he knew was very dark.

"Oh," she muttered, writhing a little.

This was too good. That erotic nub of tissue had already swollen and without the restrictions of his own anatomy he could massage it from all angles, and press inside her.

But she isn't leaping away, he thought, knowing that one small look would tell her he wasn't sleeping, or not so deeply that he didn't have an erection growing into its own small Mount Vesuvius at eruption time.

Her breasts were high and round, and very full, the nipples large and pink, and distended at their centers.

He sighed and turned his head to the side. And he passed over the sides of her breasts like a warm breeze, back and forth until the breeze became a very physical feeling brush.

Fingers of sensation started at the outer edges and slipped inward, stopping at the edges of her nipples. Fortunately he had very long fingers. He must not smile, just in case.

With the projection of his fingers and thumbs, Sykes took hold of her nipples. He pulled carefully, wiggled, touched a fingernail over the very tips until she cried out.

"Sykes—"

Before she could finish, he returned to the swollen place between her legs and with a dozen lighter feather strokes, he reduced her to a panting, helpless creature spread eagle on the bed. She pulled up her knees, but he didn't stop. In seconds, she climaxed a second time.

He thought he heard a scream choke off in her throat.

"How are you doing that?" she gasped out, moving deliberately, kneeling beside him and taking his face in her hands.

He didn't answer.

She shook his head so hard he opened his eyes. "Mean," he said. "Is that the way to repay a beautiful experience?"

Her smile was beautiful. "No. I'm very bad, but I'm going to make it up to you. Will you promise to lie absolutely still and not interfere with the exercise I'm about to show you?"

Low in his belly, everything turned. His shorts must resemble a tent.

"I promise," he whispered. But he pulled her face to his and kissed her, turned her onto her back and opened his mouth to devour her lips, pull them inside his; used his lips and tongue hard enough to rock her head. And she kissed him back, matching move for move, sighing, moaning, shivering with the intensity of their powerful reactions to each other.

"I'm glad you're naked," he said. "Did you get too hot?"

"Oh, yeah," she agreed.

He paused and before he could start again, she whipped out of reach to the floor at the bottom of the bed. "Where was I?" she said but her voice was unsteady and the rough edge spoiled her attempt at teasing.

Poppy went back to licking the sole of his foot and this time every nerve in his body was on alert. Only his fear of hurting her kept him still.

Slowly, she kissed her way to his knee while she ran her hand up his other leg.

"I love your legs," she whispered. "They're all man, just like the rest of you."

He didn't say anything—couldn't. Control was costing him all the energy he had.

Poppy knelt between his legs. With her forefingers and thumbs she squeezed the muscles in his thighs and made them jump. He heard her little laugh and smiled.

But she wiped that smile away and replaced it

with the tossing of his head. She moved fast, pulled aside a leg of his boxers and sank her mouth over him.

He reached for her.

"Ah, ah," she said. "You promised." His boxers were skimmed down his legs and over his feet and Poppy's body lay, his penis buried in her mouth, stretched over his legs, her nipples pressing into him. She reached up to stroke his chest, feel the shape of his mouth, play with his hair.

"I can't," he said, appalled at his croaking voice. "Poppy, have a heart."

He climaxed, and his shout seemed so loud he wondered if everyone around the Court heard it.

"I have a heart," Poppy said, letting him slip from her lips. She scooted up his body, dragging every erotic bit of her over his scorched skin.

He had his own brief laugh when her breasts encountered the hair on his chest and she couldn't catch her breath for seconds.

Sykes lifted her, slid her upward until he could replace anything else with his mouth and teeth fastened to her breasts.

Her shudders came in waves until she sat astride him and he looked up at her breasts. Running his eyes downward, he took in that small waist and flared hips. He glanced back at something hanging around her neck and touched it. "What's this?" It was soft, like velvet.

"A beautiful little bag Wazoo gave me. I love it."

"What's in it?"

"I don't know. And it's none of your business."

"And you still have the ring Pascal gave you?" He ran a thumb over it. "Beautiful thing."

"He won't let me give it back, but I'll find a way."

Now wasn't a time when he wanted to talk too much, but she was his. He would never let her go. He was crazy about her like this, but he was crazy about everything she brought into his life.

"Ready, lover," she said.

He opened his mouth to protest, but nodded his head, yes, instead.

She settled the wet center of her over his still throbbing parts. "I can feel that," she murmured, raising her hips until she could guide him inside her.

He bounced her upward, so hard she had to hang on to his shoulders. "Sykes!"

"Your fault," he said, not easing off at all.

It was too soon when their climaxes broke again and she fell on top of him, struggling for breath. He let her lie there, stroked her all over, kissed her hair.

"Not enough, Poppy," he said when he couldn't wait any longer.

"Animal," she muttered, sitting on him again.

But he flipped her over onto her hands and knees. "I want you to feel me everywhere you can."

Holding her hips, he carefully pushed himself into her vagina and leaned over her back. The rhythm settled until all he heard was the slap of her bottom on his belly.

"Oh!" Poppy dropped her head and shoulders onto the mattress. "Sykes. I never—"

"It's got to be right, sweetheart. Everything's right with us."

His release was like a spear piercing him from groin to navel and it went on and on. He heard when Poppy started to cry.

"I'm hurting you?"

"No," she said. "I've never been so happy. This is so right."

"I can never be without you," he told her. "If you decide you hate me one day, you still won't get rid of me."

They collapsed, arms and legs entwined, their bodies slick. And they kissed again before she pushed her head beneath his chin.

"There will never be another man for me," she told him. "Only you—ever."

31

Poppy chose not to accept the invitation to be at the Millets' meeting about what she and Sykes had found the night before.

He had not been pleased when she left.

She would always be independent and if he

267

couldn't accept that, their road ahead would be rocky.

A black Mercedes limousine stood at the curb in front of Fortunes.

Poppy stopped in the act of turning down the alley that led to the side entrance she used. Limousines were rare at Fortunes—she couldn't remember the last one she had seen there.

Curious, she went through the vestibule and pushed open one side of the double blue doors into the main part of the club. The house band noodled on the stage, the pianist, fedora tipped over his eyes, rocked his head in time to rapid riffs.

Bart Dolan, Ward's PR guy, was the first person she noticed. He shouted at Otis across the bar, "Do what I goddamn tell you to do, and get her here."

Otis saw Poppy at the same time and continued polishing a glass at a measured pace, holding it up to the light from time to time.

"Shit," Bart said with a lot of feeling. "Am I supposed to believe this?" He looked at other customers at the bar, who all kept their eyes on their drinks.

"Look," Bart said, puffing with the effort of trying to calm down. "I know you're probably busy. Perhaps one of Poppy's brothers is available."

Much as she would have liked to watch the show a little longer, Poppy didn't want Liam or Ethan disturbed, if they were in, and Otis needed a break.

"Looking for me?" she said brightly, walking

toward the bar. "You'd better watch your carbon footprint."

"Huh?" Bart said, and she wondered how good a PR man he was. Looking like the all-American golden boy went just so far.

She laughed. "Sorry. Did you come in the limo outside?"

"Uh-huh," Bart said.

Poppy shrugged. "Forget it. What can I do for you, Bart?"

"Ward wants you at his place. He sent me to get you."

The faintest curl of annoyance attacked her stomach. "I'm not free right now. A business like this takes some running."

"There's three of you and you got plenty of help," Bart said, sounding irritated, petulant and pushy. "Ward wants you. He had me bring the limo for you. Special."

Poppy didn't go around reading the auras and brain waves of everyone she met but there were times when something caught her attention and she concentrated. Bart Dolan was no Einstein, she decided, but he was determined. Blue dots coalesced, interspersed with gray and they trembled. Bart was the kind of man who followed directions to the letter and expected others to fall in with whatever he needed to please his authority figure.

"Sorry," she said, irritated. "Can't do it now."

"But—"

"Did you put in that order for liqueur glasses, Poppy?" Otis said. "No problem if you didn't, I'll phone it in myself."

"It went in," she told him.

Bart walked close to Poppy. He shook his head, sighed and looked at his feet before staring her dolefully straight in the eyes. He lowered his voice. "Ward isn't doing so well."

"I thought he'd gone out of town."

"He got back this morning. The talk about the murders isn't doing him any good. You know how it goes. Once they read bad publicity in a paper or see it on TV, they convict."

Poppy wasn't sure who "they" were. "There's absolute proof that Ward had nothing to do with that."

Bart shuffled a bit. "He needs to tell you about it himself. I hate to see a man with his potential cut off in the prime of his career."

"It won't be," Poppy said. She made up her mind. "Okay, I'll come with you but I can't stay long." And she would prefer if Sykes never found out, or her brothers.

It wouldn't be fair not to let anyone know where she was going.

"Otis," she said, as offhand as possible. "I'm going to visit a friend, but I'll be back shortly."

Otis grunted and gave Bart a hard look.

Riding in the back of the stretch limousine felt

ridiculous, especially when they weren't going far.

On St. Louis Street, Bart drew up in front of a pink-washed house next to the one where Poppy had been to the party. He got out and opened her door. "The boss is in here today. The cops still keep running in and out of the other place."

He let her into the very pretty building and led the way through rooms furnished primarily in overstuffed but well-done Victorian style to a conservatory at the back of the house. A small but elegant garden was visible through the windows.

"Poppy, you came!" Ward leaped out of a white wicker chair with green cushions and strode to meet her. "I'll call if I need you," he told Bart.

"Hi," she said.

Ward took her by the hand and studied her face for so long her awkwardness swelled to painful proportions. What he wanted from her she couldn't give but she needed inspiration to make him get the message.

"I came back early. I missed you."

"Bart said you ran into trouble," she responded without thinking.

"Yes. Let's go into the garden." He took her by the hand and led her outside. A path of broken stone went between lawns and flower beds. The surrounding walls were covered with blooming creepers and climbing roses.

"This is lovely. Why do you have two houses next to each other?"

"I like the idea of privacy. I own the one on the other side, too."

He withdrew his hand and put the arm around her shoulders. "You are such a gentle thing."

He didn't know her well.

"I feel as if I have to handle you like porcelain or you'll break. Maybe that's because you're good, and I feel that in you."

The water was getting deeper.

"Let's sit on the bench, on the other side of the rose beds."

The bench was of ornately carved white marble. Ward stood and so did Poppy. He kept on standing and looking at her until she gave up and sat down.

Today she was into auras. Ward's showed he was intelligent, but she already knew that. And that he believed he had a right to get what he wanted.

That revelation unnerved her.

But he wasn't completely certain of himself.

A jagged yellow pulse, just one, surprised her. Had she seen it before? He sat beside her and she kept looking at him, waiting for the pulse again. It didn't come. Perhaps she had imagined it.

She stopped reading him. Getting out of here without hurting him was the only thing she wanted—that and making sure he didn't keep pursuing her.

"It's been hard," he told her quietly. "Sometimes the biggest disappointments come from people you thought you trusted."

Poppy felt trapped. She crossed her feet, fiddled with her fingers in her lap.

Ward sighed. "My folks sent word for me to put in an appearance. That's where I went."

"Where do they live?"

"It doesn't matter. Not anymore. I've embarrassed them."

Impulsively, she took his hand in both of hers. "I don't see how. You haven't done anything wrong. They should be proud of you."

He smiled slightly. "You would say that because it's the way you think. You don't know my folks. They don't want to see me again unless I'm elected to the senate. They figure that if I am, it'll prove they don't have to be embarrassed anymore."

Appalled, Poppy moved closer to him. She inclined her head and felt tears of sympathy well in her eyes. "You probably misunderstood, you know. Sometimes we hear what we expect to hear. Are your folks pretty tough on you, usually?"

"They always have been."

"There, you see. They couldn't have been as blunt as you think."

He put a palm against her cheek, threaded his fingers into her hair. "I don't care about them. No, I don't mean that. I won't let myself go into mourning over this. Either they'll come around or they won't. If I've got you on my side I don't need anyone else."

Her stomach took a dive and she glanced away.

"You are on my side?"

"Of course I am."

"This is for you." He put a square black box into her hand. "Open it."

Horrified, she did as he asked and almost fainted with relief when she looked down on a gold pin set with large diamonds. W. W. "I . . . I . . ."

"Put it on. You know how much your support means to me."

"This pin would buy a lot of campaign pamphlets," she said and immediately regretted her words. "I mean, it's too much. Gorgeous but outrageous." There had to be four or five carats of stunning white diamonds in the thing.

Ward took the box from her, removed the pin and attached it to the neck of her dress.

She looked down at it, amazed and uncertain what to do.

"Remember the little gold ones we gave out at the meeting?"

"Yes," she said. "One of those would have been fine."

He laughed. " 'Win With Ward'? I knew you'd think that's what yours meant. Wrong. 'Ward's Woman.' " He held her hand again, kissed her fingers. "The only woman I'll ever want in my life."

"I'm not what you need, not good enough." She hadn't meant to say that. "I mean you need a woman from a different background than mine."

Preferably someone who wasn't paranormal, not that he knew about that apparently.

Ward laughed. He was irresistible when he laughed. "You need a course in self-esteem, my darling. Better yet, you need me. You are incredible. With you I can do anything. I'll do it for both of us."

Coming had been a mistake but she had hoped she could make him understand. "Please, Ward, wait—"

He kissed her softly, cutting off what she'd been about to say, but the kiss was light, quick and undemanding.

From a pocket he took another box, this one navy-blue velvet. She tried to latch on to some hope because it wasn't square.

"If you don't like these, I'll have someone come in and bring you more to choose from."

Her hope dwindled.

This time Ward opened the box and the glitter from inside sent shafts of light in all directions. Rings, an engagement ring and two wedding rings. One for her and one for him.

Poppy had never seen a canary diamond as large as this one. Huge, princess cut, the band was studded with deep-set white and canary diamonds. It was a beautiful thing. The woman's wedding band was plain platinum, as was the man's.

"You like them," he said quietly with a smile in his voice. "You don't know how relieved I am."

She couldn't speak. With her fist to her mouth, she couldn't stop tears from falling. She hated doing this to anyone who was sincere.

Ward removed the engagement ring, took her by the finger and began to slide it on. "Marry me quickly, darling. I can't wait for you any longer."

Poppy jerked her hand back and put it behind her back. "Ward. I can't."

"Of course you can. I love you."

"And you deserve someone to love you back."

She took off running and glanced back only once when she heard him behind her. Driven by a kind of mad need to escape, she closed and locked the door behind her. Her throat burned and she heard her own sobs.

A last look at Ward showed his face twisted with confusion.

And she saw the single, crooked yellow pulse —just once—again.

32

"What is this?" Sykes called to Nat who paced back and forth outside the morgue. Gray had been summoned to come, too, and they both needed to be at Millet's.

"The shit's hit the fan," Nat said succinctly when they reached him. "Must have. Look at that lot."

Sykes and Gray followed the direction of Nat's

finger. Every coroner's van and medic vehicle in town must be parked beside the building.

"What the hell," Gray said. "What happened that we didn't hear about?"

"Come on," Nat said, walking into the building. He stopped just inside the door, and Sykes hopped sideways to avoid walking into him. "Will you look at all this?"

The corridor teemed with activity, technicians in scrubs, boots and rubber aprons hurrying to and fro but oddly, no talking.

"I've never seen more than a couple of people here," Gray said. "Have we had a disaster or something?"

They advanced, staying close together, until a door on the right opened to spit out Blades. Sykes frowned. The man actually seemed agitated.

"You three," Blades said. "Come with me."

"Good evening to you, too, Dr. Death," Gray muttered.

Nat glared at him. "Inappropriate."

"How do you know?" Gray came back. "So there's a lot of people around. Doesn't have to mean the sky's falling."

Blades swept through a swinging door, and Sykes barely caught it before it would have hit him in the face.

"Nice," Gray whispered, to no one in particularly.

Nat actually gave a lopsided grin. "Some things never change," he said.

This wasn't the usual autopsy room Blades used. It was much larger with two rows of steel tables.

Most tables bore a sheet-covered body—or partially sheet-covered in some cases.

"Oh, shit," Nat said.

"Is that your word of the day?" Sykes said, but his insides clenched. Blades hadn't called them just to see how the place looked when it was crowded.

"They started arriving late last night," Blades said. He went to a far corner and stood with one rubber-booted foot crossed over the other.

"You've got a lot of help." Gray nodded to the people at work in the room.

"This takes more than one pathologist, if we want the job done before the stench gets a lot worse."

"Where did they come from?" Sykes asked. He engaged his third eye and realized there were no drifting shadows of people passing. "That's not normal," he muttered.

Blades looked at him sharply. "What does that mean?"

"Nothing."

"They showed up in different places all over the Quarter. Mostly just dropped in the street. We've got twelve so far."

Sykes worked his jaw.

"Anything to link them together?" Nat asked.

"Take a tour first," Blades suggested. "Get familiar with our corpses."

"Fun," Sykes muttered, but he started down one row of tables at once, pulling sheets from any faces that were covered. "So? Or do I have to look at the whole bodies?"

"We'll get to that. The faces will do for now."

Sykes looked up and caught Nat's eye. The detective stood between two tables and went back to looking from the face on the left to the face on the right before moving to the next two.

Settling in to get the job done, Sykes found himself starting to compare the victims.

"I'm damned," Gray said. "Do you see what I see?"

"What do you see?" Blades asked.

Gray didn't answer. He raised his brows and looked to Sykes and Nat.

They returned to the corner they had left and Blades joined them.

"It's strange," Nat said. "They all look so similar."

Blades nodded. "They're ordinary. Not one of them stands out. You wouldn't look at them twice. The first ones who came in—right after the woman—they were distinctive and we know who they were."

"What does that mean?"

"Not one of these people has been reported missing."

Nat inclined his head. "If you don't know who they are, how do you know if someone's looking for them?"

"In the last twelve hours we've had one missing person report and it turned out the woman who made the call killed her husband and set fire to his car with his body in it. There haven't been any other calls."

"So what are you thinking?" Sykes had very bad feelings.

"Take a look at this." He pulled two sheets down from male bodies to expose the genitals.

"My God," Gray said. Sykes took a quick look and turned away.

"Do they all look as if they were mangled in a big sharpener of some kind?"

"Yep. And the women are the same as Sonia. Deliberately lacerated inside."

Sykes crossed his arms and tried not to feel sick. "So what do you think it means, Doc?"

"Embran," Blades said. "Mass attack this time."

Sykes nodded. "That's what I think, too. And they want us to know they're here, so they devise another of their sick killing methods."

"We're running more tests," Blades said. "If my hunch is right, Embran are killing Embran. What I don't know is why. Unless they think they can throw us off by having these . . . these . . ." He waved a hand. "These whatever they are left lying around."

Sykes looked at the rows of bodies. "You mean they may be Embran?"

"I mean they may have been Embran. They

don't know much about the way the human body works. They might as well be nothing now."

"Just a minute." Sykes turned back and took another look at one of the last two bodies he'd seen. He stared at the face. "Look at this one."

"What is it?" Blades moved fast to look at the body with Sykes.

"We're going to have to check with Poppy and Liam about the man they identified on the tape. I think this is the one who killed the singer."

33

Ward Bienville wore a white terry robe and sat in a black wingback chair facing away from the door.

He had been here twice before and sworn never to return.

Anything capable of enslaving a man could make him weak.

Need could change a man's mind.

Now he needed—badly—to give in to his lust for violence.

The room wasn't large. Black and purple with a small soaking pool on one side, he considered it all a joke, designed to look as some fool thought a room of its kind should. They didn't know it could have been empty and served just as well— as long as there was no question of interruption.

He was an inventive, imaginative man.

A rap sounded at the door and he smiled. "Come, Ilsa."

The door opened, closed and the lock snapped shut. "You've disappointed me, Craig." He wasn't Craig and she probably wasn't Ilsa but it didn't matter, anonymity did.

He didn't answer her.

"I don't like to be ignored," she said. "And I don't like sulking."

Anger had swelled in him for hours and, just as he had planned, it boiled now.

Her hands settled on the sides of his neck and she ran her fingers under the robe. She worked the muscles in his shoulders firmly, then, in one vicious move she dug into the tendons, drove her nails down and pinched with her thumbs.

He let his head fall back and absorbed the pain, the numbing sensation that weakened his arms. And the anger grew. It simmered.

"Mmm," Ilsa said. "I think you're ready to tell me how sorry you are for staying away so long. You hurt my feelings. I thought perhaps you weren't pleased with what Ilsa can do for you. I can make you feel like no one else can. And when I have, you will stop sulking."

She posed as a masseuse. She *was* a masseuse but with a unique flair. She was massage fusion.

"Where do you ache, my friend? Tell me where you have pain and Ilsa will use it."

He knew what she meant by *use it*. She wanted

instructions and if she didn't get them, she would decide what would happen. Tonight he would let her decide—or think she was deciding.

"I am in your hands, bitch."

"Mmm-mmm, I think we shall have a spirited time. But my hands will do what needs to be done. Stand up."

He did so.

"Face me."

Again he did as she asked. Her black hair streamed over her shoulders almost to her waist. Knowing exactly what she looked like was impossible given her theatrical makeup and the black-leather mask she wore. Her lips were the red of blood.

Ward studied her from head to foot. And his cock responded to every inch. A leather bustier trimmed with lace pushed up overflowing and ample breasts. Her waist was small. The leather chaps she wore over a transparent thong disappeared inside boots with unbelievably high, thin heels. She turned and looked at him over her shoulder, ran her pointed tongue around her lips. Her ass was naked, high and hard but her hips flared in a way that was all female.

She approached him and undid the belt of the robe, she pushed it from his shoulders and let it fall. Her eyes settled on the abbreviated triangle of his black thong underwear, tenuously clinging to the end of his hard-on.

Ward swung his hips and Ilsa pushed her mouth out in a pout. "Off," she said, pointing to the thong.

"Anything for you," he said and stripped it away.

"In the hammock."

Steps were provided and he climbed up, expertly stretching out in the string contraption.

He saw Ilsa go to a wall where equipment hung. She chose a whip, a long whip and backed away from him.

Ward heard the whip snap on the floor, saw it wave sinuously like a snake. Then without pause she changed her aim and the braided leather wrapped around and around his body, effectively tying him to the hammock. It hurt like hell but she knew just how hard to hit without breaking the skin.

"Ilsa, you are a wonderful witch," he said, knowing it would please her. "I've changed my mind."

The whip unwound from his body and she cracked it across the floor. "Whatever you want."

He hopped from the hammock and reached the floor. The mask didn't matter. He didn't care what she looked like. He walked around her, sizing up the outfit.

The chaps closed at the back. He slid down the zipper, spun her around and whipped them off. They came free of her boots and he grinned.

"Cute," he said.

Her belly, slightly rounded, her pubic hair just visible above the thong, she swung her hips then strutted in her bustier and boots.

Ward ran his eyes over the "toys" on the wall. He liked a short cat-o'-nine-tails. An efficient tool that meted out punishment fast.

Another zip disposed of the bustier and a tug tore off the thong. He grinned at her. "I like the boots."

She tossed back her hair and he thought he saw an unfamiliar gleam in her eyes through the slits in her mask. Perhaps she was brighter than he thought. Perhaps she could feel danger.

"You need something special," she said and spread her legs, bent her knees. She massaged herself and showed him how damp her hands were. She beckoned him.

It would be so easy, but it was a risk he couldn't take. Today his pleasure would find a different release. He pointed to the ladder and the hammock. "Your turn."

He heard her swallow and took pleasure in her fear. Women came in two groups. A man used them both—one to look good on his arm, have the requisite children and even to love. He flinched. The other type were to be used only for sex and anything else that made a man feel good.

Ilsa climbed slowly up to the hammock and climbed in.

"Legs over the sides," he told her.

She hung her legs, displaying her sex. They were good legs and the boots turned him on until he hurt.

Before she realized what he intended, the vicious tool was in his hand and the first strike made. Weighted at the ends, the pieces of twined leather curled rapidly around her thigh.

Ilsa screamed, full-throated and pained.

He expanded his lungs. Another benefit of this place was that no human sound caught the interest of passing ears. He had heard more than one of the rooms vibrate with shouts and wails, of all kinds.

In the hammock, Ilsa lay with her arms crossed over her waist. She kept her face turned up to the ceiling.

Ward checked his watch. "I have ten minutes," he said, "so I must work fast. Ten minutes can seem a lifetime. Enjoy yourself."

The next stroke landed on her belly, wrapped over her hip.

The next striped her arms and hands where they gripped her middle.

The next ripped into the collarbones and upper chest.

The next . . .

Exposed concrete on the floor was deliberate. Carpet would have muffled sounds, the cracks, the smacks. Noise was important in Ilsa's business.

She lay on that cold concrete in a curled ball.

Her eyes opened as the door closed firmly

behind Craig, the man with maddened eyes. When he had come before he had liked his time with her rough, but nothing like the nightmare she had just been through.

The lights were on and she struggled to sit up, her arms around her calves to stop her from tipping over. Her flesh bled through the wounds he had made. Not once had he touched her with his hands or any part of his body, only with the tails.

She felt her swollen mouth and looked at more blood on her fingers. The mask felt as if it would cut her, too, and she tore it off.

Craig?

He would suffer for this and not in any way he would be expecting, not from a woman he considered less than human.

When the door opened again, she cringed and tried to lie down again so he would think she was unconscious.

There wasn't time.

But it wasn't Craig.

A woman stared at her for an instant before shutting the door behind her and hurrying to kneel beside Ilsa. "My God," she said. "What has he done to you?"

Ilsa didn't answer.

"You must soak the wounds." She looked at the sunken pool on one side of the room where water bubbled constantly.

Some clients could only perform in the water.

"Take these off." The woman unzipped the boots and eased them from Ilsa's feet.

At least she had managed to take a gouge out of Craig's back with one of the heels. The thought made her shudder with pleasure.

"I saw that beast leave," the woman said. Her perfectly arranged dark hair was pulled back with a tortoiseshell comb on either side and her makeup had been carefully applied. "He must be caught and punished."

"He will be," Ilsa said, starting to smile then sucking in a breath as cuts in the corners of her mouth stung.

"Let me help you. Are there salts? Not with perfume—that would hurt."

"We avoid perfumes for that reason," Ilsa said. "On the side, see? The white jug."

The salts poured in an easy stream from the lip of the jug into the water. They didn't turn to suds but whirled in opaque white circles.

"Come on. I'll steady you."

Ilsa took her hand and stepped down into the warm water with difficulty. She closed her eyes as the warm softness enveloped her. Even the sudden smarting pain of the salts felt good.

"We should not let too much time go by. I'm Jacqueline, by the way. I will get you clothes and we'll go to the police."

"What are you doing in this place?"

"I heard screams," Jacqueline said.

Ilsa laughed a little but doubled over, coughing. "I never thought I would go to the police but I'm finished with all this now and I have a score to settle."

"I don't blame you."

"I know who that man is and I'm going to make sure everyone knows what he is."

Jacqueline nodded. "I know how it feels to be abused by a man. That's why I never go anywhere without this."

From the large purse she had dropped to the floor she took what looked like a squared-off metal tube folded into three with a handle at one end. She snapped it open and laughed, looking it over. "This can do so much harm."

On one end was a pincer that opened and closed when Jacqueline squeezed and released the handle.

Ilsa laughed despite the pain. "I can think of a number of things to do with that."

"So can I."

Jacqueline rammed the pincer end of her contraption over Ilsa's throat and squeezed it shut. On her knees, she held Ilsa under the water until her flailing grew weaker.

Then she pushed her to the bottom of the little pool and held her down by the pincer around her neck.

Little bubbles rose from the nose and mouth. The eyes stared.

Ilsa's arms and legs went still.

Her eyes remained open.

The little bubbles ceased.

34

When Poppy opened the door to her apartment Sykes leaned his elbow on the jamb and looked down into her face. He drove his fingers into the front of his hair. After this bizarre day he needed to be around her.

"Sykes?" she said in a puzzled tone.

"I think I just want to stand here and look at you," he said. "It's been a long day without you."

She blushed. He had never seen her blush before and it made him happy. Poppy's was the only face he wanted to see.

"I just came from the morgue. Blades needed me or I would have been here a lot earlier." He wasn't ready to overload her with what was there, or talk about one of the bodies in particular.

"You're here now." She took him by the hand and pulled him inside, shutting the door behind him. "I need you," she said, taking him to the couch and pulling him down beside her.

"Pascal had to know every detail of what happened last night—several times. He's convinced the reason I was the one to find the pages was because I'm supposed to take over his position with the family. He wouldn't give it up. Marley backed him up, and Gray."

Poppy watched his mouth while he talked. She

rubbed his forearm and threaded her fingers in his. "What will you do?"

"I don't know. Ask me again when everything becomes clear."

"When you find the Harmony?"

"Maybe then."

She turned the ring Pascal had given her around and around on the middle finger of her right hand. "I don't think I should keep this," she said.

He kissed her, holding back, keeping it soft. Then he said, "If you want to break his heart, try to give it back. I think he's already got the two of us together forever. That looks like a hint to me. He sees you as a member of the family."

Poppy withdrew her hand and slid to sit against the back of the couch. She continued to play with the ring. "I'm looking for a way to tell you something. But I don't want you to get mad at me."

"What is it?"

She shook her head. "I made a mistake."

"What mistake?"

"The wrong choice, Sykes. I should have said no."

He took her chin between finger and thumb and turned her face toward him. She kept her eyes lowered.

"Poppy, what is it?"

"I sort of wondered if Pascal would want David to take over eventually," she said, her voice so small it was hard to hear. "They seem as if they'll be close, and—"

"Poppy, please don't do this to me. Don't change the subject. What's wrong?"

"Ward sent Bart over here. When I got back he was in the club looking for me."

Sykes figured they would get further, faster, if he let her do the talking.

"Bart persuaded me to go and see Ward. He'd been away and his family gave him a hard time."

"My heart bleeds for Ward Bienville," Sykes said. He knew sarcasm wasn't what Poppy wanted to hear. "Sorry. Families get into it sometimes. I know that too well."

"They told him he's embarrassed them. I felt sorry for him. I . . ."

"Yes, you would, honey." He didn't like the way he felt. There was much more she wasn't telling him. "You know I don't like the idea of you being on your own with Ward."

She nodded her head yes. "I told Otis I was going."

"Did you tell Liam and Ethan? How about calling me?"

"I couldn't face all the arguments. I decided to go and get back quickly—I felt guilty for ignoring him, Sykes."

He stood up because he couldn't sit still. "Ward Bienville knows what he wants and intends to get it. You don't have the kind of ambition he does, if you're not single-minded. He intends to get you. You haven't encouraged him and the more you try to turn him off the more he comes after you. I hate his guts."

Sykes ran a hand around his neck and paced.

"It was awful," she muttered.

"What do you mean?" He stopped in front of her. "Tell me what that means, now."

"Don't shout at me. Regardless of what we may feel for each other, I don't belong to you. I had to do what I thought was right."

"But you were wrong."

Her jaw worked before she said, "You're making this so easy on me, aren't you? Okay, let me get this out."

"What's that?" Sykes said. He bent over her to look at a diamond pin at the neck of her dress. "Are those real diamonds?"

"I'm sure they are." She touched it as if she had forgotten it was there. "He gave it to me."

"And you accepted it?"

"I didn't accept or not accept." She was on her feet now. "He put the thing on me and I was too surprised to react. I can't just throw it away but I'll send it back."

"W.W.?"

"It's his motto or something." Her eyes avoided his.

"Is it?"

She didn't answer.

"What else? There's more, isn't there?"

"I had to run away from him."

Muscles in his back hardened. He shrugged his shoulders and waited.

"He asked me to marry him." She looked horrified. "He had this extraordinary ring and the wedding bands and everything. He wanted me to marry him right away and, when I said I couldn't, he kind of went a bit crazy."

Sykes's heart beat faster. He visualized Ward's face and came close to sending an unpleasant message in the man's direction. The last time he had sent a dart into someone's face at a distance, he had been a teenager dealing with a bully. He was too mature for games like that now.

"Did he put a hand on you?"

"No. I ran away."

Sykes boiled. "Does that mean he would have done something to you if you hadn't run away? And how come he didn't catch you—he's got to be faster."

"I made it to the house and locked him outside in the garden. Then I got away."

"You went to his house alone. My God, Poppy, what were you thinking?"

"I still thought I owed him a break. He had never been anything but nice to me. Sykes, there's something about him I don't understand."

"Big surprise."

"Please go with me on this. He's not used to being turned down. But I saw something. In his brain waves. I've been thinking about it ever since and I think I know what it was. He could be mad, Sykes, as in crazy. Just for an instant, he wasn't—he wasn't in any control of himself."

He held her face and brought his own very close. "I don't own you, but will you promise never to go to him again? And don't think he won't keep trying to see you. I know a persistent man when I see him."

The doorbell buzzed and Poppy went to look through the peephole, happy for the reprieve. She threw open the door. "Gray and Marley. Wow, you're the last people I expected to see, and the people I'm happiest to see. Come on in, please."

Gray ushered Marley in front of him and she promptly sat down on the nearest chair. "I'm fine," she said. "Just tired. Boy, I thought Pascal was never going to wind down today."

"Yeah," Sykes said.

"Can I leave Marley with you?" Gray said.

"Oh, Gray," Marley said, looking embarrassed.

He rubbed her shoulder. "Pascal and Anthony went out and Nat called me in. I don't want Marley alone, not now."

Sykes stared at Gray. "*Now?* What is there about now?"

"Nat will tell you all about it," Gray said. "Let me get going."

"What do you know?" Sykes said. He automatically requested to enter Gray's mind but got a muddled reaction. Gray was still a neophyte with his psi skills.

"You need to tell them," Marley said. "And stay calm, Gray. I'm just fine and all of this will work out."

"I should let Nat decide who knows or doesn't," Gray said. "Okay. Ward Bienville's been arrested again and he isn't likely to get out in a hurry this time."

Sykes watched Poppy's reaction. She took a step toward Gray, stopped and wound her hands together. "Why? I saw him this afternoon," she said. "He wasn't happy, but there was nothing wrong. You've seen that tape. You saw the man who killed Sonia. Have you found him yet?"

Gray hesitated, looking at Sykes. "Maybe. Look, take care of Marley for me. I've got to get going."

"Finish what you started to tell me," Poppy said. "Why has Ward been arrested?"

Gray looked uncomfortable.

"Tell me," she said. "Please."

"He's staying in a house next to his primary home," Gray said. He rubbed his face and looked tired.

"He owns three properties in a row there," Poppy said distractedly.

"Well, he's running out of places to live, at least on St. Louis Street. That or he'd better stop waking up to find dead bodies in his house."

Poppy paled.

From the way Marley kept her eyes on her hands, Poppy could tell she already knew all of this.

"A woman's body was found in Bienville's conservatory. They think she was drowned—that would be after she was horribly beaten.

"Bienville says he was upstairs sleeping. Sound familiar? He reckoned he was tired from traveling."

"He has been traveling," Poppy said, but her voice broke. "Did they pick up anything on the cameras?"

"There aren't any in that house," Gray said.

"This is horrible," Poppy said. "Who is the woman?"

"Tentative identification suggests she was Ilsa Semmers. She worked as a dominatrix."

35

"A prostitute," Poppy said. She couldn't stop her hands from shaking. "It's going to be the same as last time. Someone's trying to frame Ward."

She didn't want to look at Sykes, but he said, "You're probably right. This is too much of a coincidence."

Poppy smiled at him, trying to convey her gratitude—and how much she loved him just because he was Sykes.

Another knock at the door startled Poppy.

"Come in," she said, and all eyes turned expectantly to see who would arrive next.

Six-and-a-half feet tall, hazel-eyed with dark brown hair curling past his collar, built like an agile heavyweight boxer, though no boxer had the kind of straight nose Nick Montrachet had, Poppy's latest visitor wasn't smiling.

Liam and Ethan came with him.

"Nick!" Poppy smiled. She had always liked Nick and the rest of the Montrachets a lot. "This is great. Welcome."

He gave her a bear hug and she got the full force of that piercing hazel stare. Nick's mouth was, according to some female friends, something that should be against the law.

"Sykes," he said, looking past her. He nodded to the rest. "This isn't a social call."

Poppy's tummy dropped. She didn't know how much more tension she could shrug off.

"Liam and Ethan brought me up because I asked them to. There should probably be a lot more of us here. I know what's going on. Did you ever intend to contact the rest of the families?" He spoke to Sykes.

"Sit down," Sykes said.

"I'd rather stand."

Poppy sat down instead and didn't like the troubled expressions on her brothers' faces.

"I intended to talk to you," Sykes said. "We're going through some crazy times."

"But you don't think that, since they implicate all the psi families, you should have included us?"

Sykes bowed his head. "Mea culpa," he said. "Guilty of carelessness. I got so tied up in what's going on I only thought about sorting it all out. I'm sorry."

"So am I," Nick said, but the lines of his face softened a little. "I do know how it is to get caught up with things. I know there's big stuff going down in New Orleans and it has the families' names all over it."

"How do you know?" Poppy asked.

Nick glanced around, taking in all players. He singled out Gray. "You're married to Marley?"

"I am," Gray said.

"Okay. I had a visitor, someone who apparently decided it was time to involve me. Disaster time has arrived, kiddies. He was a dude in old clothes—said he was Jude and I think he was one of yours, Sykes. He looked like you. He told me a long story, very long. He brought me up to date on the Embran?" He raised a questioning eyebrow and continued when everyone nodded. "This has been going on for months."

"I hoped we could clear it up without spreading panic," Sykes said.

That got him a very direct stare from Nick. "I don't panic. We need this Harmony, or whatever the Ultimate Power is that it holds." He pointed and kept his finger extended.

Four small gold keys shimmered in the air.

"To open this."

A gold globe appeared above the keys.

"Still the good, old powerful Nick," Sykes said. "I get the picture. You're involved and we'd better not forget it again."

Nick lowered his hand and the visions disappeared.

Absolute silence followed.

"I'm glad Jude came to you," Marley said. "The more of us the better. We think we could be on the edge of an explosion of these Embran."

"Something's been puzzling me," Poppy said. "We do have four keys but according to the missing pages each of the seven families should be holding one. Just about all of them turned up in the Court of Angels."

"My grandfather told me about it," Nick said before he turned sharply to Sykes. "You saw the missing pages? Where are they?"

"They're safe but the Harmony isn't with them."

Nick nodded. "My grandfather told me about a meeting long ago. And about the keys. He said he had no proof but he'd heard rumors that some of the keys had gone missing."

"Like the fifth, sixth and seventh ones still are," Poppy said.

From his pocket Nick took a small leather bag. He pulled out two keys just like the others. "Only the seventh is missing," he said. "My grandfather gave these to me before he died. He was afraid some of the keys would be missing because so much time passed. Could be a bunch of them were kept together in the end."

There was a collective sigh.

"I guess we start rounds of the families," Gray said.

Nick shook his head. "Not immediately. We should all have stayed closer so we knew enough to trust each other. Jude told me about the deaths, the earlier ones and the ones this time. This time it sounds like they intend something on a big scale."

"So why not go to the other families?" Liam said.

"Because we've got to be sure none of them is involved with the Embran in some sort of power thing," Sykes said.

Nick murmured assent and Poppy felt so cold she chafed her arms.

A cell phone rang and for a moment no one reacted. Then Gray started on the second ring and pulled his own phone from his pocket. He checked the readout, switched on and said, "Gray. What's up."

Whatever was up took a few minutes to explain and Gray put on his poker police face. His eyes weren't quite so expressionless.

"We'll be there," he said, and put the phone back in his pocket. "Ethan, please stay with Marley. Don't leave her even for a moment."

Ethan nodded.

"Nick, would you stay, too, in case something comes up." He gave the big man a significant look.

"While the rest of you go off and hide something else from me?" Nick said.

"We're not going to hide a thing. This is about the first killing that happened—the singer. Poppy and Liam think they saw the killer and we may have an ID. Sykes was with all of us earlier. Once we're done we'll make sure you're all the way in the loop."

Nick grinned. He sat in a chair and made it look small. "Thanks, but now I know what's necessary, I'll be in the loop. I'll make sure of that."

36

Nat wished he didn't feel the approach of doom. A seasoned detective wasn't supposed to panic and he wasn't, but mounting agitation wasn't fun. And it didn't help a thing.

"That wasn't any fun, I know," he told Poppy and Liam.

"At least we know where he is," Poppy said.

He had decided to show them the actual body of the man they thought had been on the surveillance tape from Ward Bienville's primary house. Photo identification might have been enough, but the real thing was available—if deteriorating fast—and there was no substitute for that.

They walked along the basement corridor to his office where Sykes and Gray waited. Nat had already been filled in on all the mumbo jumbo about keys and globes and books and . . . a lot of unlikely stuff. Unfortunately he believed it all.

He opened the door for Poppy and the three of them went in.

Sykes got up and put an arm around Poppy at once. Gray looked on expectantly.

"We've got a positive," Nat said. "Not that it helps much."

He saw Poppy's reproachful glance and said, "Sorry. That didn't come out right. Bienville will like the news."

"I wish we knew where he fits in," Gray said. "Even knowing someone else placed the singer in the foyer, doesn't mean the same guy killed her. So it doesn't let Bienville completely off the hook."

"Ward Bienville is either a killer or he's made a really bad enemy," Sykes said.

The worried pucker between Poppy's brows didn't explain either the deep frown or her evident jumpiness.

"Do we have enough chairs for everyone?" Nat asked, and Sykes promptly made sure they were all sitting.

Liam leaned his forearms on his thighs. "Shoot, I don't recall any mention of a key—not by any member of my family," he said. "Where is it?"

"Probably among the ones we've already found," Sykes said, sucking in the corners of his mouth. "Unfortunately. You could ask your folks, though."

"They won't know," Liam said, and his sister nodded agreement. "We'll have to see what we can find."

"Do that," Nat said. "Meanwhile forgive me if I concentrate on things I can see and touch. Like complaining spouses. And people walking into the street like zombies. And a growing body count."

He had their attention. Absolute.

"I haven't been updated on that body count in the last hour, so who knows how many there are now."

Gray was the only one who didn't react.

"What does all that mean?" Sykes said. "What zombies?"

"You saw the bodies in the morgue earlier," Nat said. "They've been coming in ever since. Only now people are seeing them die. They just fall down and die. We had twenty-two the last I was told."

"Horrible," Poppy said.

"We don't know who they are. They're all mutilated the same way and they're gradually rotting away."

Poppy covered her mouth.

"Blades says they're not human, they're Embran as far as he can see. Some of them gradually take on other forms, but they still disintegrate."

304

"So many of them," Liam muttered. "Why are they dying? Will they all die?"

"We don't know how many of them are here," Sykes pointed out.

"Blades did make one very interesting observation," Nat said. He looked at the Fortunes. "In the past they've always had eggs with them. Eggs with young Embran inside. Apparently that's the way they're born, or whatever they are. They ate the eggs and the little creatures inside."

"Oh, don't!" Poppy shuddered.

Nat continued. "We found bits of the eggs wherever there was an Embran crime and with the first one we encountered in Bolivar, who manifested like a Komodo dragon, and attacked Marley. The weaker he got the more he stuffed down the eggs but they weren't working."

"So it's fair to assume they've given up on them?" Sykes said. "Hell, let them be dying out before they get any closer to doing what they came to do."

"At the same time we're getting calls from hospitals about people coming in with similar symptoms—and similar recent social contact," Nat said.

"The calls from the hospitals. Why are they contacting the police?" Liam said.

"In every case a husband or wife, or some relative has taken the patient in with amnesia. At first it's total, then it gradually fades in a fairly short space of time."

"You think there's a connection between what is showing up in the morgue and these people with temporary amnesia?" Gray said. He had the edgy look of a man who wanted to be somewhere else and Nat knew where that was.

Nat took a deep breath. He shouldn't be looking forward to this but he was. "They start remembering but only to a specific point."

He had everyone's rapt attention.

"Their last recollections are either of being in a movie house down by the river—at the same movie, same day, same time. Or they were at one of the fundraisers for Ward Bienville. I think Embran moved in to use them as host bodies. Then, when Embran felt themselves deteriorating they vacated the host bodies again and tried to go for help. It was too late for them but the hosts are returning to normal—except for gaps in their memories."

37

"It's a conspiracy to keep us apart," Sykes said, shoving his cell back in his pocket.

They had left Nat's office and were almost at the shop. Their plan was to go by the Court of Angels to check in with Pascal then go to Poppy's for . . . just to be together.

"What is it?" Poppy said.

"Blades wants me back at the morgue."

She made a face. "I hope I never have to go back there," with a wicked grimace she added, "alive."

"Not funny." And he really didn't think it was.

"At least Gray's gone back to Marley," Poppy said, and they passed the shop to set off for Fortunes. "You don't need to take me back to my place. It isn't far."

He pulled her arm under his, happily accepted the shiver that went through him, and laced their fingers together. "Yes, I do and I don't want you out alone. That's why I prefer to see you home."

He felt her bristle. "I won't push it now, but I am not going to behave like a scared rabbit, Sykes. I can be careful and I'm not without my own skills."

"What would you say if you were attacked? 'Let me take a look at your aura.' That would scare off the bad guys."

"You'd be surprised what I might be able to do. And you don't have to be rude."

He had a hunch that whatever Poppy could do it wouldn't include fighting off a stray Embran. "It's my mouth," he told her. "It's got a mind of its own. Sorry."

She gave that some thought, then smiled at him. "We haven't had a chance to talk about the famous sealed room—not just the two of us— since you were with your family. I've got to admit I was hoping you'd find some treasure behind that wall," Poppy said. "Preferably fabulous jewels and hunks of gold."

He would tell her soon what he had hoped for. "That would have made you all happy."

"Not as happy as seeing your face when you found those missing pages. Are you worried about the seventh key?"

"Yes," Sykes said. "I'm going to follow Mario around and hope he produces it."

"That could be a long shot."

"I know. Pascal seems more worried about it than the rest of us. He gets agitated every time it's mentioned."

Poppy looked sideways at him. "Maybe he's afraid it's the Millet key you don't have yet."

"I already thought of that." Not that Pascal's turmoil helped. "What do you think of my cousin?"

She took a double step to keep up with him. "That's right. David's your cousin. He seems like a great kid. What do you think?"

"He's growing on me. Bit of a shock though, huh? Pascal's son turning up."

"I wasn't sure this was the first time they'd been around each other."

"Yeah," Sykes said. "David showed up looking for Pascal who now remembers the boy's mother—he hasn't told him he'd forgotten her. The birth certificate has Pascal's name on it and he and the mom were both working for Habitat for Humanity at the time."

"People are fascinating," Poppy said. "I think

that part of life's lovely. The unexpected. Pascal should be a father. And from the look of Anthony, he's loving the idea of the kid being around, too. I bet he'll have him bulked up in no time. Lift those weights. Lift those feet—run—no walking on the treadmill. Poor David."

"Poor David, nothing. He's got a terrific dad."

"Did his mother die?"

Sykes paused and looked at her. "I don't know. It was his stepfather who beat him up and I get the feeling it wasn't the first time. You wouldn't think David would leave his mother alone to deal with that." He shrugged. "Could be he thinks it'll make it easier if he's not there. Pascal will say something sooner or later."

"You really don't have to walk me home," Poppy said as they passed Sugar Daddy's where the level of laughter almost made you want to look inside. "It isn't even completely dark yet."

"Soon will be. I'm going the same way. We might as well go together."

"We're not going the same way. You're a control freak."

He tightened his hold on her fingers and kept striding along. "Piffle, as the men say in those Jane Austen stories."

"How would you know?"

"I've read them all. That woman knew how to write a romance. Sexual tension on almost every page."

Poppy put her tongue in a cheek. "I bet you don't tell your friends you read them."

"I would if the subject came up. I'm all for glowering, heated, I-can-see-through-your-clothes stares." He looked her up and down and took in a slow breath through his nose. "Oh, yeah. I did tell you about that being something else I can do, didn't I?"

"Wow, we've got a talent in common," she said, returning the visual favor. "You shouldn't tell fibs."

He made sure his smile was as evil as could be, which was pretty evil. "You don't know if I'm telling a fib or not."

Sidestepping in front of her, he took Poppy by the shoulders and held her there.

"What?" she said, but she looked seriously into his eyes.

"I'm glad," he said, massaging her upper arms.

Poppy frowned. "Glad about what?"

He shook his head. "You do this to me. My mind goes to mush and I can't finish a sentence. I'm glad you and I found each other, girl. I've been alone a long time and I didn't expect that to change."

She took her bottom lip in her teeth, but not before he saw it tremble.

Gently, he wrapped her against him and rested his chin on her head. He rocked her from side to side, absorbing every frisson of reaction between them.

Her hands slipped around his waist. "You are the last thing I thought would ever happen to me," she said.

"Mmm. Darn Blades anyway. He wouldn't even say why he wants me. We should already be enjoying wine."

"And your etchings."

He kissed her hair.

"But we can't now, and you have to keep this lovely appointment. Or, do you?"

"Yeah, sweetheart." Reluctantly he released her and took hold of her hand. "We can't forget what we're dealing with. I'll get back as fast as I can."

"I keep looking for someone to drop dead," Poppy said. "I haven't so far, have you?"

"You're impossible."

They reached Bourbon Street where the good times weren't just rolling, they were pouring, crashing and exploding in every direction.

"You want a daiquiri in a plastic cup?" Sykes asked, nodding to one of the daiquiri bars with its row of machines churning icy drinks in psychedelic colors.

Poppy elbowed him.

She had fallen silent and he noted her expression changed. When their eyes met, he felt a jolt. Poppy's passion glowed.

"We've never really talked about . . . physical feelings," he said. "How intensely do you feel it when we touch?"

"Sometimes it's like I imagine a burn would be," Poppy said.

Every fresh eruption of neon from a window or doorway streaked her shimmering dark hair with colored light and intensified the intriguing lines of her face.

A dangerous question it might be, but he asked, "Have you felt that with anyone else?"

"No." She frowned slightly. "It's a Millet thing, isn't it?"

"Yes. But only when we meet someone who should have special meaning for us. Ben and Willow Bonded because they were like this together. It meant their lives were entwined forever. Gray and Marley, too."

They got to St. Ann Street and almost to the alley where Poppy preferred to enter Fortunes.

"I don't want to leave you," Sykes said. The feelings he had for her were new territory for him. It seemed as if, minute to minute, he crossed another barrier he had not even known existed in his mind.

Poppy paused. She studied his face for a moment. "I don't ever want to leave . . ." Her voice trailed off and he knew she was afraid of overwhelming him. "I'll come with you and find a place to wait," she finished.

"No, honey. I know you don't want to be anywhere around the morgue." He led her to the doorway in the alley. "Is it okay if I come back?"

They stood with their arms around each other again and she turned up her face to kiss him.

Poppy would never be in the forgettable kiss category. She nibbled and licked and when he returned her nip for nip, reaching tongue for reaching tongue, he wondered if the singed-all-over sensation he had was the same for her.

"Mmm, of course," she murmured on a quick breath break. "Come back for me. I've got an excellent assistant general manager. Except for final approvals he just about runs the place anyway. I don't tell him that because he already knows it."

Sykes knew how hard he was, and that Poppy knew it, too. She clamped herself too him and squirmed just a little. "You are an answer to my dreams," he told her.

"What kind of dreams?"

"You know darn well." He cupped her bottom and eased her even closer, pressing her into the perfect gap between his spread legs. "I want you so badly," he whispered in her ear.

"No!" She glanced into the gathering darkness and the St. Ann Street end of the alley and placed one of his hands on her breast. Immediately, she slid her own fingers down and squeezed him rhythmically. "I wouldn't have known you wanted me if you hadn't told me. Weird, I want you, too, Sykes." She kissed him again, her mouth wide open.

"Whoa." Sykes almost leaped back. He stood beside her and leaned on his straightened arms against the wall. "We're going to have a disaster here if we don't stop."

"Or something beautiful," she said, smiling.

"Get inside, you hussy," he said. "I'll be back."

She opened the door and went in, leaning out again to say, "Bye. Later. Yum, yum."

He hurried away.

Poppy waited only a couple of minutes. She knew where he was headed. She would follow and surprise him by whisking him away the minute he was through with his appointment. Surprises were good things. Anyway, she couldn't bear just waiting around in the club for him to come back.

She gave him four minutes altogether. He was so tall she'd be able to pick him out under the lights and she couldn't afford to get too close.

Poppy slipped out of the door and closed it behind her. She felt mischievous and excited at the same time—and very, very sexy. What Sykes had let her feel right here in the alley should not be wasted for long.

She headed back out. St. Ann's had its share of nighttime traffic. Poppy reveled in the atmosphere of slight madness and the determination to enjoy every moment of a city that existed for good times.

"Hey, Poppy," someone shouted behind her. "Wait up a sec."

She turned and slowly started back toward a man who looked familiar. "Who is it?" she said.

"Marcus. We spoke in the club the other night. I've been trying to catch you. Can I talk to you for a minute?"

"Okay." She didn't remember any Marcus and didn't think she wanted to talk to him anyway but turning off customers was something she tried to avoid.

She drew close enough to see his face, or she could have if he hadn't just pulled a stocking cap down to his chin.

Poppy spun around to run, but the man took her by the neck, pressed his fingers into the soft flesh on either side of her windpipe.

She couldn't shout or scream.

The pressure grew and her head spun.

Her arms didn't work the way she wanted them to.

Harder, he pressed and she started to choke. Kicking back at him did nothing. The grip was an iron vise.

Sound faded and her legs buckled. She fell straight down, her sight flickering out.

38

Gray was not surprised to see Nat walking toward him outside the morgue. It wasn't usually necessary to have both of them there at the same time, but these were extraordinary circumstances.

Blades had called Gray when he was taking Marley back to their flat.

"Hey," Nat said. "Command performance, huh?"

"Seems like it."

They went in together. This was not a place that was ever convivial and welcoming, but in the evening it seemed particularly somber.

"Nat? Gray?"

Sykes came through the door and walked briskly to join them.

"Looks like a party," Gray said.

"Yeah," Nat said. They all turned their mouths down. "Let's find the man. I've got other things to do."

"Hot date?" Sykes said, and Gray winced.

Nat's face lost any expression. "Let's get on with it."

Gray peered through the reinforced window into Blades's domain. "Shucks," he said. "I thought he'd called us down to show us what the new interior decorator did."

At that, Nat laughed and pushed the door open.

White light, stainless steel, chrome and white, white, white met them. And even more sheeted bodies than earlier, even though many of the ones they had seen must have been moved by now.

The night watch must have started because there were only two men present, both in scrubs, masks and caps. They washed their hands at a row of sinks behind the autopsy tables.

"Can I help you?" one of the men said.

"Dr. Blades asked us to meet him here," Sykes said.

"He's having dinner," the guy said. "I don't know when he'll be back."

Gray muttered something and "Dr. Death" was mixed in with whatever he said.

"There's a lounge. Last door on the right. Wait there, if you like."

Nat thanked him and they filed out. "I don't like," Nat said. "He's an arrogant bastard to call like it's an emergency, then not be here when we arrive." But they found the unappealing room the lab assistant had indicated and settled into green plastic-covered chairs with stuffing poking through slits and punctures.

"Look on the bright side," Sykes said. "He probably has something really important to tell us, and we'd all like that."

"He's getting as frustrated with these cases as we are," Nat said.

"No, he's not," Sykes told him. "He doesn't have the kind of personal involvement some of us do. And I'm not talking about you. I figure you've got a lot riding on this, too."

The sight of David Millet walking in silenced the rest of them.

He skidded to a halt, his black duster almost at ground level. Gray noted that he had a faint bristle of dark red hair visible on his scalp. The dark glasses were in place.

"Blades called you?" Sykes said. "Why the hell would he do that?"

"Who's Blades?"

Gray gaped at the kid. "What are you doing here?"

David swallowed loudly. "What are all of you doing here? What's happened? I saw . . . felt. Um, I caught sight of Sykes coming in here, so I followed. The guy down the hall sent me here. This is the city morgue." He glanced anxiously around. "Who did you come to see?"

"Dr. Blades," Nat said dryly. "He's the head honcho around here, the chief chopper-upper."

David neither shuddered nor laughed. "Just tell me who it is."

Gray realized the boy was even more pale than usual.

"Settle down," Sykes said. "No one you know, thank God. That's the problem, isn't it? You think we came to identify someone we know."

David fell into a chair and let his head hang back. "Yeah. Stupid but I thought it could be . . . my . . . Pascal. He gets so mad about things he could have a heart attack."

"Well, he didn't. This is police business." Sykes gave him a significant look. "Have you been following my—you know?"

David's mouth set in a firm line and he didn't answer.

"Nat," Gray said. "Sykes has forgotten his

manners. This is David Millet—Pascal's son, Sykes's cousin."

There was no missing the disbelief on Nat's face before he covered it up and nodded. "Hey, David. Your dad's quite a guy."

"I know," David said and actually smiled.

"So where's Blades?" Gray said. "I don't want to be too late back to Marley. She worries."

Gray was just as worried about her. She had calmed down but there was no question about how she hated his new career development.

Silence became long and awkward.

Gray cleared his throat. "Did you know Pascal got himself a cat?" he asked the other men. "Damn great orange thing. Marigold, if you can believe that."

"That's because she's the color of marigolds," David said defensively. "She's a great cat. Slept on my bed all day. I like her and so does . . . Dad."

Gray hid a smile.

"I met her," Sykes said. "I still bear the scars on my legs."

"She didn't scratch you on purpose," David said, frowning. "She paws because she's happy. Dad thinks she had a hard time before he found her."

"That's probably why she weighs about twenty pounds," Sykes said.

"Only eighteen," David cut in. "I weighed her."

"What's with everyone in this family finding overfed, abandoned animals?" Sykes said. "If some critter comes after me it'll be hauled off to the humane society or whatever."

Gray smirked. "I guess you'd do that. I see how much you hate Winnie and Mario."

Sykes looked at the ceiling. "Yeah. Mario and Marigold. Cute."

"Where the fu—were is Blades, dammit all." Seeing Nat's color heighten wasn't easy, but there was a definite bronzed glow over his cheekbones.

As if he heard the call, Dr. Blades came into the room. He carried his gray cotton jacket in one hand and a hamburger in the other. A large bite was missing from the hamburger and he chewed steadily, working the purplish hollows in his emaciated cheeks.

When he'd swallowed he said. "Company, huh? I'd offer you dinner, but there isn't enough." Another major bite went into his mouth and the chewing action also made the prominent bone where his eyebrows should have been move up and down.

"What's going on?" Nat said.

Blades crooked a finger and set off.

"Bloody Pied Piper of Hamelin," Gray muttered. "Doesn't he need a flute or something." They went single file.

Into the morgue itself they went, and Blades held the burger between his teeth while he shrugged into his coat.

He removed the food and waved it, more expansively than Gray had ever seen him do anything. "We've got another pattern and you're not going to like it."

"I haven't liked any of them so far," Nat said, deadpan.

"No nicks and scratches this time. Not a puncture or a cut like the other times. That's different. I've been trying to figure it out."

Gray saw Sykes cross his arms and frown. "Then maybe this isn't what we thought it was," he said. "Doesn't have to be Embran."

"Oh, yes. They're Embran. You really ought to look at what's happening to some of them. Turning into weird monsters and they're falling apart —we've seen their kind before. But things have changed for them. If it hadn't, they wouldn't be showing up the way they are."

Nat tapped a toe. "We were saying earlier that there hasn't been any sign of those eggs this time. You haven't found any pieces, have you?"

"No. I was going to mention that. You saved me the trouble." Blades's nostrils flared with his indrawn breath. "Remember me talking about allergic reactions? One person to another?"

"Yeah."

"Okay, don't wimp out on me. The problems are on the inside."

They looked at each other, and David swallowed loudly again.

Blades seemed to notice him for the first time. "Who are you?" he snapped.

"He's my cousin," Sykes said promptly. "This is family business and I want him with me."

David gave a small, pleased smile.

"Cousin?" Blades said, obviously confused.

"My dad is Pascal."

Blades actually laughed, a hollow sound, before he cleared his throat loudly. "That's interesting," he said. "Is he likely to pass out on us?" He directed this to Sykes.

"No," Sykes said promptly. "Quit building the mystery."

"Do you know what an *auger* is?" Blades asked.

"Like *Jack and the Beanstalk*," Gray said. What was Blades getting at?

"Like a tool you make a hole with," Blades said sounding disgusted. "Not an *ogre*. They come in all sizes for clearing obstructions in joined pipes. Some are big enough they're fed down from a crane. But there are manual ones to bore different-sized holes. They look like pointed screws only usually bigger and with a handle in the middle to rotate around and around, three-sixty."

"Oh." Sykes nodded. "You said something off the wall about rotators or something."

"Yeah, only now I know more about it. I know what happens—at least to the women."

"Good," Gray said. He always seemed to talk under his breath in Blades's company.

Blades glanced at David and it showed that the boy's presence made him uncomfortable.

"He can take it," Sykes said.

Gray figured he was thinking about the kind of life David had lived and assumed he had seen a good deal.

"There was intercourse. Or it was made to look that way."

David didn't even blush, Gray noticed.

"So the things that have all been mutilated have been Embrans. Who's doing this to them and making them decay? Humans? That's the allergic reaction?"

"I'm talking about allergic reaction because of what was left behind afterward. Skin, some tissue, and it started to show unnatural signs right away. After the intercourse, that's when the auger came in." Gray was surprised to see the pathologist show distaste. "I think the cause of death was shock again, this time because the vagina was, er, destroyed. Same for the penis, only the tool had to be different."

"Which is the reason for the smart comment about a pencil sharpener?" Sykes said.

"Yeah. We're working on finding out if there's something portable that would make a screw." Blades had the grace to fight with an urge to make some other comment at that.

"Jesus," Nat said. "Are you sure?"

"Wanna take a close look?"

"Not unless I have to before this is all over," Nat responded quickly.

"Let's pass for tonight," Sykes said.

Gray felt sickened. Again he checked David over. He looked a little green but was holding up better than most would.

"Look," Blades said. "It's late and I want coffee before I clear up one or two things I've got to do. If you want more information in the morning I'll be happy to talk to you then."

Gray saw both Nat and Sykes tighten up and said, "Gotcha. We're all past ready for dinner." Although he wasn't sure he'd be eating tonight.

"For the record," Nat said, "you did assemble this little gathering tonight. We didn't just barge in for a chat."

Blades's deep-set eyes narrowed to slits. He raised his forehead, sending ripples of creases upward into his high, bald dome of a head. "I assembled it? As in, I invited you over?"

"Yeah. You said earlier you'd want to see us again."

"But I didn't ask you to come tonight."

"The hell you didn't," Sykes said. "I got a call."

"So did I," Gray said. "Marley and I were almost home."

Looking around at them, Blades didn't look happy. "I never contacted you tonight. I didn't ask you to come here. Or you, Nat."

Seconds moved like hours filled with whirling thoughts—and encroaching fear.

"They got us out of the way," Sykes said, striding for the doors. "This was a setup."

39

Poppy didn't know how long she was unconscious. She didn't think it was long because she could hear familiar street sounds, music, hawkers, people yelling.

Tied up on the floor of some sort of vehicle she tried to move her hands but they were bound behind her back. Her ankles were tied together and her head was covered, a head that ached and buzzed.

She wasn't dead. If "Marcus" had wanted to, he would have killed her and left her in the alley.

He wanted her for something else.

Poppy's stomach turned. Her heart beat hard and she broke out in a sweat. A gag tied between her jaws made her gorge rise.

The vehicle stopped but the engine kept running.

She saw a wash of red glow and the vehicle slowed. Had to be a traffic light. Poppy did her utmost to raise herself in hopes of being seen by someone in another car.

A slap on the side of her head sent her sprawling again. She hurt so badly all over.

"Make it easy on yourself," a voice she didn't

recognize said. "Don't move. Do what you're told to do when you're told to do it and it'll go easier for you."

The gag was soaked and she tasted blood. She let herself lie where she was and tried to pretend she had passed out again.

"She okay?" a different voice said.

"Yeah. But she won't be." The first man laughed. She thought it was Marcus. "Has she passed out again?"

A hand beneath her chin turned her covered face up and she made sure her neck was loose so her head fell back heavily when released. "She's out," the second man said. "You didn't go too far, did you? The boss won't like it if you did."

"We never even seen this boss," Marcus said. "Maybe we ought to get a lot more for her than he's offering. I'm not afraid of anyone."

"If you're planning to roll the dice on a double cross, count me out."

"We were sent to do this job together," Marcus said. "If I go down, so do you only that's not going to happen. I know what I'm doing. Don't forget that."

"You threatening me?"

"Take it any way you want."

They ran out of conversation and drove without speaking. Poppy had no idea how much time passed or which direction they were headed. She didn't expect any success but she pulled enough calm together to reach out to the mind of the man behind the wheel.

He came in loud and clear.

Almost at once she shut him off. Money was on his mind, and sex. He was seeing her legs in the dress that had ridden up beyond the level of her panties. And he was weighing his chances of fucking her before he had to hand her over. He'd let his partner have a turn, so there would be no worry about being given away.

This boss, whoever he was, wouldn't listen to anything the woman said, not that she'd have enough wits left to try complaining.

Poppy struggled against tears. They would only help choke her and achieve nothing. But tears ran down her temple nevertheless. She had had mild success contacting Sykes psychically but she didn't have any idea where to direct her efforts.

She considered all the behaviors others would have found weird. As Sykes had said, aura reading—and brain wave patterns come to that—would be useless. What else could she do?

Nothing.

Poppy held very still and fought to quiet down and think. She had strong hands, really strong. When she was little, eight or nine, her brothers had called her "numb knuckles." It had all been a joke for a while but they had impressed on her that the only reason she could make an arm or leg—

belonging to someone else—go numb by knuckling it was because they pretended it worked.

She had forgotten that but then, they were probably right and she'd given up the whole thing after a few months.

When she had pressed her knuckles into Liam's leg he fell down. Or pretended to. They had learned as children that each of them had a method of self-defense and for a while she had thought that was hers.

But her hands were still unusually strong.

Poppy felt so sick, she wanted to faint. This wasn't the time to make a fool of herself by pressing her fingers into desperate people and waiting for them to fall over. Anyway, they would only get up again.

She felt the little green velvet bag Wazoo had given her and wished she could touch it, just for comfort.

These apes had her completely incapacitated.

She thought about the bag and how Wazoo had told her to wear it always, which Poppy had. It comforted her to imagine Wazoo's spirited little presence and she hoped she would see her again.

If she ever saw a friend again.

"You worked for this guy before?" the man in the passenger seat asked.

The other one grunted.

"Is that yes or no?"

"It's mind your own goddamn business. I'm

going to pull over just up here and go in behind some buildings I know. They're abandoned."

"Why?" The passenger sounded anxious. "I didn't see this boss of ours, but that weird guy who talked to you said the guy he works for is a scary dude. We shouldn't keep him waiting."

"We're running early—thanks to my quick work." Marcus didn't sound as sure as he wanted to. "We've got a little time to enjoy ourselves."

"Enjoy . . . You hungry or somethin'? I wanna get paid and get away."

"Why shouldn't we have some fun with the lovely lady before we hand her over?" Marcus said.

The other guy made an explosive noise. "Straight there, straight back and make sure you don't hurt her. Those were the instructions."

"We're not going to hurt her, just make her happy."

"Sure. And when she tells them what happened, what then?"

Marcus laughed, not a pretty sound. "There was a big struggle and she got banged up—trying to escape. You saw how bad they want her. They won't be listening to her, anyway. The man wants something from her and he doesn't care about any complaints she could have."

Something thumped against the rear of the vehicle and it swung.

"Shit," the passenger said. "Watch where you're driving. All we need is to blow a tire."

"You will be in on my plan?" Marcus said. "Up to you. If you just wanna get your jollies from the show it's okay with me."

Poppy couldn't settle her mind. Terror messed with every thought she had. Terror and revulsion.

"Damn, you hit something else."

It was as if the rear of whatever they were in dropped down, dragged, then continued on.

"I'll stop," Marcus said. "You get out and check."

"Nothing doing."

"Do as you're told, unless you're tired of living."

"Don't threaten me. They want both back, remember? They're not stupid, they want us watching each other and doing what the big man wants done. Nothing more, nothing less. Let's get her where she needs to be."

"Damn you," Marcus growled. "It isn't every day you get a chance at one like her."

But he kept driving and Poppy dared to hope he wouldn't stop after all.

The vehicle slowed down.

"Now what?" the passenger said.

"I'm just going to check her over and make sure she's okay."

"Shit," the other man said again and with feeling. "Too bad you can't keep it in your pants."

"Shut up and remember I've got the gun and the keys." Marcus swerved to the right over bumpy ground and slammed on the brakes. In minutes his door opened and Poppy heard more noises. Then he was on her, his hands all over her, tearing open the front of her dress, his rough fingers scraping up her thighs.

He knelt behind her and used her torn dress to start yanking her onto her back. And Poppy ground the knuckles of both hands into his calf, the only part of his legs she could reach. She twisted and shoved as hard as she could. If nothing else, his muscle wouldn't feel so good afterward.

Marcus grunted. He released her and squirmed around, moaning.

The vehicle started to rock, to bounce up and down until Poppy heard something snap.

"Get yourself up here," the second man yelled. "This thing's falling apart on us."

Marcus rolled away from Poppy and she could feel him lying beside her, breathing hard and moaning.

"What the fuck's the matter with you?" the second man said.

"Get yourself in the driver's seat." Marcus's voice came in bursts. "And keep your mouth shut."

Again a door opened and the springs moved as Marcus got out. Poppy heard him cry out and curse. Then there was weight on the front of the vehicle again as he must have got in, or dragged himself in.

She realized her mouth was open with shock and closed it. "Numb knuckles" had done it. Those brothers of hers had put her off from using a life-saving skill and they were going to hear about it.

"What's the matter with you?" the man who was driving asked Marcus.

"Leg gave out on me. Cramp or something. Get where we're going and not a word about any of this."

Poppy heard keys change hands.

"You got it," the man said, sounding relieved.

They drove on, a scraping sound following them. "You sure we shouldn't get back there and check this thing?" the new driver said. "May only be the exhaust crapped out on us, but—"

"We're almost there," Marcus said, gasping. "Let's do this and get the hell out of here."

More silent minutes passed, silent except for whatever bounced and scraped along behind them.

"They're waiting," the driver said. "Damn, I told you we couldn't waste any time."

"Shut up and stay that way," Marcus said. "When they open the gates drive only partway in so they can't shut us inside. I don't trust these crazies. They can get her through the side door."

The swinging of large gates was unmistakable and the man behind the wheel drove forward only a couple of feet before they stopped again and the brakes jammed on.

Poppy felt air through an open window, and

Marcus yelled. "She's behind my seat. Slide the door open."

She couldn't hear the response.

"We got engine trouble," Marcus said. "We gotta get this baby to the shop. Take her out. We'll get a loaner and be back to settle up."

More unintelligible conversation.

"Okay," Marcus said. "So we'll take her back with us and get here again when we can."

The slam of a sliding door jarred every nerve in Poppy's body.

She was picked up gently enough and carried in someone's arms.

It had to be a man who had her and he seemed to do his best not to jolt her as he walked swiftly. What she heard next was unmistakably gunfire and she started to choke on the gag. The man who had her broke into a run and didn't stop until they had gone through what seemed like several doors. At one point his shoes stopped clipping a hard surface and she figured they were on carpet.

"Get that off her head," a huge voice roared. "What have they done to her? My instructions were that she was to be treated with absolute care."

"This is how she was delivered, Protector." Her feet were set on the floor and more than one pair of hands unfastened the bag from her head, slashed the bonds at her wrists and ankles and rapidly straightened her clothes.

The room was dim.

"Get that away from her." Looming before her, a massive head of carrot-colored hair, and a shaggy beard and mustache to match stopped the breath in her throat.

But the gag was cut off and she covered her face, her aching jaws. The corners of her mouth hurt and she felt blood there.

"Put her there." Long silver robes swished as the huge figure turned and pointed to an opulent couch, suddenly illuminated by spotlights.

Swept from her feet again, she was carried and set down as if she might break. Silken pillows supported her head and more silk settled softly over her body.

At last she spared some attention for these other people. Insignificant, a small number of ordinary people in ordinary clothes, their faces bore no expressions, their eyes must see but did not register reactions.

"And the two who brought her?" the red-haired one asked. His shaggy eyebrows moved dramatically with each word. Heavy gold rings shone in his ears. The hand he extended toward her showcased long, curved nails encased in solid-gold covers chained together at thick wrists.

"Dead," a flat voice announced. "They tried to leave, and we saw they had touched the woman."

His attitude and the atmosphere around him thunderous, the great creature approached her, frowning down, eyes glowing.

"Get out," he told the others. "Take the bodies of those two and have them thrown to our sick. They will enjoy some vengeance, even if only on two dead humans."

The whispering of people departing very quietly followed.

"You have an important purpose," the big man said to Poppy, his voice vibrating from the walls. "You will help save my people."

"What?" Poppy could just croak out. Was she unconscious again and having nightmares?

He gave a vast laugh. "Through you I will get what I must have. You and all the humans' greatest weaknesses will get it for me—their empathy, their honor and conscience, their ability to love.

"Allow me to introduce myself. I am Zibock, Protector of the Embran. I am here to do what I can no longer trust to others. You will become my . . . what do you call it? My accomplice."

40

Poppy wasn't at Fortunes.

With Liam and Ethan, Sykes stood in the living room of her apartment. Tension boiled in the atmosphere.

"I watched her come in here," Sykes said.

"So you've told us," Liam said. "Several times. But that was hours ago and no one here has seen her."

Sykes opened and closed his hands. "She could have gone to Royal Street."

"Already called there," Liam said. Muscles worked in his jaw. "No luck. I'm going to ask Ben and Willow to come back from Kauai. Ben's gonna want to be here for his sister, and so will Willow. We need everyone we can get."

"Nick Montrachet will be with us," Sykes said. "We'll have to figure out how to contact the other families—and fast. But I'm going to find Poppy first, then worry about the rest of it."

Two sets of footsteps ran up the stairs outside but they were too heavy to belong to a woman.

Nat Archer came in with David.

"At least Marley's at home with Gray and Pascal, but it's going to take both of them to stop her from sneaking out and trying something dumb," Nat said. "She's muttering about ushers or something. I think she's lost it."

Sykes met David's eyes by accident and realized the boy wasn't hearing about the Ushers for the first time. "Did you see Marley?" he asked. "Is she all right?"

"She thinks she ought to travel," David said obliquely.

"Travel where?" Liam asked.

David raised his shoulders to his ears and kept his eyes on Sykes. "She said she was waiting to be told where."

"That's not going to happen," Sykes said.

David shook his head no. "I guess not. They're getting a doctor in."

"Jesus." Sykes paced around the perimeter of the room. "I've got to reach Poppy. Her skills are patchy, though." He glared at Liam and Ethan.

Both men looked uncomfortable.

"Mind if I join this party?" Nat said. "When I got the news I started a search going. At this point I can't do anything more than have officers alerted to keep an eye out for her."

Sykes paused his walking. "At this point?"

"There's no evidence that anything's happened to Poppy."

Sykes spread his arms. "Do you see her anywhere? There's no sign she ever came back up here after I left her and we were all lured away so we wouldn't be around to stop anything."

"We weren't," Liam pointed out.

"I was," Ethan told his brother. "She didn't come back here. I've tried her phone a dozen times."

Liam gave a hollow laugh. "I wish she would answer but we both know how likely she is to have the thing on."

"We'll be lucky if she has it with her at all." Sykes didn't look at the brothers. "She's starting to communicate. I don't know when she got convinced she could only receive but not send. It might not make a difference now, but at least it would be a chance. I could try."

"Yeah," Liam said. "We should have helped her

with that but she was always the little sister and I guess we never stopped treating her that way."

With downcast eyes, David left. He didn't say a word, just closed the door behind him and clattered down the stairs.

"Damn, you people are oddballs," Nat said. He looked at the ceiling. "Come home, Poppy. Just show up and we promise not to beat the crap out of you."

No one cracked a smile.

"We need the Harmony," Sykes said. "We're supposed to have it by now. I know we are." He thought about the little angel gradually emerging from stone in his studio. Why had he been unable to work faster? Why did the piece seem to evolve only at its own pace?

"And we need another key, and the Ultimate Power," Liam added. "The time has run out. You said we were warned to hurry, Sykes."

"Okay," Nat said. "We go over everything again. Go back to when you left the Court of Angels, Sykes. Switch on all those extra senses of yours and look for any little thing you might have noticed. Someone who seemed out of place. Are you sure you weren't followed?"

Sykes gave him a pitying look, which he quickly softened. You couldn't expect someone who wasn't psi to know how off the wall that sounded.

"Earlier than that," Nat continued blithely. "The call you got about going to the morgue. Did you hear anything or anyone in the background. Was the caller identified?"

"No identification. When he said Blades wanted to meet with us I assumed the secrecy was because of his job. Didn't hear anything or anyone in the background."

"How about anything on the way here?"

Sykes thought about the walk from Royal Street and the woman he had held and kissed. Nothing unusual? Nothing he wanted to share. "I didn't see a thing. It was getting pretty dark. The crowds were out. Everything was normal."

"You saw her come into this building?"

"I've told you I did." He looked down and away. Very distant, very faint came the suggestion of a voice. He held up a hand for silence and listened. And listened. It didn't come again.

"You're sure she was inside?" Nat said.

"Yes, goddamn it."

"This is my job and I know how to do it," Nat said. He wore no jacket and planted his fists on his hips. The sleeves of his white shirt were rolled above his elbows and every muscle and sinew flexed in his forearms. So did the ones in his jaws.

"Then do it," Sykes said under his breath. He kept all channels open so wide he heard a scuffle of small animal feet, very small. He wondered if Poppy knew she had a mouse in her wall.

"We have to be able to do more than stand here," Ethan said.

"We're going to." Sykes looked around. "Anyone got a city map?"

"I don't need one," Nat said through his teeth.

"There," Liam said, nodding toward a bookcase where a row of guidebooks were lined up. He pulled out one of several for New Orleans and unfolded a map of the city from inside. "This is the one I use when people ask directions. We all think it's the best."

"Got a highlighter?"

Liam took one from a cup of pens and pencils on a side table.

Spreading the map on the same table, Sykes pored over the area. "I don't know what else to do, so I'm going to search. Who's with me?"

"We all are," Nat said, sounding tired.

"Then we divide this up and off we go."

Nat said. "I don't like waiting around any more than you do. But we don't have an idea where to start. Someone will have seen something—believe that. We'll get a lead."

David arrived back in the room, unusually flushed for him. He had taken off the shades and his eye looked worse than ever now, the range of colors was so much broader.

"You walked her back here and down the alley," he said to Sykes.

"I've already told everyone that."

David looked away. "I didn't know before."

Of course he didn't. "Sorry. Yes, that's what I did."

"You, er, stood outside the door. First facing each other, then side-by-side with you pointed toward the wall."

Now he had everyone's attention. "That's right," Sykes said.

"You left. You turned back a couple of times."

"I waved," Sykes told him.

"And Poppy had gone inside about then?"

"Yes."

"You went to the morgue where I found you, right? Straight there?"

"Straight there," Sykes agreed.

David looked miserable. "I'm not sure of the order, but Poppy came out of this building and walked down toward the street, then she turned and walked back. She got just so far and she turned around again and tried to run. Someone came up behind her. She was dragged. Her heels made grooves in the gravel."

Sykes wiped sweat from his eyes.

"It was probably a van that backed in. The size of the wheel base looks like it. Or a small pickup. Someone got out and went around to the passenger side. Got back in again. The footsteps from behind Poppy were heavier, like he was carrying something. He stopped a bit, then got in the driver's seat and drove away. That's all I've got."

"What the hell?" Nat gaped. "How would you know that?"

Sykes said simply, "Patterns?"

"Patterns," David agreed. "Yours, because I know them—Poppy's, too. Others are just marks to me like hundreds of others—nothing I remember seeing before."

Sykes massaged his temples. Once more there was a whispering voice very far away. He couldn't be sure, but he thought it said, "Hear me."

41

It was the biggest egg Poppy had ever seen. Cradled in a red bowl, from end to end the shell must measure about eight inches.

"Eat," Zibock cried with gusto. "It is the best of the best and I'm happy to give it to you. They are rare now and must be used sparingly. But it will make you stronger. I believe you have been misused on my account. This, I regret."

She sat on her silk bed, with pillows propped all around her, while Zibock, his own red bowl in the palm of one huge hand, stood over her. Her bowl was on her lap.

Whatever she did must be thought through carefully. To antagonize this bizarre person could be lethal. She knew this without his having said an unpleasant word to her.

Poppy swallowed. She didn't give up easily but she couldn't get around the conviction that she would die here.

He fixed her with his glowing eyes. "Eat," he said.

She looked up at him and realized she was frowning.

Then he laughed, a big laugh that shook his oversized body. "Aha, it is your first of its kind. I shall show you."

He sat on his haunches, put one end of the egg between his pointed teeth and bit down. The shell cracked open at the top, breaking off a large, ragged piece. First he sniffed the interior, then nodded. He chewed what he had bitten off and fastened his mouth over the hole in the shell. Up he tilted the egg and with a loud sucking sound appeared to inhale the contents.

Small strings of gummy material streaked his beard and little . . . bones?

Finally, he shoved the entire shell in his mouth and crunched, gulped, then sighed with pleasure. "Now you," he told her.

Poppy figured this was part of a test and she had better manage to at least make a start on her sickening meal. She raised the egg, surprised at how heavy it was, and opened her teeth on the end.

"Soon you will oversee the production of our young," Zibock said. "You will be able to get the secret to our renewal from your kind. We will work together." He laughed again, his body quaking.

The doors to the hall flew open and several of the nondescript people she had seen before marched into the room. Among them was one with a head resembling a bloated, hard-shelled insect although the rest of the body appeared human. She tried not to look at the thing.

"Protector," the one in the lead said, "we understand there are problems with some of our subjects. They have been unable to remain with their host humans and have emerged again and terminated."

"What?" Zibock pounded a fist on a column and the gold chains attached to his hands rattled. He paced, throwing his robes behind him each time he turned. "An error has been made. There is something we did not get quite right. By the honor of our predecessors, we cannot afford to waste more time. Bring them all in and we will regroup."

"But they are all over New Orleans," the man said.

"And every one of them can be located on our system," Zibock thundered. "Get started."

"There is another unexpected occurrence." The spokesman snapped his fingers and the creature with the bug head went back to the door. It opened and a figure shot into the hall, propelled by a female Embran whose ears jutted from the top of her head.

"There," the woman said. "She was trying to find a way inside. She will not say why." With that she threw Wazoo forward and she sprawled on the carpet.

"Wazoo?" Poppy threw aside the red bowl, the

egg and her silk covers to rush and help the other woman up. "How did you get here? Are the others—"

Wazoo pressed a finger to her lips, silencng Poppy, but her heart beat fast and she felt the first hope in too long.

"What others?" Zibock asked, advancing on them. He pulled Wazoo from Poppy's grasp and studied her. "You are a different kind."

Drooping as if she was ill, Wazoo didn't say a word.

"You are of the New Orleans sect. The one as old as time."

Coughing, Wazoo sagged.

"What's the matter with you?" Zibock asked.

"We think she came to take the Protector's new partner away. Her movements were stealthy. It was only by chance she was seen," one of the helpful minions piped up.

Zibock threw up his hands. "Foolishness. We are unperturbed by this voodoo or whatever it is you people practice," he told Wazoo.

He looked at Poppy. "You disappoint me. I had thought you would be flattered at my offer to take you as my partner."

"She didn't know I was coming," Wazoo said.

"I cannot dally with you now." He indicated Poppy. "I note that this one rushed to help you, which suggests she was glad to see you. Take them both to the indoctrination cell and lock them in.

Do not go near them. I will decide what is to be done when I have dealt with our other problem."

"One of our subjects told me he could not meld," a man said. "It happened at one of the gatherings for your representative. Twice the subject attempted to enter and assume the body of one of the guests but he encountered resistance and had to make sure he could not be found afterward."

"What do you mean? He couldn't meld? He met resistance?"

The creature appeared nervous. "He followed the man into a small room the humans always have and walked at him to become one with him. Instead of entering the other's body and brain, he was met with a blow that threw him back. He said the other one had a mark on his face afterward but he remained impenetrable."

Poppy remembered the story of Liam at the rally gathering and had no doubt that event was what this Embran spoke of. They could not take over the bodies of paranormals. But who did they mean by "your representative?"

Ward.

Instantly she saw again the yellow flash from his aura and knew what it meant. Ward was insane, and capable of inestimable cruelty. It didn't automatically make him other than human, but she had not considered that humans could be conscripted by Embran.

She felt sick and weak.

"I would have spread the powers of the Embran before you," Zibock told Poppy. He turned to his creatures and shook his great head and rolled his eyes like an animal in agony. "Get these two. Both of them."

The others bowed and backed away, until one looked up and said, "Not all will return. More than one have terminated. They lost their hold on the hosts, separated again, and . . . they terminated."

"The fools!" Zibock pointed to the doors. "Get as many as remain. And secure these two."

It took only one of the Embran to drag Poppy and Wazoo from the hall and along corridors, turning and turning until Poppy wondered how big this place was.

She considered trying to use the strength in her hands on the Embran. But who knew how many more would come to replace him, and perhaps she and Wazoo would be better trying to figure out another escape.

The next corridor ended at a door with a small window. "Like a prison," Poppy murmured.

The lock was a broad band of steel that slid through a bracket and buried deep into the metal doorjamb. "Simple but effective," the Embran said, opening the door and pushing the two women into a brightly lit room. The walls and floor were covered with some soft material in pure white. There was no furniture.

"Sleep," the Embran said, pointing at the floor. "You will find it comfortable."

He took a step backward and as he did so, he burst from the simple men's clothes he had worn to assume the form of a huge spider with fangs. "I will return," he said in the same voice as before. "But in time the Protector will also return—to deal with the indoctrination. Afterward you will be changed for the better. Think of that while you try to sleep."

42

"You can't go on any longer," Ben Fortune said.

Sykes wrenched his arm from the grip of Poppy's oldest brother, who had accomplished, as only he could, an almost immediate transfer from Kauai in Hawaii, to New Orleans, together with his wife, Willow. Willow was Sykes's younger sister.

"Please sleep for a little while," Willow said softly, her red hair caught back in a band and her green eyes luminous in an unnaturally pallid face. Even her weeks in Kauai hadn't been allowed to tan her skin. She was naturally very slight and ethereal but her appearance made her look ill today.

Sykes sat on the edge of a couch in the living room at his St. Peter Street house. He couldn't face the chaos at the Court of Angels anymore.

He covered his face with his hands, scrubbed them back over his hair and looked up at these two frantic people.

"She's been gone almost twenty-four hours. With every hour we're less likely to find her alive. I need to do my own thing and that doesn't include sleep. Please give me a little space. I'll join the rest of you soon."

"You've got an idea," Ben said promptly. Another big, dark-haired man with navy-blue eyes that could skewer you, he moved in closer to Sykes. "Come on. Don't keep anything from me."

"Just accept what I'm asking, okay?" Sykes said. "There's something I need to do on my own."

"Dammit!" Ben shouted.

"No, no." Willow found her husband's hand and pulled him gently. "We're not helping. Come on."

Ben looked ready to argue some more, but instead he turned on his heel and left the house hand-in-hand with Willow.

Waiting only long enough to hear the front door close, Sykes shot to his feet, went to lock the door and ran to his studio at the back of the house.

He arrived in front of the angel on her plinth. Each time he looked at her, she appeared more detailed, more finished. Frustration overwhelmed him, brought a film of sweat out on his exhausted body.

Yanking the respirator over his head, he went for a fine-point chisel with a carbide tip and a hammer, pulled on shock-resistant gloves and leaned over the little figure. Almost all of her appeared perfect, all but the tips of the fingers on her right hand and a shapeless mass above this area.

Why was it so resistant to his efforts?

He took up a hammer and began work on the hand.

Twenty minutes later there was almost no change.

Sykes's heart slammed in his chest. The thud echoed at his temples. It all took too long and told him nothing.

He took the hammer and smashed in down on the rough piece of stone above the hand. Immediately he stood back, horrified. The piece cracked. As he watched, part of it began to break away. He tore off the respirator. The beautiful figure was nothing like the pieces he chose to make, mostly for private consignment, but she was exquisite.

It was there. The ball that could only be the Harmony balanced at the end of the now-completed hand. Step by step he drew close and stared down on it. There was no angel in the courtyard like this. No ball all but suspended in air above an elegant hand.

Bringing his face very close, he examined the ball and almost stopped breathing. A single digit curved down from the top of the ball. Closer, he looked. What he was seeing was a claw with a talon and he could tell that the rest of whatever should be above the ball lay in crumbled pieces on the floor.

He had probably destroyed the final clue to what they must have to find the Ultimate Power.

The sound of quiet whining broke through the churning of his mind.

Mario sat looking up at him.

"They left you behind," Sykes said. The dog had come with Ben and Willow. "I want you to go. Go home." He heard his own ridiculous rant at a dumb dog and shut up.

The dog whined again and Sykes saw something glitter in his teeth.

One of the keys? He checked the pouch he now carried in his pocket at all times, praying Mario had the seventh and final one they needed. "Damn you," he hissed. "How did you get it?" One key was missing from the pouch.

"Give it to me." He made a grab for Mario and missed. Kicking up his feet, breaking into a run fast enough to make his legs resemble locomotive wheels, he took off.

"Stop! Right now. Right where you are."

Mario didn't stop, and he didn't make for the locked front door. Instead he leaped from chair to counter in the kitchen and launched himself through an open window.

Sykes tore after him, dashing to the front of the

house and down the lane after the little renegade, pelting through the streets and dodging people who grumbled at being shoved out of the way.

Then he knew where Mario was going.

Back to the Court of Angels. The gate would stop him.

The gate wasn't closed, dammit. And Mario leaped through a gap that should have been too small. Going after him so fast he would have fallen if he had tried to come to a halt, Sykes yelled at the dog repeatedly, tracing him between the planting beds, the angels, the fairies, the rustling bamboo—and the excited and unmistakably familiar whispering of the Ushers.

The entire courtyard took on a hazy mauve glow.

Pascal, David and Marley came from the back of the shop. Sykes saw them from the edge of his vision. Liam Fortune was there, then Ben and Willow. But Sykes didn't stop—until Mario leaped at the patched wall in the row of storage spaces at the back of the courtyard. He planted all four feet, fell down and made another jump as if he were trying to batter the wall down.

"Got you," Sykes said, reaching to snatch up the dog.

Too late, Mario rushed into the storage room to the right and before Sykes could make any headway, the red monster had disappeared behind the wall that hid the entry leading to the hidden room.

"What the hell's happening?" Ben cried. "Why are you chasing our dog?"

"Your damn dog has stolen one of the keys. If he loses it, we're finished. More finished than we already thought we could be."

Sykes made for the gap but when she saw him squeezing in there, Willow went after him. "Let me go first. I'll be faster."

He stood back and then followed her.

All but Marley made the trek through the narrow tunnel and down into the foul-smelling room on the other side.

"Don't you frighten him," Willow said, facing them all. "If you do and he drops it we could lose it anyway. And you're not to frighten Mario anyway."

"Patience," Sykes muttered to himself.

He stood quite still, his hands to his head, and closed his eyes.

"My God, are you ill, man?" Ben said.

"Sit down," Liam commanded. "Take some deep breaths."

Sykes waved them away. He heard his name, very faint, very distant and in a cry begging him to hear. "I think Poppy's trying to reach me," he said and sent an answer. *Poppy, where are you?* If she was as far away as he thought she might not have the power to keep the channel open.

All the others remained silent, watching him.

He kept his eyes closed and concentrated. The

hand that settled on his arm squeezed tight, a very big hand and he knew it was Ben.

"Nothing," Sykes said. "But if I did hear her, she's . . ." He couldn't finish.

"She's alive," David said. He had shed his sunglasses and, with a fine brush of auburn hair showing, there was little doubt about his identity.

"Yes," the rest of them chorused.

"The Ultimate Power could be all the help we need now," Pascal said.

Sykes turned back to the dog. "Get the key from him," he said.

"Not that it'll do any good," Liam said. "Not without the Harmony."

Mario leaped to the ledge where the box of papers had been. He began to scratch at the wall. His movements became frenzied and he barked, and barked, gouged at the plaster and howled.

"Get that key," Pascal said. "Before he swallows the thing."

Liam took hold of Mario to pull him away, but claws on one of the dog's paws were stuck into the plaster. Prying open Mario's jaws, Liam reached inside his mouth. Slowly, he removed his fingers. "He's already dropped it. Or swallowed it."

And the claws remained stuck in the plaster.

Pushing her way past the men, Willow put an arm around her dog to support him and worked his foot free—and with it a chunk of wall.

"Mario," Willow reprimanded. "Naughty boy."

Sykes aimed his flashlight on the hole Mario had made. "What if he's managed to get the key in there?"

"It was probably gone before he made the hole," Liam pointed out.

David went closer and looked. "There's glass in there. Colored glass." He hooked out more plaster, but carefully, making sure nothing fell inside. "There's those lead lines. Stained glass."

On his hands and knees, Sykes searched among the debris on the floor.

David continued to break away the wall.

"Sykes!" Liam said urgently. "Look at this. Have you seen anything like it before?"

Liam focused his flashlight on the big opening David had now made.

Getting up slowly, Sykes went to stand beside David. What he saw, created in vivid green, purple and gold, was a stained-glass window depicting an angel, the angel standing in his studio.

"She was meant to show me what to look for," he murmured of the piece in his studio. Carefully, he broke away more pieces of plasterboard until a full view of the angel came into view. Liam and Ben went to help and gradually the whole piece was revealed.

The claw Sykes had seen in his studio belonged to a red griffin.

"A griffin?" Willow said. "I don't understand."

"I do," Sykes and Ben said together and they

raced to get out of the room with the others scrambling behind them.

Leading the way, Sykes went to the stand of bamboo and parted it, pushing his way through. "There it is," he said, pointing at the red stone griffin.

He scraped soil away from its base and others joined him. The statue was buried deep and they worked frantically.

At last it came free of the earth with a sucking sound. The light was failing yet a gold ball attached to the base of the griffin glowed.

Sykes carried it into the shop, into Pascal's office and put it on its side atop the desk. He took out the bag of keys while Ben worked the Harmony loose. "They moved it," he said. "They were afraid it would be taken so they hid it." He shook the five keys he still had onto Pascal's blotter.

A clink at his feet made him look down into what looked like Mario's grin. His mouth was open and he panted as if laughing. On the floor lay the key he'd swiped earlier.

"Don't you say anything mean to him," Willow said. "He wanted us to see the window."

"Or smelled a mouse in there and fancied a snack." Sykes gave her a small smile. "I'll have to wait to congratulate him."

The keys fitted into tiny locks at the top of the ball and had to be moved from one to another to find the right ones, the ones that clicked open specific segments.

"Will we break open the last one?" Pascal said.

"We could jeopardize something." Sykes clicked another key.

"But—" David came closer. "Those are the keys? I didn't see them before. I thought they'd be big."

Sykes sighed. He began to struggle against defeat.

David reached inside the neck of his sweater and pulled a leather cord over his head. On the cord hung a key that matched the other six. "My mother gave this to me years ago. She said Dad gave it to her the night I was . . . that night. When I came here, she said I could show it to him if he didn't believe I was his son, but he does."

With a long look at Pascal, Sykes fitted in the final key that clicked smoothly in its lock.

"You gave it to her," David said to Pascal in a very small voice.

Pascal put an arm around him and didn't say anything.

43

"Thank you," Sykes said quietly, watching the segments of the ball fall open in his hands. "Just let us know what we're supposed to do next."

"We'll know," Marley said. "It will show us."

Inside the ball lay yet another box, this one deep purple velvet and oval. Willing his hands to be steady, Sykes picked it up and snapped it open.

Empty!

He looked at the ring of blank faces, watched horror fill every pair of eyes.

"It's been stolen," Sykes said.

44

"Whatever it takes, we're getting out of here," Poppy said. She walked the edges of the padded room, pressing the walls. "How did you find me?"

Poppy looked over her shoulder at Wazoo who sat on the floor staring straight ahead—lost in thought.

"Wazoo?" Poppy said. "How did—"

"I was going to see if I could find you—to talk to you about—something. I was almost at Fortunes and a van came past. You were in it."

Poppy frowned at her. "I was on the floor in the back. You couldn't have seen me."

"Show me the velvet bag around your neck."

Patting absently, Poppy closed her fingers over the bag and pulled it from the neck of her dress.

"That's how I knew. I felt you. It sent your fear to me, and when the van slowed down I jumped on the back and held on."

"And nobody tried to stop you?"

"In the Quarter at night?" Wazoo laughed. "The

bumper dropped down but that only made it easier for me to balance and hold on. That and our connection. You held me to you. You have to get Sykes to come. He'll bring Nat . . . and all the others."

Poppy leaned against the wall. "I heard him," she said, dejected. "I called Sykes and he answered. Then I couldn't concentrate and he went away."

"You can talk to him?" Wazoo stood up, her dark eyes blazing. "You *will* talk to him. You're going to guide him here."

"I don't know where we are."

"I do. Concentrate. Speak to him."

"You're psychic," Poppy said. "You try, too."

"Psychic but not telepathic."

Turning away, afraid to fail, Poppy reached the door. She peered through the window and recoiled. "There's someone out there. I think he's dead."

As she watched, the figure sprawled on the floor of an otherwise empty corridor shrank. It coiled like a spent firework and Poppy saw little pieces break off. They were hairy and she realized this was the shape-shifting spider they had seen earlier.

"Wazoo," Poppy said urgently, "I think they're in trouble. I think they're being overtaken by some sickness."

"Let me see." Only Wazoo wasn't tall enough to see through the window.

"Here, jump." Poppy caught her under the arms and hoisted Wazoo.

She sailed past the window and rose all the way to the ceiling. Grabbing her before she could fall, Poppy lowered her carefully. "It isn't that bouncy," she said, shaken.

Wazoo screwed up her eyes to study Poppy. "I didn't even get to jump, girl. You threw me up there. You don't know your own strength."

Turning back to the door, Poppy slid her fingers under the padded edge to peel a piece back. The entire door covering stripped away.

"Holy Halloween," Wazoo said.

Poppy cleared her throat. "I've always had strong hands."

"That's more than strong hands."

There was no knob on the inside of the door. Expecting nothing, Poppy worked the fingertips of her right hand into the crack between the door and the jamb at what she thought was the level of the bolt.

A deafening sound of metal tearing made her stop. She turned around to Wazoo who said, "You're gaping. It's not pretty."

The edge of the door had buckled and they could both see where the wide bolt slid into its deep slot.

"Can you get at it?" Wazoo said.

Hooking two fingers under the steel bar of the bolt, Poppy worked to get enough purchase to slide it undone.

The entire bolt snapped free, the sound like a bullet in a confined space, and Poppy grabbed at her hand muttering, "Ouch, ouch, ouch." The ring Pascal had given her had dug into her finger.

She shook off the discomfort and they eased open the door.

"Where is everyone?" Wazoo whispered. She looked at what was not a small pile of spider detritus and sucked in a breath. "What did it do, eat itself?"

"Anything's possible with this group," Poppy said.

"Now we find a hiding place and you start talking to that scrumptious man of yours."

Poppy looked at Wazoo and felt helpless.

"Or I can just send you running through this place tearing everything up," Wazoo said. "Shouldn't be a problem for you."

"I want to know what's going on here before I start knocking my brains out."

She slipped from the room with Wazoo behind her. They passed through empty corridor after empty corridor until Poppy heard a mounting sound in the distance and flattened herself to the wall. She shot out an arm to halt Wazoo who immediately yelped.

"What?" Poppy said.

"You nearly knocked me out," Wazoo said, rubbing the back of her head. "I hit the wall."

"Sorry. Can you hear the noise?"

"Sounds like a riot," Wazoo said. "I think it's coming from that great hall."

They crept around another corner but drew back again. Pouring from somewhere they couldn't see, a whole army of people, or part people, part bizarre creatures in many cases, advanced through the massive double doors Poppy recognized as the entrance to the hall.

"I want to see in there," Poppy said.

"Not until we establish contact with Sykes, or anyone else you can talk to."

"They're coming out again," Poppy squeaked.

"Start talking."

Slipping out of sight of the jostling Embran, Poppy slid to the floor with her back to the wall and tried to concentrate. *Sykes, I need you. We need you. Wazoo is with me.*

Wazoo knew enough to sit and listen to Poppy's silence.

Poppy heard nothing and began to sigh, letting her head hang forward.

"Dope," Wazoo said. "You don't just give up. Keep at it."

Poppy?

She jumped and her eyes flew wide open. *Sykes? Where are you?*

"Where are we?" she asked Wazoo.

"In a compound by the river. A big warehouse. Near Algiers Point. There's a building with C & O Mills on the front. It's written all the way across.

The compound is huge. We're in the big building."

Very carefully, Poppy kept still, tried to relax, and repeated Wazoo's directions.

She waited for a response but none came.

Her eyes felt moist.

"No losing your nerve now," Wazoo said. "Answer me one thing first. Do you think Nat and I should try to be together? That's what I was coming to ask you."

"Of course," Poppy said.

Wazoo nodded. "Get back on the job, then. Concentrate. Go inside your mind or wherever it is you talk to each other."

Sykes, please hear me. Poppy strained, her head beginning to ache. Again she gave him their coordinates. *And Wazoo's with me.*

Don't let it be too faint for him to hear this time.

Good. Now, be quiet until you hear from me. Stay hidden. No heroics and that's an order. I love you.

Poppy almost collapsed. She told Wazoo what Sykes had said.

"I told you that was one outstanding example of the male of the species," Wazoo said. "Too bad he saw you first. I'd have snapped him up."

"Nat—"

"Not if I'd already seen Nat, of course. We gotta make sure a bunch of those turkeys don't suddenly come on us. But I want to see what they're all up to."

"How's your sense of direction?"

"Fantastic. We'll see if we can get around from the other side of the hall. There has to be another way out of this place."

Crouched, they began to move again, away from the front of the building. "If we could get outside our chances of not being seen might be better," Poppy said.

"You're not hearing her right," Nat said, for Sykes's ears only. "What would Wazoo be doing with her?"

"And I should know?" Sykes stared at him. They were driving in Nat's unmarked car toward the waterfront. "She told me twice, so I don't think she's making it up."

He looked in the rearview mirror. Spread out behind them, more vehicles converged on the directions Sykes had given them.

"That place always looks well maintained," Nat said. "Polite watchmen. Trucks coming and going. No problems. Never a call about any trouble. I hope they've got the right place."

"They have," Sykes said, and he was convinced.

He flexed his hands and rotated his shoulders. The sensation traveling through him was new. If he didn't know it was impossible he'd say they had somehow come upon the Ultimate Power even if they hadn't seen it. He felt invincible—

and his nerves leaped about at the same time. He wanted to see Poppy, to touch her.

Sykes. There are many, many of them here. They don't all look the same. Can you hear me?

Yes!

Something's gone really wrong with them. They're dying, I think, but a lot of them are still very strong. Let Wazoo and me try to find our own way out. It's too dangerous for you to come in here.

He looked sideways at Nat. *Stay out of sight. Don't try being heroes.*

"They're telling us what to do," Poppy told Wazoo.

"And that surprises you?"

"There's a door ahead. I don't see anyone."

When they reached it and pushed lightly, the door cracked open and the moist warmth of the night hit their faces. The sound of many shouting voices came from the distance. Poppy inclined her head at Wazoo and they slipped outside.

Dodging from one hiding place to another, relying on shadows, they made their way to a back corner of the building, then, very cautiously, around the side.

Wazoo pulled Poppy's arm and whispered in her ear. "Those big drums over there. If we could get behind them we could see the front of the building and stay out of sight."

Nodding, Poppy set off, racing to a stack of crates, then a Dumpster, a parked truck. The drums were actually just beyond the side of the warehouse and Poppy knew the last leg to get there would be dangerous.

I wish we could be invisible like you can, she communicated without thinking.

What are you doing?

Getting where we can see what they're doing. And we're going no matter what you say, so don't try ordering us around.

She listened to heavy silence and knew he was deciding what to say next.

We'll talk about this later, he said. *Put your arms around each other and hold on tight. Look at the place you want to be and put your faces on each other's shoulders. Do it now.*

Poppy grabbed Wazoo. "Don't ask," she said, holding her close. "Keep your face down on my shoulder."

There was no sensation, other than disappointment.

Poppy opened her eyes and almost gasped aloud. They were next to the drums. Wazoo caught her hand and hurried them both completely out of sight.

"Neat trick," Wazoo said.

"It was Sykes."

"Surprise, surprise. Now we can see everything. Look between these things."

Poppy peered between the oil drums at a gathering in front of the warehouse.

Under the standard lights it was Zibock who commanded the center of the scene, his carrot-colored hair aflame, the gold on his hands flashing. He stood twice as tall as the rest with his silver robes shining almost white. And he bellowed at all around him.

"Now is the time to test you all. We must call in all our resources and correct whatever we did not expect to encounter."

A blue glow, shot with green, illuminated the space around Poppy. She blinked, expecting her eyes to react, but there was no discomfort. "Do you see that?" she asked Wazoo.

"He is a pompous bag of disgusting waste," Wazoo said, staring through at Zibock.

"No, this. The light."

Wazoo looked at her. "Out there you mean." She pointed toward the overhead lights.

"Okay." So Wazoo couldn't see it. The colors radiated out from Poppy and stained everything around her.

Another vehicle arrived, this a familiar, long black limousine. Ward erupted from inside and marched forward, only hesitating when he saw the masses in the compound. He frowned around. "Who are they?"

"Ward," Poppy said. "I thought he was tied in with Zibock."

"They are my subjects," Zibock thundered. "Why are you here? You were to wait until I contacted you again."

"Wait while I was blamed for the murders of women I hadn't touched?" Ward said. "Hadn't killed?"

"Sounds like there's a distinction to me," Wazoo said quietly.

Zibock had no immediate answer. The gaggle had grown much more quiet.

"He isn't worthy!" Bart got from behind the wheel of the limo. "I am the one who should be your representative. He makes mistakes. Let me go back and wait in his place, Protector."

"You are Embran," Zibock said in a low, fearsome voice. "I need a human as a placekeeper until I can take over the place of power. We are to get him elected—"

"He never will be," Bart said. "They have released him only on what they call a bond. I made sure both women were found dead at his home. Joan helped me with the second woman."

"Shoot," Poppy muttered. "They're all crazy. We gotta get out of here."

Ward launched himself at Bart and began to fight with his fists while the other one darted out of his way, laughing.

"Look," Poppy whispered loudly. "Outside the gates."

"What?"

"They're all coming. Sykes in the front, and Ben, Liam, Ethan. There's Nick Montrachet and his brother and Pascal with David. Willow, too. She must have sneaked out. Gray. They keep coming, fanning out. All the paranormal families. Some I hardly recognize, I haven't seen them for so long."

And around the advancing army of friends, the same light that enveloped Poppy also glowed. She could see Sykes's eyes, gleaming, deadly, as if he were only an arm's length away. He swept ahead, looking from side to side, searching.

He was searching for her but she dared not draw attention to herself.

Poppy glanced at Wazoo and realized she couldn't see their own people coming. But then she smiled and said, "There's Nat. What is he doing?"

Poppy saw him, too. Hanging back, speaking into a collar mic, he crouched, absolutely still.

"He can't come in here on his own," Wazoo said, her voice rising.

"Don't worry, he won't." She squeezed Wazoo's arm. "Just be ready to run when and where I tell you."

A yell split the night, a curdling yell. Poppy searched for the source and found it too quickly. Ward lay, bleeding from his head and unmoving. Bart stood over him, an arm that now glinted like a cylinder of dull metal raised in the air. He smashed it down on Ward again and the man's body would never, Poppy knew, move again.

She felt an odd distress. In a way Ward Bienville was a pitiable figure, destined for failure. But she didn't think this should have been his end. He wasn't a killer.

Zibock took one step forward and felled Bart with a single stroke of his gold-studded hand. Parts flew, metal and flesh, in all directions.

"This isn't a good place to be," Wazoo said.

Poppy was not in the mood to be flip. She feared for Sykes and the rest of them. *Sykes, go back. Take them all back. It's too dangerous.*

Only his eyes moved, but toward her. She knew without any doubt that they looked at each other.

We can't go back yet but we will win, Poppy. Zibock is the one who keeps the rest of them together. Wait there.

He would be invisible to make his move, Poppy remembered with relief. And Ben could do the same. But not the others as far as she knew.

Gradually noise built again among the crowd.

Zibock held up his arms as if in triumph, and the Embran roared approval.

Then Poppy saw Sykes start forward. Around him, the blue-green light pulsed and he advanced until he stood within feet of the giant.

Poppy's heart twisted so hard she felt pain in her throat. "Can you see Sykes?" she asked Wazoo.

"Yes," Wazoo said quietly. "I fear for him."

Which meant they could all see Sykes. She started forward but Wazoo threw her arms around her. "Don't. You'll only make it all worse. Can they be shot?"

It took Poppy a second to realize Wazoo meant the Embran. "I don't know. I doubt it." Then she realized what Wazoo was thinking. "It can't hurt for Nat to have a gun with him."

Sykes put his fists on his hips and the light around him went out. At once Poppy realized that Zibock saw him. The light alone had made him invisible to other than those with special sight so all the other members of the families must also be invisible.

But now Sykes stood before Zibock, legs spread and flexed, his hair lifted away from his strong neck by the warm wind and his chest and shoulders massive inside a black T-shirt.

"You can't do it on your own," Poppy moaned.

Wazoo continued to hold her although Poppy knew she could shake her off if she had to.

Zibock began a step toward Sykes and paused, returning his huge foot to the ground. Poppy saw how Sykes fastened the full force of his gaze on the other man's eyes. Sykes, utterly still, seemed to grow larger as she watched him.

His arms fallen to his sides, Zibock made unintelligible noises.

All of his "subjects" had fallen silent.

Neither man moved but there was a change in

Zibock's presence. He began to sway, just slightly. Sykes got closer, never breaking his eye contact.

"He's killing him," Poppy said under her breath. "Hypnosis."

"Go hypnosis," Wazoo said. "Kill the creep."

"He will make his brain die," Poppy whispered. "He must not feel he has done the wrong thing. Sykes is so principled."

Zibock crumpled slowly. He twisted a little and gradually sank until his knees gave out and he dropped that far.

Sykes bent over him, never touching him, never looking away.

When Zibock fell, it was backward from the knees and Poppy saw his bulbous eyes, sightless and filmed with white, rolled back in his head.

The members of the other families burst forward, all of them bringing their concealing light with them. Only when they struck down the enemy did they show themselves, giving each opponent a chance to react to what was coming.

The Embran went down like stalks of wheat before a threshing machine. When they collapsed, they morphed into dozens of forms that gradually shriveled.

"There you are! Come out." Nat reached Wazoo and hauled her into his arms. He kissed her and kissed her again and she wrapped her arms around his neck. When he swept her up into his arms she didn't make a peep, and Poppy didn't hear a single word about Wazoo's independence or a demand that she be put down.

"It's over."

Poppy swung around and looked up at Sykes. He took hold of her right hand and held it up. "See."

She looked and did see how a mind-numbing brilliance seeped out from the ring Pascal had given her. When she caught it in the door it must have snapped it partway open and now the power was free to shine upon them all.

"We've been blessed," Sykes said. "But most of all, I've been blessed." He locked his arms around her so tightly she could hardly breathe. "Let's see if I can do this again," he said.

45

Sykes and Poppy clung together in his darkened bedroom in St. Peter Street, breathless, laughing and soaked—and racked by their reaction to one another.

And maybe they were a little hysterical, she thought.

"We came through a storm," Poppy said, unnecessarily. "It wasn't raining at that place." Her hair hung wet over the shoulders of her sopping dress.

Sykes held her face in his big hands, looked into her eyes and listened. Rain pelted the window and thunder rolled in the distance. The night was warm, steamy. "It's raining here," he said. "Sounds good." His lips parted and he stared at her mouth. He raised his head, gasping, his eyes closed and she pressed a hand to her own fiery mouth.

"Wow," she said. "Ben is going to feel threatened when he finds out how well you're doing with this traveling around."

"I didn't ask where you wanted to go," Sykes said, serious again, indicating his house. "Tell me if you want to be somewhere else and I'll do my best to get you there. As long as I can come with you."

"I love this place," she said. "Sykes, the last couple of days have been hell."

He muttered something she didn't understand. "What?"

"And heaven," he said clearly. "I'd be a liar if I didn't admit that with all the fear—and, lady, you have frightened me—I've never been happier in my life. I think it had something to do with you."

"I've been scared for you," Poppy said. "Is it all over?"

He pushed her wet hair away from her face. "I think so. I think this was their last attempt but something went really wrong for them. And they asked for it."

"Yes." She couldn't feel pity for the Embran. "Do you think there could be more humans they got over to their side? Other than Ward?" She lowered her eyes.

"It wouldn't matter if there were, would it? They didn't really change him. He was just doing what they told him to."

"Because he wanted what he thought they'd give him. Power."

"Try to forget all that."

She didn't think she would ever completely forget, but the memories would fade. "You're really wet," she told him. "You need to get into some dry clothes."

"You, too. Take what you want."

"I don't want anything," she said. "But you."

Hugging again, not caring how sodden they were, they kissed. Sykes opened her mouth with his, kissed each of her lips, sucked on her tongue. Poppy met every move. She shook constantly but couldn't stop and didn't care.

"I think you're shocky," Sykes said.

"Uh-huh. It doesn't matter. Are we Bonded?"

He held her by the shoulders and laughed. "How can you ask?"

"You never really told me."

"Of course I did. From the first moment we were really together we were Bonded. But don't think there won't have to be more ceremony down the line—for those who expect such things."

"My brothers will want it, and my parents, I suppose."

She kissed his neck and he let his head fall back. She kissed the beard-rough skin on his

375

throat again and again, reached to nip at the lobes of his ears.

"The ring," she said, growing still.

He looked down at her and took her right hand from around his neck. "It's quiet," he said, as if it were alive and perhaps it was. "That's because it's done its job, don't you think?"

She stared at it, still quietly glowing in the shady room. "I've damaged it. That's why it broke open."

"It was meant to. Everything fell into place."

"Where can we put it?"

"We'll put it back, but not tonight. Poppy, will you sleep with me tonight, and every night—and maybe every morning and afternoon?"

She squeezed her eyes shut and felt hot shudders chase, one after another, through her body. "We are Bonded, Sykes."

"Get out of those clothes," he said, stepping away from her.

They separated, each stripping until they were naked. Poppy stood with her back to him but might as well have been pressed against him. At her core she was moist and aching. A subtle but sharp throbbing began.

When she turned around, Sykes stood on the other side of the room, the gray shadows through rain-spattered glass passing over him, the rises and dips where his muscles tensed. His eyes glinted. And she knew he must see her in much the same way.

"Come to me," he whispered.

She took a step toward him and he matched it. They moved like that, small step by small step until she could feel the heat of his body.

A few more inches and her nipples brushed the hair on his chest. She sucked in a moan and Sykes turned his head aside, something close to exquisite pain on his face.

"Closer," he said.

They both did what he said and fitted together as if they had been made as two halves of a whole.

Kissing her shoulder, Sykes stroked the backs of his fingers up and down the sides of her breasts. His flat belly and hips rocked into her. He bent his knees and bounced subtly, once, twice, until she parted her legs and let him slide between the pulsing folds hidden there.

Poppy felt as if her nerves were stripped and raw. She longed for completion, yet dreaded it, too. Even knowing they were together, they hoped forever, she didn't know how she would bear not being joined with him even for a few hours.

I feel the same way.

She jumped and forced his face up. His hands roaming over her back, her waist, her bottom, made it hard to concentrate but she was getting good at this now. *You didn't ask permission to come in.*

Yes, I did. You just weren't aware of it.

Fibber. Oh—Sykes.

Here's to a wonderful life.

"You're teasing me," she told him, returning his favor by molding her hands to his unyielding buttocks. With her thumbs, she traced the indent where they met his thighs, then ran her fingertips softly up the cleft in his rear. "I don't want to move, but I want more."

"Try and stop me."

Catching her by the waist, he hoisted her a few inches and she wound her legs around him. Slowly he let her most tender parts slide down his belly until she gripped his shoulders, drove her nails in. Almost without warning a climax ripped through her.

Sykes sighed. "Perfect. Let go, darling."

She had no choice. If he had taken his arms away she would have fallen. Her hips jerked helplessly against him and she absorbed wave after wave of searing release.

Sykes contrived to bend until he could suck a nipple into his mouth. He played the tip of his tongue over the hard flesh and the tension between her legs mounted again.

"I want you," she said, almost desperate.

"I'm all yours, lady." Once more he raised her a few inches and this time he drove her unerringly onto him, buried himself inside her. They began to move and each stroke was white hot.

Her back came in contact with the wall.

He entered her again and again, faster and harder

and their bodies remained twined together until she dropped her legs and took her weight on her toes.

"You are my love forever," he said. Holding her hips, he strained together with her and in the end they both sobbed out completion. With the final thrust, Sykes fell against her, pulled her to him and supported them both with one hand against the wall.

Seconds passed when their hearts hammered so hard that Poppy thought she could hear them. Sykes picked her up and put her on the bed. He lay on his side, his head supported on a hand, staring down at her.

"This is sort of a wedding night," he said, and she saw his lips curve in a smile. "May we have many more. But do be prepared for Pascal's ceremony. It'll be in the Court of Angels. He's a stickler for these things."

"I'll like that. But I want to say whatever we say in front of the beautiful angel window. It will have to be treated with great care."

"It will be." He kissed her, planted dozens of small kisses on her face and body. When he moved lower she grabbed him and urged him back up where she could see him again.

"You don't like that?" he said.

"I can only take so much amazing agony at one time. At least without a little break. Do you think all the others are safely at home?"

"I know they are."

"Of course you do."

"I'm surprised you didn't say anything about . . . I thought it would make you afraid of me."

"What happened to Zibock had to happen. I could never be afraid of you."

In the darkness, they listened to the rain. Finally lightning shattered downward sending white light through the room, across Sykes's almost savagely wild features. She only wanted to look at him forever.

"Do you hate poetry?" she said, a little self-conscious.

"I don't go to poetry readings, if that's what you mean. But I have my favorites."

" 'How do I love thee? Let me count the ways.' "

Sykes took up one of her hands and kissed the base of each finger before pressing her palm to his mouth. He watched her, his eyes full of waiting.

"Elizabeth Barrett Browning," he said, rolling to his back and gathering her on top of him.

He must feel her tears on his neck.

"I do, you know," he said. "I always will."

"We always will."

Epilogue

J. Clive Millet, Antiques
The Court of Angels
Royal Street
New Orleans

Greetings:

It was never my intention to communicate with you directly. Of course, I've known you were there, watching and listening and mistakenly thinking I wasn't aware of you. Well, be assured that there is very little, if anything, that goes unnoticed by Jude Millet.

I think of you rather as I do that useless creature over there on the chair, the orange cat my relative calls Marigold. Curious, constantly needing to be fed with whatever, and unsuitable for carrying out tasks requiring advanced psychic skills.

Do you know that she now comes flouncing up here when she can't find Pascal, David or Anthony? She feels quite proud of walking through the door, as in, *through* it while it is closed. Her one dubious accomplishment. But could she be relied on to carry out the smallest task on cue? Absolutely not. How grateful I am for the return of that brilliant dog, Mario, to say nothing of my own brilliant move in encouraging Wazoo's involvement in things.

What a woman!

One wonders if she will settle for the policeman, honorable as he appears to be. He is certainly not her equal in talent.

There must be a reason he's writing to us, you are probably thinking, sneering as you do so. You're right. A great deal has transpired here. I am pleased with the eventual revelation of the Ultimate Power, even if those dolts took forever to find the window.

I should explain that I didn't actually know about the window, only that such a depiction existed and that it would lead them to the Harmony and the Ultimate Power. The stone I sent to Sykes had been with me a long time and my own father had told me he believed it had special properties that would be useful one day.

Sykes almost messed that up.

So what of Poppy, hmm? Exotic-looking thing and bright, I suppose. Yes, I admit she performed extraordinarily well when everything was in the balance and we could have faced failure. Mmm, quite extraordinarily well.

These descendants of mine are all notable. They have faced trying challenges well—I might even say I'm proud of them. Well then, I am proud of them.

That's enough of that.

What I really wanted to warn you about was the possibility that I have discovered more was expected of me than I had thought. Having had dealings with members of the paranormal families other than my own, I am persuaded that our beloved Court of Angels may not be done with me yet—or should I write, done with us?

There is much more to the Fortunes than meets the eye, and the Montrachets make me positively nervous. Even more disturbing is the evidence that I have been appointed to watch over all of these younger members. How that happened, I have no idea but when I find out, heads will roll.

I think that when all is finally quiet tonight and I'm sure it will remain so for a while, I shall wander in the Court of Angels. If I can control the unruly excitement of the Ushers, I think they may have more to tell me. They may well know if you and I should continue to be vigilant and to watch for danger stalking our families in the French Quarter.

Ephemerally yours—I hope,

Jude Millet

Center Point Publishing
600 Brooks Road ● PO Box 1
Thorndike ME 04986-0001 USA

(207) 568-3717

US & Canada:
1 800 929-9108
www.centerpointlargeprint.com